A Spy to Die For

KRIS DeLAKE

Published by Sourcebooks Casablanca, an imprint of Sourcebooks, Inc.
P.O. Box 4410, Naperville, Illinois 60567-4410
(630) 961-3900
FAX: (630) 961-2168
www.sourcebooks.com

Printed and bound in the United States of America.
VP 10 9 8 7 6 5 4 3 2 1

For Dean

for getting us through a dark year

Chapter 1

FOR REASONS SHE NEVER UNDERSTOOD, SKYLIGHT Jones loved the Starcatcher Restaurant. The restaurant had the best bacon double cheeseburgers that Skye had ever tasted. The fact that the restaurant was on Krell, possibly the grimiest space station she'd ever been to, and the fact that the cleanliness in the Starcatcher matched the station's really didn't bother her. If anyone had asked her (and no one ever had), she would have said that the dirt encrusted on the hamburger made it all taste better.

She had arrived on Krell about three hours ago. She'd taken a transport because she didn't want anyone to notice her, and one of the best ways to get noticed in a place like Krell was to bring your own spaceship. Particularly the kind of spaceship that she could afford on her Assassins Guild expense account.

The Guild thought her a valuable asset, so she had one of the largest expense accounts they'd ever devised. A normal person could live off Skye's monthly expense allotment for two years.

And the other nice thing about the Guild was that they paid the expense account money in advance. Because Skye's missions were always secret, even from other Guild members, she couldn't very well charge everything to some Guild account.

She kept one month's expenses at the touch of her

finger and banked the rest. The Guild usually wanted an accounting of what she spent, and damn, if that accounting didn't show that she spent every last bit of that money. Yes, she lied.

It was the least she could do, since she was still working off what she called her indentured servitude. If the Guild wouldn't let her go until she had finished seven-plus years of practically free work for them to pay off all her childhood debts, then she would keep the extra from the expense accounts and never tell a soul.

Besides, she didn't need a lot, even when she was on a job. She liked grungy, cheap places like this. They felt luxurious to her. The Guild was so clean and bright and regimented.

The Starcatcher had probably been here since Krell was built. It had started as a little hole in the wall, literally, and had become a medium-size hole in the wall, with an "open-air" section to the restaurant.

Skye hated the "open-air" part.

First, there was no real air, because they were on a space station. So the air wasn't fresh or windblown or anything. It was recycled, like everything else on the place. And second, it wasn't open, because no part of Krell (outside of the docking ring) had a view of space.

So what "open-air" actually meant was that the patrons got to eat in the wide concourse that everyone walked through on the way to somewhere else.

Not Skye's idea of relaxation.

So instead, she sat at a table in the very center of the restaurant, her back to the grimy faux-wood wall. She had a clear view of the door and of the kitchen. The other thing she liked about the Starcatcher was that it had actual human chefs. They fried the burgers (or whatever the hell this stuff was) themselves. No machine flipped the patties, no grill shut off when the meat was cooked. Just juicy frying fat, that actually sizzled so loud that she could hear it in the front part of the restaurant, over the conversation.

If there was conversation.

Because at the moment, there was only the waitstaff and her. The waiter kept glancing at her like she was a bit of garbage that needed cleaning. (Not that anyone here ever really thought of cleaning anything.)

They wanted to force her out, and she wasn't going.

She had arrived half an hour before closing, and apparently it was a slow day, because the open-air part of this silly place had already shut down, chairs up and locked to their tables, the gate sealed shut.

The fact that there was an actual waitstaff meant that the place needed to lock its doors as well. Usually the Starcatcher got by with talking serving trays or little mobile robots. Those things couldn't work the last half hour due to Krell regulations. Apparently thieves came through a while back and stole all the robotic servers just before shutdown, and no one noticed for the eight hours the restaurants were closed. Whoever that was had made a hell of a haul.

Skye didn't mind. She liked annoying people, especially in service of a great burger. Hers was nearly done. When it finished sizzling, she would eat it slowly, savoring it, since she hadn't had a good meal for the last five days. She didn't care how hard the waitstaff tried to get her out of this place.

She glared at the water glass in front of her, so

smudged that she actually had to peer over the lip of the glass to see if the liquid was the water she had ordered or not. If the burger didn't get here soon, she might break down and drink that stuff.

Then the door opened, and a man leaned in. Skye couldn't quite see him; he was so hunched over that his face was obscured.

"Can I get some service out here?" His voice was marvelously deep and musical. It sent little shivers through her.

"We're closed," the dried-up tired-looking woman on the waitstaff said without looking at the door.

"She's lying," Skye said. "They got another ten minutes before they're allowed to turn away customers."

The woman glared at Skye, and Skye smiled sweetly. Usually she tipped well whenever she encountered human waitstaff. But this woman was pushing her luck.

"Great!" the man said without moving. "So, can I get some service out here?"

"Nope," the dried-up waitress said. "That part of the restaurant *is* closed."

The man said, "You gotta be kidding me."

"Not kidding," the waitress said.

"I'll pay extra for service out here."

"Nope," the woman said.

Skye frowned. What was the big deal about coming into the restaurant? Yeah, it smelled a bit gamy, but so did most places on Krell. In fact, with a frying burger on the griddle, the Starcatcher was probably the best-smelling place on Krell at the moment.

"How about something to go?" the man said in that delicious voice. "I could wait out here—"

"No." The waitress crossed her arms. "In here or nothing."

The man remained in that hunched position for a moment. He actually seemed to be having trouble making a decision.

Skye was curious now.

"You can sit with me," she said. "I wiped this table off my own self."

Another glare from the waitress. Skye couldn't tell if it was because the waitress didn't want the man in the restaurant or if it was because of the dig about the filthy table. Or both.

"Well, I can't refuse that offer." The man's voice had amusement in it. He came in the door and still didn't stand up straight. Skye finally understood what was going on.

He was huge.

She had never seen a man that large before—at least, not out in space. Space stations, spaceships, space resorts, anything space-related was built for the compact body. Like hers. She barely topped five feet on a good day, and she was average height for a woman who spent most of her time in cramped ships or cramped bunks in tiny space resort hotels.

She was thin too, which took some work, considering what she liked to eat and the fact she didn't like using enhancements to keep the weight off. She actually exercised. She wasn't good with weapons—at least not conventional ones (which was one of the many reasons she wasn't an actual assassin)—but she was strong enough to fight anyone off in hand-to-hand combat.

Provided that she caught him by surprise, of course.

Like this guy had caught her.

He couldn't stand upright. He had to bend at the waist just to get inside the door, and even then, the top of his head scraped the door frame. He had black hair that seemed a touch long, but she couldn't really tell because she couldn't see his face yet.

At least he was thin. She couldn't imagine how a tall fat guy would survive on a space station like Krell. The doorways were as narrow as they were short.

The man somehow managed to wend his way around the tables and found a path to her little bit of wall. As he did so, he said to the waitress, "Bacon double cheeseburger, extra cheese, extra bacon, extra crispy. And a Krell special soda. Keep that funky water away from me."

"Yes, sir," the waitress said sarcastically. "Should I salute too?"

"C'mon, Delores," he said, surprising Skye by knowing the waitress's name. "It's already been a tough week."

He pulled a chair to the side of Skye's table and sat down so hard that the chair actually groaned. He straightened his back. It cracked as he did so. Then he brought his head up.

Skye's breath caught. She hadn't expected him to be so handsome or so young. He had moved like an old man—probably because he had to hunch to get into the place—so she had just assumed that he *was* old.

She had assumed wrong.

He was probably in his early thirties. He had high cheekbones that accented the hollows in his cheeks. His nose was angular and pointed at that marvelous mouth of his, not too big and not too small. It was curved up in a smile now, a smile that made his unbelievably blue eyes twinkle.

"Thanks for sharing your table," he said. "This place is so crowded, I can see why Delores didn't want to serve me in the open air."

Skye laughed. "Well, you know. It's me and the piles of dust."

"I don't think there's dust here," the man said. "Dirt, maybe, but not dust."

Skye tilted her head just a little to concede the point.

"Yet," she said, "it must not bother you. You come here often enough to know the name of the waitstaff."

"Just Delores," the man said. "She's been here longer than the dirt."

"I heard that," the woman—Delores—said from the back.

"I was hoping so, darling," he said. "You know how I hate stepping inside this place."

"It's not my fault you're too big to fly in space."

"Honey," he said, that smile growing, "I don't fly. That's what ships are for."

Skye was smiling too. She couldn't remember the last time she had felt this amused.

"You are the tallest man I've ever seen off-planet," she said, agreeing with the grumpy Delores. It had to be hard for him, traveling in places built for people like Skye.

"Yeah, I get that a lot," the man said. "Most people let height regulations discourage them. Me, I just pretend to be shorter."

"Does it work?" she asked.

"You just saw how well," he said. Then he extended his hand. "Jack Hunter."

She hadn't expected introductions. She stared at his hand stupidly for a moment, thinking that a) his hand was big (*nice*) and b) his hand was big. Then she took it in her own, noting calluses which meant he did some kind of physical labor.

"Skye," she said, conscious that she wasn't giving him her last name. She never gave out her last name, since she wasn't really sure what it was. Her parents had used Jones the last time she had seen them, but before that, they'd been using Anderson, and before that, Ngyen. The Guild had stuck her with Jones, but she had identification in anything except Jones.

"Skye," he repeated. "As in 'skies of blue'?"

As in the color of your eyes, she thought, but didn't say. She was not about to tell him her name was Skylight. People always wanted to know where that name came from.

"As in skies of gray, maybe," she said. "I tend to reject anything that's black and white."

"Or colorful," he said.

"Or colorful," she agreed. But he seemed colorful, and she wasn't rejecting him. In fact, he still held her hand. Or, if she really wanted to be accurate, his hand enveloped hers.

She rarely felt small, but next to this guy, she felt truly tiny. And her hand was lost in his.

In a good way.

She rubbed her thumb against his palm, and his cheeks actually flushed with surprise. His hand twitched just a little, and she wondered if he had nearly pulled away from her.

But his gaze never left hers. If anything, his eyes seemed to become a deeper blue.

"You seem colorful to me," he said.

"Only every other Thursday," she said.

He smiled. It softened his features and made him seem even more approachable. How long had it been since she'd seen such a handsome man?

All right, that probably wasn't the question to ask, since she'd seen a lot of handsome men. But none of them had attracted her. This guy, he made her relax, maybe a bit too much. Spies should never relax.

"It's my lucky day then," he said so softly that she almost didn't hear him.

Banter rose in her mind: *Mine too*. Or *maybe we could both get lucky*. But she didn't say either of those things because she suddenly felt awkward. That "lucky day" comment seemed sincere, and she distrusted sincere.

Delores showed up with a steaming burger, something that resembled fried potatoes, and a tray of condiments. She slammed it all on the table, narrowly missing Skye and Jack's still-entwined hands.

He let go of Skye's hand and she glanced at him, startled. She hadn't even thought of letting go.

Oh, yeah. Sincere was very dangerous.

His cheeks still had spots of color as he reached for the hamburger. Delores slapped his wrist.

"The sandwich, you overgrown monstrosity of a man, is for the young lady."

No one ever called Skye a lady, and very few people called her young. Both terms applied to weaker, more polite people than she had ever been.

"Yeah," Skye said, sliding the plate toward herself. "You wouldn't like it. I prefer my bacon wiggly."

And the banter again: *Unlike my men. I prefer them hard.*

But she censored that as well.

He glanced at her, a small movement, almost unnoticeable. Jack Hunter, huh? She had never heard of him, and she wondered why not. A man like him would be hard to miss no matter where he went. Since he was comfortable in the Starcatcher, he came to Krell a lot.

She should have heard of him—not necessarily by this name, but just because he was so big. People talked about anything unusual, and his size made him very unusual.

"Well, then," he said, his hand retreating to his side of the table. "I guess I'll have to wait for mine."

Skye could hear the burger sizzling, so it wouldn't take very long.

"What about my special soda?" he asked Delores. "I'm thirsty as hell."

"I shut down the fountain," she said. "Drink her water."

"No one should drink that water," Jack said. "I swear it's another life-form."

"Naw," Delores said. "But I wouldn't bet against other life-forms living in it."

She wiped her hands on an apron as filthy as the table, then stalked to the back.

"I want the soda!" Jack yelled after her.

"I want some handsome prince to rescue me from all this," Delores shouted back. "I doubt either one of us will get our wish."

"You can have my water," Skye said to him. "I don't mind."

He was still looking toward Delores. Then he turned his attention to Skye and she felt the power of that face again. He wasn't the most handsome man she had ever seen, but something about him took her breath away.

"I'm sure you don't mind if I have your water," he said. "I'd pour it out if I didn't think it might melt the floor away and Delores would charge us for it."

"I heard that," Delores yelled.

"And I heard that comment about a handsome prince," he yelled back, then added just loud enough for Skye to hear, "and that gave me some imagery I'll never get out of my head."

Skye chuckled. When had she last chuckled? This man was fun in addition to being attractive. She wasn't even sure when she'd last had some fun in her life.

"Eat your burger," he said, "before I do."

She reached for it, but he touched her arm, stopping her. His mood seemed to have changed in an instant.

"You have eaten here before, right?" He sounded worried.

She wasn't used to answering direct questions, even questions as seemingly innocuous as that one. "Why?"

"Because, as good as the burgers are, and I think they're the best in the sector, they do have added bits of—um—shall we say… unidentifiable material? Usually added after cooking, in the transfer to the plate."

"Or from the plate itself," Skye said. "If I thought there was a more antiseptic way of serving these things, I would have asked for it."

He grinned and leaned back, again removing his hand so quickly from her skin that he seemed to be afraid she'd burn him. His tone was calmer than his movements.

"Ah," he said, "so you have eaten here before."

"Of course," she said. "And I make it a point of eating here whenever I can. Because I agree: these are the best burgers in the sector."

The sentence had barely come out of her mouth when her breath caught. *Whoa*. She had been paying attention, and she had still said too much in that simple response. *You want to find Skye on Krell? Go to the Starcatcher. She's traveled all over the sector, eaten burgers all over the sector, and she comes here as often as she can.*

You want to find Skye anywhere? Burger joints.

She grabbed the burger off the plate and squished the bun against the meat. The bacon curved upward. She was going to pretend that she hadn't just revealed a ton of stuff about herself, pretend that her lack of caution didn't bother her, pretend that she was just an average woman flirting with an average (if tall) man.

He didn't seem to notice any of the revelations. Or if he did, he didn't seem to care.

Which was exactly what she would have done if she had just learned something important.

She mentally kicked herself. She was acting like an untrained rookie, and she knew it.

She just didn't know how to stop.

Check that: she knew how to stop. She had never acted like this, not even as an untrained rookie. But then, she had never met a man whose sheer attractiveness had fritzed out her brain before.

He was looking at her in pleased puzzlement. "You know," he said, "I have never met a woman who likes to eat here before."

Skye didn't believe that for an instant. Her heart sank just a bit. Was he exaggerating? Making conversation? And why should it matter if he was?

She really wanted him to be as attracted to her as she was to him. That's why.

"Delores likes to eat here," Skye said, deciding to go for the banter after all.

He mock-frowned, and shook his head. "Delores doesn't eat here. Are you kidding? She knows what goes into the food."

His eyes were twinkling, and suddenly Skye understood. He was deliberately playing with her, because she was holding her burger but hadn't eaten it. He was trying to put her off her food, maybe to see how far her own bravado went.

She tilted the burger at him, then slowly eased it into her mouth. Juice dripped onto her tongue and lips, and some ran down her chin. So much for being provocative and sexy. Now she was just going for the teenage gross-out.

And since she was committed, she went all the way with it. She took the biggest bite she could and savored that burger. There was a lot to savor: the charred meat (she still wouldn't say categorically that it was real hamburger), the cheese (which, despite its bright orange color, *was* real), the squishy bacon (could also be fake), and all those unidentifiable (and a tad too crunchy) other things hidden inside that bun.

Jack watched her eat as if he'd never seen anyone eat before. Maybe he expected her to gag and grimace. Instead she chewed slowly, her stomach growling. She really had been hungry, and she really had wanted this burger.

She didn't even set it down all the way, although she did shift it to one hand as she groped for the napkin to clean off her chin.

He handed her a folded napkin. She could see the stains on its surface, and wondered when it had last been washed.

If it had been washed. For all she knew, the Starcatcher simply refolded the napkins before putting them on the table, tossing them when they started feeling too crusty.

Not even that thought bothered her enough to stop cleaning the burger juice off her chin.

She'd helped assassins hide dead bodies, hidden in garbage scows to get information for the Guild, spent a month on a cargo ship with barely enough water to drink and certainly not enough to bathe in. It would take more than a filthy napkin and some hamburger juice to gross her out.

"Good?" he asked.

"Goo," she replied, nodding, her mouth filled with the second bite.

He grinned. "You're not like any other woman I've ever met."

She sure hoped he meant that as a compliment. But she was too busy devouring that burger to ask.

Then Delores showed up with his burger. It was taller than hers—the extra bacon, probably—and the cheese looked like an orange patty all by itself. He thanked her and tossed her a credit chip, something Skye hadn't seen in years. She didn't think anyone used credit chips anymore. How old-fashioned of him. Or maybe he was just cautious.

Delores pocketed her chip and said, "You got fifteen minutes, or we'll lock you in."

He hadn't taken a bite yet. "Special soda, and I'll give you another chip."

"No," she said. "I mean it. I've been working thirty-six hours straight, and I'm done with you people for the next forty-eight."

Then she stalked off.

Skye set down the remaining section of her burger and wiped her mouth with the back of her hand. The back of her hand had to be cleaner than that damn napkin.

"Sounds like she does mean it," Skye said.

"She does." Jack took the top part of the bun off his burger and added condiments—multicolored condiments. She'd guess that they were ketchup or mustard or mayonnaise, but that was presuming too much.

Besides, watching him do that made her stomach do a slow flip. She didn't mind the filthy restaurant and the mystery substances on her fried/grilled/cooked burger. But those condiments might have been in those containers for a year and left completely untouched.

He clearly noted her skeptical expression. "Don't worry," he said. "They're as fake as the meat. There's nothing in these condiments that can spoil."

"I don't like to think that the meat is fake," she said.

"I don't like to think that the meat is real," he said. "Where do they get it out here?"

That stopped her stomach from spinning. She'd grown up with budding assassins, for heaven's sake. She knew how to gross out someone better than this Jack Hunter ever could.

She finished her burger, even though she now felt like she was in an eating contest with him. He was going through his quickly, the condiments dripping off onto the plate and table.

When she finished, she handed him the dirty napkin. He held it in one hand and finished feeding himself with the other. Then he wiped off his mouth with a flourish.

"Two minutes to spare," he said.

She tapped a chip on the back of her hand, showing her the time. She hated the "useful" augmentations that put that stuff just inside the eye.

He was right. They had two minutes to spare, and they certainly weren't going to spend that bussing tables. The only reason anyone bussed a table in this place was to have a place to sit down.

"Amazing," she said and then burped. So ladylike. Ah, well. She hadn't acted politely since she met him; wasn't time to start now. She didn't even excuse herself.

His grin grew, and his eyes twinkled. God, he had a pleasant face. She really liked that.

"How about getting a drink?" he asked. "I still want that special soda."

She'd never had the local sweetwater, as a friend once called it. She had no idea how they made the special soda here on Krell, and she was afraid to find out that the stuff wasn't boiled or sterilized or pasteurized or whatever the hell companies did to purify liquids way out here. Not that they'd want anyone to get sick here, but public safety regulations really weren't Krell's strong suit. That was one of the reasons why so many shady characters showed up here on such a regular basis.

She counted herself as one of those shady characters.

"A drink sounds good," she said as she stood. She extended a hand to help him up and to her surprise, he took it. For a half second, she thought he was going to tower over her, but he hunched.

"Good," he said, not letting go of her hand. Instead, he used it to drag her out of this place. Did he actually believe Delores would lock them in?

Perhaps he did. But then, he knew her better than Skye did.

They made it outside—if, indeed, the concourse could be called "outside"—and the door locked behind them with an audible click. Skye turned slightly and saw Delores frowning at her through the window.

Jack still held her hand, but he hadn't moved. Skye glanced at him and was startled when her gaze hit his torso.

He had stood up. Upright. To his full height.

Which, she had to admit, was impressive.

The top of his head nearly bumped the concourse's ceiling. She had thought he was tall before, but he was *really* tall. She had never seen a human in space who was that tall, bar none.

She craned her neck, saw the elegant line of his throat and the underside of his chin. He had just a bit of growth. It gave him a rough, careless look. She suspected if he cleaned up a bit, he would be so handsome everyone would remember him.

Not that they could forget his height.

"How in the universe do you manage?" she asked him, her neck getting just a little sore from looking up at him.

He was scanning the area—probably for open bars. "Manage what?"

"This," she said. "Space stations. Space*ships* for that matter. Being out here, where everything is built for people like me."

He looked down on her. How many people had done that in the last few years? She could probably count them on one hand.

It made her feel like she was on Kordita standing next to a tree.

"It's not so bad," he said.

"Not so bad?" she asked. "You have to watch your head all the time."

"As if that were possible," he said with a smile. "I can't see my head."

He went back to scanning.

She got the message. He didn't like talking about his height. Interesting. Well, everything about him was interesting. *Everything*. She squeezed his hand.

"Drink?" she said.

"Yeah," he said slowly. "I suppose you want alcohol."

"I don't care," she said. "I generally avoid the stuff."

He looked down on her again, those blue eyes suddenly serious. "You like crusty Starcatcher burgers, you burp like a cargo jockey, and you don't drink. What *are* you?"

Her heart twisted a bit. She was always a surprise to people. She wondered if he no longer found her attractive. (Had he found her attractive? Or had she just imagined that? Still, he was holding her hand…)

"I'm clearly not a girl, right?" she said. "Or at least one you'd find in polite company."

He chuckled. "Like there's polite company on Krell."

"Good point," she said.

"Come on," he said. "There should be a place across the way which, if I remember right, is open continually."

Then he dragged her forward and she went. She had to walk fast to keep up with him. That surprised her. They maneuvered around the open-air part of the restaurant, with its locked chairs, across the actual concourse to the other side, with its other open-air sections.

Most of them were closed. The shops had locked up and so had the restaurants, but the bars were open.

Three had revolving "open" signs in their windows, but only one had an open-air section. It was close to the exterior walls of the bar, and there were only a few tables, but she knew that Jack would choose to sit there.

And she couldn't blame him. He didn't have to worry about hitting his head.

There was one available table, but she had a hunch it wouldn't be available for long. She squeezed his hand and said, "You get the table, I'll get the drinks."

Then she slipped her hand from his and pushed her way inside the bar.

It was crowded and smelled of beer. The actual bar itself had a self-serve section, and she was grateful. People pushed against her, talking, laughing, trying to find room to stand.

She glanced out the door. He had gotten the table and was watching her.

Her heart pounded. When was the last time she had been this impulsive?

When was the last time she had had fun?

She couldn't remember.

She smiled at him, then turned to the bar and ordered their drinks.

Chapter 2

SHE WAS BEAUTIFUL. JACK HAD TO GIVE HER THAT. The mysterious and forceful Skye was one of the most beautiful women he had ever seen—and he had seen a lot of beautiful women.

She negotiated her way through the crowd inside the bar, working her way to the self-serve section. She looked tall in there next to all the space jockeys. Tall, and thin, and stunning.

She wasn't tall. She was, in fact, a tiny little thing. Her hand had felt fragile in his.

Her black hair was cut short around her head, forming a cap around her face. She could hide behind that wedge of hair if she had to. Her eyes were as black as her hair, blacker maybe, like pieces of space that starlight couldn't reach.

Yes, he was waxing poetic over a woman he had just met. And yes, it scared him.

He tried to ignore women whenever possible. They were trouble. But this woman was impossible to ignore.

She came out of the bar holding a drink in each hand. She had gotten something yellow and fizzy. He had gotten the special soda, which was just root beer, made with both wintergreen and real cherry tree bark that got shipped in.

Or maybe the combination of all the artificial flavors mixed just right. Maybe it was all hype. Whatever the case, he liked the special soda on Krell almost as much as he liked the Starcatcher's burgers. Less than he already liked this woman.

Whose last name he didn't know.

She set the drinks down in front of him then climbed into a chair. It was noisy here, with the conversation inside and out, plus some pounding music that he didn't recognize.

"Not good for talking," he said.

"Then why talk?" she asked and leaned forward.

Before he knew what had happened, she kissed him. Her lips were warm and firm. She hesitated for just a minute, as if asking his permission.

He thought about pulling away—he couldn't remember the last relationship he'd had (well, he could, and he didn't want to think about it)—but he waited too long. Besides, his mouth opened slightly, and she took advantage of it, her tongue sliding in and exploring his.

She tasted like lemon, and he realized she had taken a sip of her fizzy drink. Then he stopped analyzing and just kissed her back. Somehow his hand left the table and cupped that wedge of soft black hair, somehow his other hand caught her shoulder and pulled her just a bit forward, somehow he leaned in so hard the table slid aside.

Her hands cupped his cheeks, holding him in place. The kiss took forever—a good forever—the kind of forever in which time slowed down and each second felt like an hour. He savored the feel of her, the taste of her, the way she threw herself into the kiss, just like she had thrown herself into that burger.

He had never been kissed like that, not once in all of his thirty-two years, and then, suddenly, it was over.

"Wow," she said, her cheeks flushed. "Screw the drink. You want to see if you fit in my room?"

At first, he wasn't sure if he heard her right. She didn't seem like the kind of woman who propositioned a man after an hour's conversation. Then he realized he didn't know what kind of woman did that. He had assumptions, and apparently she didn't fit into them.

He swallowed, still tasting her, not sure how to respond. Her room? Here?

She sighed and shook her head slightly. "I surprised you."

"Yeah," he said.

"And you're probably involved with someone."

"No." He sounded stunned. He probably looked stunned too. No woman had ever done this to him before, not so fast, not—at least—without one of his friends behind it all or as part of a job (her job). Hookers weren't uncommon on space stations like this, but then, hookers almost never looked like Skye. At least, not on space stations like this.

"And you've got scruples or something," she said, the light going out of her eyes.

"Um, yeah, I mean, no, I mean—ah hell." He didn't know what he meant. He didn't know what she meant.

"Look," she said, leaning toward him, her elbow on the table, her hand dropping down dangerously close to his thigh. "I travel a lot. I spend a ton of time alone. I've learned to take things when they present themselves. You presented yourself, and I thought—well, you know what I thought. I didn't mean to insult you."

"You didn't," he managed. "Insult me, that is."

She raised her head, looking surprised.

"You startled me." He didn't want to admit that no

woman had ever come onto him like this before—at least, not since his early years, after he left Tranquility House, the horribly misnamed government home for orphaned and abandoned children that he had gotten stuck in. During those post-Tranquility years, there had been a lot of drinking and a lot of posturing and a lot of morning-after regrets.

He couldn't drink now, not with his job, not the way things were—not that he'd ever enjoyed it—and he hadn't put himself in a position to be around interesting women in a long, long time, and even then—

"Ah, hell. I just..." There it was, the near-admission. He didn't want her to know that other women never found him this attractive. "I just wasn't thinking..."

"I hope you weren't," she said with a tentative smile.

He smiled back. "I mean, I—we—were flirting, and I thought it wouldn't go beyond that."

"Because you have someone back home, wherever home is. Because you don't travel much. Because you're worried that this'll get back to her, and you'll get in trouble, and—"

"No," he said. "I travel a lot."

Why he responded to that, he'd never know. He could have objected to anything that she said. It was all wrong.

"Then you understand that sometimes you just have to take the leap because you'll regret it for the rest of your life," she said.

"I'm a leap?" His brain was still working sluggishly from that kiss.

She grinned. "Yeah. You're a leap. One I'd love to try."

His cheeks warmed.

"The universe is a big place, and we probably will

never get this chance again. I'm not asking to go to your place. Hell, I'm not even asking what you do. If you don't want to go to my room, we can get one for both of us. I'll even pay…"

Her voice trailed off. Then she sighed.

"I'm embarrassing myself, aren't I?" she asked.

"No," he said. "No, you're not. I just—um—you know, normally, I'm a really articulate guy."

She smiled.

"But I don't have words." He took her hand. "So screw words. Let's go to your room and see if I fit."

Chapter 3

JACK HAD NEVER SEEN A ROOM LIKE THIS BEFORE, NOT on Krell. The first time he'd come here, nearly a decade ago, he'd rented a room and it had been as filthy as the Starcatcher. The bed smelled like the previous occupant (maybe the dozen previous occupants) and he had slept in a chair that night.

From that moment on, he slept in his ship.

This room, though, this room... wasn't a room. It was a suite. Two rooms and a bathroom. Two *clean* rooms and a bathroom. So clean the place actually glistened. The air still smelled of lemon—not because of Skye's drink, but because of some kind of mix in the room's environmental controls (a mix she had probably chosen)—and there wasn't grime or dust or dirt anywhere to be seen.

She walked in ahead of him, and her presence made the room seem big. She stood like a princess among the matching couch and chairs, her back silhouetted against a wall screen that she had shut off.

The room had no windows, which was not a surprise, since there weren't many windows anywhere on Krell. No one wanted to see out, and no one wanted any incoming ship to see in. Most people came to Krell on business they didn't want anyone else to know about, so seeing and being seen were not high on Krell's priority list.

Still, he had no idea that a rented suite like this existed

here. Although he should have known it. A lot of rich criminals spent a lot of time here, and those people liked being comfortable.

Jack hovered at the door. Skye smiled at him. The smile lit up her black eyes. It made him want to smile back.

He didn't. His heart pounded.

He knew nothing about her. And she was in one of the expensive suites. She said she traveled a lot. What if she did so for her work—her illegal work?

She tilted her head slightly. "Are you changing your mind? Because I think you will fit."

Her hand brushed her thigh ever so slightly. She wasn't talking about the room; they had both known that from the beginning.

He could back out now and fantasize about this forever. Or regret it forever. She had promised him no strings, promised just a moment in time, and he hadn't had a moment—a good moment—in more than a year.

He smiled, hoping it didn't look too hesitant, then ducked under the door frame and stepped into the living room part of the suite. He could stand upright, but the top of his head brushed against the ceiling.

"Wow," she said. "I would have thought you'd have to bend just a bit."

He was bending. He was bending all of his personal rules. His heart pounded—not just from nerves, but from her nearness. He wanted to touch her, but for the first time since he met her, he felt shy.

"Are you changing your mind?" This time, her tone was different. The teasing quality had left. She looked serious for the first time since he met her. That seriousness aged her just enough to make him realize she was closer to his age than he thought. She had a lot of experience, just like he did.

"I… um… don't do this usually," he said.

Her eyes sparkled. "Most women would think that a good thing."

"You don't?" he asked.

She grabbed his hand and pulled him toward her. "I think we're stepping out of our lives here, so what we usually do and don't do doesn't matter."

His breath caught. She didn't normally do this either? Was that what she had implied?

He took her other hand and bent his head. She tilted hers toward him, and his lips touched hers.

This time, the kiss was gentle. He explored, tasting her, softly touching the inside of her mouth. She opened to him and didn't move—not her hands, not her body—just her tongue answering his.

He took her arms and wrapped them around him. Then he tugged her as close as possible, feeling her athletic form against his. Her hands rose up his back, pulling him down just a bit more.

But if he bent farther, he couldn't feel her against him, and he didn't want to lose that. So he lifted her, settling her on his hips, letting her feel how aroused he was.

And he was aroused. He couldn't remember ever feeling like this. He wanted to slam her into the wall, pull off her clothes, and take her right here, but he didn't. He needed to move slowly, to remember this, to take it one step at a time.

She shifted against him, her thighs pulling her even closer. He could feel her through her very thin pants.

"Hurry," she said against him.

"No," he breathed. Then kissed her again.

"Please," she said into his mouth.

He shook his head, deliberately taking his time, shaking with the effort to maintain control.

She yanked her head back, slid her hands around his front, and opened his shirt. Her palms pressed inside, her skin warm on his, and he nearly lost all control right there.

"Now," she said.

"Bed?" he asked, not sure if he could handle more words than that.

"Couch," she said decisively, then unwrapped her legs from him and put her feet on the floor.

He felt her loss as if he had lost part of himself. She tossed off her shirt, revealing small upturned breasts. As he reached for them, she slapped his hands away with a smile.

"You said slow, remember?" she said. Then she wriggled out of her pants. She was trim except for her wide hips. A small wedge of black hair pointed the way.

He reached for her again, but she danced out of his grasp. It took his sluggish brain a moment to understand: she wanted his clothes off as well.

He yanked off his shirt, opened his pants, and nearly tripped as he stepped out of them. His penis bobbed forward, announcing itself, and he wondered, with a flush, if he was too big for her. She looked so much smaller without clothes.

She grabbed him, and pulled him into her warm and willing mouth, and it took every measure of control he had to hold on. He was going to take his time, he reminded himself. He was. He. Was.

Then her mouth left him. "Pick me up," she said, and he did.

She settled on him like she had before, only this time no fabric barred his way. He wanted to make sure she was ready, but she didn't seem to care. She slid onto him, as warm and willing and wet as her mouth had been.

Then he lost all rational thought, moving with her, moving against her. She controlled the rhythm, or maybe he did, and she came against him, adding to it. She made a soft cry—not anything like he would have expected—her head flung back in sheer pleasure, and he couldn't take it anymore.

He came too, losing himself inside her.

It felt like he was falling. Then he realized he was. His knees were wobbling, his legs giving out from the unusual effort. He staggered to the couch and sat naked on the rough fabric, her legs still wrapped around him.

She brought her head forward and nestled her face in the crook of his neck.

"My God," she said against him. "You fit perfectly."

And he did.

Chapter 4

SHE HAD SPOKEN OUT LOUD. SHE HADN'T MEANT TO speak out loud.

But she was so shocked at how good she felt, and part of that was how good she felt *with him still inside her*.

When she had first seen him without his pants, she had a momentary thought: *My God, he's as long as he is tall*. But she found that intriguing—she'd never ever really thought about tall men before or how they were built.

He was built beautifully. He didn't have an ounce of fat on him, which surprised her, since he had worn such loose clothing that she had thought him out of shape. He wasn't. He even had well-defined abs, which no one could get with enhancements. His broad shoulders accentuated his narrow hips and muscular legs.

He had to work hard to maintain that shape, and yet he had hidden it under bulky clothing. The clothing had also aged him. He looked younger naked.

Not that she'd been able to reflect on that much in the heat of the moment. In that moment, she had taken him in her mouth just to see if his length was an illusion as well.

It hadn't been. In fact, when his penis had touched her lips, it had jumped just a little, as if it were trying to grow harder.

And—sweetly—he had wanted to take his time,

probably to please her. She was already pleased, so she made sure she controlled things.

He hadn't minded. In fact, he seemed to enjoy himself.

He held her against him, their hearts beating together. Odd that she noted the heartbeats first, before she realized that they were also taking breaths at the same time.

That had never happened to her before. Nor had she ever relaxed like this before, not after having sex, not after being so vulnerable.

Not that she had ever been this vulnerable before either.

That thought made her sit up and push some damp hair out of her face. His cheeks were flushed, his blue eyes even bluer. He looked open to her, and she had thought him open before.

Such a sweet man, such a gentle man.

The sex had confirmed her impression, not changed it.

She had an ability to see people clearly. Not necessarily all their flaws and faults, but their essences, their cores. She never lost sight of their humanity either, which made it impossible for her to become an assassin.

Her parents, with the help of the man they had hired to pretend to be her uncle, had dumped her on the grounds of the Assassins Guild on Kordita when she was ten, and the Guild had both saved her life and trained her to be an assassin.

The cost of the training, and the room and board, had left her indebted to the Guild. They had done this because they thought she was angry enough and smart enough and asocial enough to be an assassin. But she wasn't. Angry, yes. Smart, yes. Asocial, no.

Something about her prevented her from seeing any human being as someone to be destroyed—no matter how evil. And she knew people could be evil. All of the targets of the Assassins Guild were supposed to be evil.

Everyone connected with the Guild, from the lowliest instructor to the Guild's director, Kerani Ammons, had told her that as if they believed it. In fact, Director Ammons's eyes had glowed with fervor, as if she had thought destroying evil was part of the Guild's mission.

It was now Skye's job to make sure the targets actually were evil. She vetted them. She had only two years left on her contract with the Guild, and then she was on her own.

She couldn't wait for that.

She ran a hand along Jack's face, the stubble on his cheek scratching her palm. She had never in her entire life been so attracted to someone. She certainly hadn't admitted anything, made careless statements like she had done with him, or even blurted out her thoughts.

He shifted beneath her, putting his hands on her hips, and she realized he was adjusting her. He was growing hard again.

He smiled, then dipped his head down and sucked on her breast. Pleasure spiked through her all the way down from her nipple to her womb. She moaned again, and tried to move his face. She wanted to taste him. He lifted his head for just a moment, eyes twinkling, then captured the other breast.

She was going to have an orgasm right there—and then, with that thought, she did. Long and slow and thrumming through her. Her breath sounded ragged. She grabbed his shoulders, holding him in place, yet somehow he moved from breast to breast as if he couldn't figure out which tasted better.

Then he wrapped his arms around her, and turned her

over without losing their connection. He slowly moved inside her, his gaze on hers, those blue eyes holding her in place as his face reddened with pleasure.

She wanted to watch him have this orgasm, but she couldn't, because she had another. The slowness triggered something deep inside her, something she'd never felt, some kind of slow-motion quake that she hadn't known her body capable of.

She tried to regain control, tried to move faster, but he slid his hands to her hips and held her there while he was on his knees, rocking in and out, out and in, until she wanted to scream.

It took longer than she thought possible—either she had several orgasms one after the other, or she had the longest one of her entire life. Just when she thought she might die from it all, he gasped, smiled half-apologetically, and poured into her, making her feel even warmer, wetter, and fuller inside.

He leaned forward, landing on his elbows, as if he was afraid he'd crush her.

"My God," she said. "What the hell was that?"

"I don't know," he said, his voice shaking. "But you may have corrupted me forever."

"Me?" she asked. "You—"

He kissed her. Really kissed her, not one of those pecks men so often gave her after sex.

"I have to move," he said, and she thought he meant he was going to slip out of her. Instead, he pushed himself up on his hands, and that was when she realized he had twisted himself into the strangest position just to stay on the couch. It was too small for him, like everything in this room.

Except her.

"The bed's bigger," she said.

"Good for it," he said as he tried to stand. Instead, he fell against the couch, then slid onto the floor.

She tilted his head back and kissed him upside down. It was such a novel sensation for both of them that rest became impossible.

They gave up all thoughts of bed and concentrated only on each other.

For the first time in her life, she trusted someone completely.

If only for a few hours. A few blissful hours she would never trade for anything in the entire universe.

Chapter 5

JACK WOKE UP BEFORE SKYE DID. HE HAD NO IDEA HOW they had gotten into the bed. He only knew that they had, and that their bodies had finally given out.

He was pressed against her back, his hands cupping her breasts, his penis against her buttocks. The thought of those buttocks made him stir, but he wasn't sure he should try anything again. She had to be sore. He might even be sore. He didn't know if men could get sore.

He never had before.

He pulled her close. He wasn't sure what would happen next. She had made it clear that she only wanted to spend one night with him, but he wanted to spend more time with her than that. He wondered if every man she had been with wanted more time with her. He had never experienced anything like the last few hours before, and he doubted he ever would again.

He had felt a connection, something more than physical. If he had to guess, he would say that she had too. The problem was that he had to guess. He didn't know her. He didn't know anything about her.

For all he knew, she slept with a different guy at every single space station she stopped at.

She had money, that much was certain. Krell had to charge a lot of money for a suite like this. Hell, it charged a lot of money for that crap-ass room he'd stayed in the first time he was here. This place had to cost a fortune.

He didn't know anyone who came to Krell who could afford that fortune without breaking a lot of laws.

That very thought bothered him, particularly with all the things he had been dealing with lately. He had left the Rovers because he couldn't work for them anymore. They had gone too far, and now, he was here, with a woman he didn't know, in a suite usually frequented by people who made their money illegally.

He should have rolled away. Instead, he didn't move. He just held her, conscious of the time ticking away.

The Rovers were a group of loosely associated assassins who, for whatever reason, refused to join the Assassins Guild. Back when they had hired Jack to vet their clients, he believed the Rovers were more ethical than the Guild. They wouldn't take jobs sanctioned by governments, they wouldn't assassinate anyone without discovering who that person was first, and they often turned down work that seemed shady.

But Jack had joined the Rovers as their main investigator more than a decade before. He had left Tranquility House with only a few skills, one of them the ability to search for things.

He had searched his entire life. That was why he had chosen the last name Hunter. He had arrived at Tranquility House with no last name at all.

He used to say that his name wasn't Jack Hunter. It was Jack, hunter, the hunter being a descriptor, not a designation.

He hadn't lost that feeling; he was still hunting, for his identity, for his work, for everything.

Only at this very moment, he felt like he had found something.

Someone.

She was right. He fit perfectly. More to the point, she fit perfectly.

And it frightened him.

He had never let his guard down this far, particularly not on Krell.

And he had never felt so confused. He honestly didn't know what to do next. Should he get up and leave? Should he wake her? Should he make love to her again?

He wanted to make love to her again. And again. And again.

He gave in. He kissed the spot where her lovely neck met her well-sculpted shoulder.

She sighed and squirmed against him.

He slid a hand away from her breast, across her flat belly, and through that small shock of black hair that he had explored in depth the night before. She was wet.

So he slipped inside her and cupped her against him, gently rocking them both. She moaned as she came awake—literally coming and waking up at the same time. Which made him come too—faster than he ever had in his life.

He hadn't thought he had anything left in him, but apparently he did.

She shifted, then pulled away from him, startling him. She hadn't done that before.

Was she angry? Did she dislike being awakened like this? Did she feel taken advantage of?

He hadn't meant to make her feel bad.

She rolled over and faced him. The pillow had creased one cheek, making her look just a little dangerous. Her black hair was tousled, her lips swollen.

She smiled at him, and to his relief, the smile reached her eyes. She put a hand on his jaw, holding him in place, as she kissed him thoroughly.

"Good morning to you too," she said and leaned back. "Although I'm not sure it's morning."

"Me, either," he said.

She ran a hand through his hair, finger-combing it. "This room has its own water shower," she said.

He felt a shock run through him. Something in her tone made that comment dismissive, not suggestive. He couldn't tell what it was, since she still looked soft and kissable.

"Do I need one?" he asked.

Her eyes became distant, even though her expression didn't change. "I just figured you'd appreciate the luxury, especially here on Krell."

"I worry what the water's got in it," he said, "especially here on Krell."

Her smile widened, and she came back to those eyes. "I've used it for two days and I haven't melted yet."

He tucked a loose strand of her hair behind her ear. Maybe he could spend more time with her. Maybe he could meet her somewhere else, just for a day. (A night.) Or just a few hours. (Or another evening in bed.)

"You haven't told me who you are yet, either," he said in the most unthreatening tone he could muster.

Her smile changed. Her lips moved ever so slightly, so that the smile didn't seem pleased, it seemed like it was tinged with an apology. He'd never seen anyone whose smallest expressions conveyed so much.

Or maybe he never noticed such things before.

"You know who I am," she said. "I'm the woman you spent the night with."

"I'd love to spend another night," he said, stroking her hair.

"Me, too," she said, and his heart actually leaped.

Then she rolled away from him, and got out of bed, all in one quick movement.

"Unfortunately, we agreed this was a one-time thing."

And she, clearly, was going to enforce it.

He sighed. "We did. I enjoyed myself so much"—which was a hell of an understatement—"that I was hoping we could renegotiate."

"Maybe," she said, and that leaping feeling returned. "If we meet again on some other crappy space station."

And the feeling fell away. He was more than disappointed. He felt… well, he didn't want to think about how he felt. He would have to use words he never used, like *heartbroken*. He didn't believe those words meant anything, especially to a man like him.

"Would you like the shower first?" she asked.

Normally, he would let her have it. After all, she was already out of bed. But he needed to get out of here. He couldn't spend any more time with her, not if she hadn't felt the way he had.

And she clearly hadn't.

"Yes, I'll experiment with that shower first," he said, getting up slowly. He was sore, but in unexpected places. His elbows were scraped. The muscles on his thighs complained, probably from that unexpected joining near the couch, where his legs finally gave out.

He smiled at her, hoping the smile didn't look as fake as it felt. Then he walked, back straight, to the bathroom, amazed at the effort it took not to grab her and hold her against him one last time.

Chapter 6

SKYE WATCHED JACK WALK AROUND THE BED. THE TOP of his head brushed against the ceiling here as well, yet he was in perfect proportion. She wouldn't have thought tall would be so appealing, and it was.

He was.

A shiver ran through her. She had been alone for her entire life, and she had just guaranteed that she would remain alone.

What would it cost to meet him occasionally on some space resort somewhere or in some hotel in an out-of-the-way city on some distant planet?

But she knew the answer to that. She had stayed awake most of the night thinking about it, and had finally dozed off maybe an hour or two before he woke her up again. Pleasantly. Sex had never been exciting and pleasant and addictive all at the same time.

The answer, she thought, forcing herself to concentrate, was that she had too many obligations to the Assassins Guild and had made too many enemies. She didn't know who Jack was or who he worked for. He might actually be someone she should have avoided.

She hadn't checked, and she wouldn't. She would do her best to forget him when she left Krell later today.

It would take a hell of an effort, but she'd made hellish efforts before.

She could do it again.

The shower squealed on. He was more trusting than she was. She had actually tested that water for contaminants before stepping into it naked. The water had been remarkably clean, probably something else she was paying for in this hugely expensive suite.

She shivered again, then yanked a sheet off the bed and wrapped it around herself. The problem wasn't with the environmental controls. It was with her decision, and she knew it.

She wanted to stay with him. She wanted to see if she could make him as addicted to her as she already was to him.

And maybe he was. He had asked exactly what she had been thinking: he had asked to meet her again.

She had to say no. Maybe she would find him when she was no longer part of the Guild, but right now, she didn't dare involve anyone else in it.

Especially someone she didn't know.

She needed armor. She trailed around the bed and found the clothes she barely remembered discarding. She slipped them on, leaving the sheet crumpled on the floor.

Then she picked up his clothes and cradled them against her. They smelled like him, all warm and safe and sexy. She hadn't realized just how erotic scents could be. Yet his was.

She made herself set the clothing on the side of the bed, then went into the living room so she wouldn't see him naked again. She would say the coldest good-bye she could, and hope he wouldn't give her that look again—the one that mixed desire with sadness. She had barely been able to stand up to it the first time.

She doubted she could stand up to it again.

Chapter 7

Skye stood in the ticket line for transport off Krell. The line wound all the way around this part of the station, with people standing patiently. Everyone knew they'd have a seat, although she couldn't say the same for folks who arrived much later.

She hated ticketing here. No early tickets because people would resell them and gouge whoever bought the seat. The transport companies had inflicted this policy on Krell, not the other way around, because too much forgery had happened and too many people ended up with matching tickets for the same seat.

She always forgot about this inconvenience until she waited in line. Usually she didn't mind. The ticket station had food and drink vendors, entertainment vendors, and everything else she could think of. All kinds of music competed for her attention, and the air smelled strongly of beer and fried foods.

But she wasn't paying any attention to any of that. Instead, she found herself looking at the door frames and ceiling, wondering if Jack could even stand in this area as long as she had. He would have to hunch.

And she would have to stop thinking about him.

Now.

Not that such internal commands had worked so far. She had barely allowed herself to look at him when they said good-bye in her suite. She had given him a cold smile, and a brief wave of the fingers, as if he hadn't mattered to her at all, as if the time they shared hadn't been the most amazing time in her entire life.

For his part, he hadn't said another word about another meeting. Instead, he had smiled at her and thanked her for the shower. If he had thanked her for anything else, she would have come unglued.

She had no idea what he thought of her. Did he think she did this at every port with a different guy every time? And did it matter if he did think that way?

She tugged on the sleeves of her sweater. She had put it on, as well as a pair of leggings because she couldn't get warm. Leaving him did send little shivers through her, and a hot shower hadn't helped.

Nothing would help. She was letting a good man walk away from her, and she was doing it for all the right reasons.

Although she had no guarantee he was good except for that inexplicable sense she got about people, the way she could see right down to their core. She liked his core. She liked the parts jutting out of his core. She liked everything about him, including the way his eyes darkened when he had an orgasm. She wondered how many women had seen that.

And then she had to remind herself—sternly, forcefully—that it was none of her business.

Jack Hunter, whoever he was, was no longer someone she needed to concern herself with. He was already a memory, albeit a very, very, very good one.

She was so preoccupied she almost missed a familiar form skirting the transport line. The form belonged to Liora Olliver, one of the toughest, hardest assassins to go through the Guild.

Skye should know, since she and Liora had tested together. Liora aced every assassin test. Skye rarely passed them. Often Skye forfeited them, unwilling to stalk someone and kill him in what she believed was cold blood.

The depth of her belief and that talent of hers which enabled her to see people clearly convinced the heads of the Guild to let her be a spy and nothing more. The Guild's director, Kerani Ammons, actually told Skye that she was unusual, that they'd never had anyone like her before.

Skye felt good about that for a few days after it happened, and then she encountered the taunts of the other trainees. Assassins in training, like Liora, had made fun of Skye in ways that still carried pain whenever she thought of them.

Liora had no reason to be here. Skye always checked to see which assassins were nearby before she arrived anywhere. That way, she wouldn't have one of those awkward "hello" moments that could derail a job—hers or the assassin's.

It was common courtesy, and it was a routine that Skye followed religiously.

So did Liora. Or at least, that was what it seemed like. But as Skye thought about it, she realized that she hadn't seen Liora's name on a manifest in months. Liora had either been out of the game or stalking very big prey.

Or both.

Yet, if it were big prey, then Skye should have known about it. Shouldn't she?

She slipped out of the line almost without thinking about it. She had discovered a lot of disturbing material in the last few months, things that pointed at some kind of plot against the Guild itself. She had sent some of the information back to the Guild and hadn't received any response.

Of course, they didn't owe her a response. They might have simply sent out some of their best operatives to investigate the threats.

Liora was one of their best operatives.

Liora was small and slender with short cropped black hair. One of Skye's constant irritations growing up was that instructors—particularly early in a course—would confuse them. Apparently they looked enough alike that the instructors couldn't see past the physical. If they had, they would have seen just how different both women were.

Both got good grades, but Liora always scored well on weapons use, hand-to-hand fighting, and willingness to go after an opponent. Skye's hand-eye coordination wasn't that good, so she and weapons didn't always get along, and she would back off if she didn't think she had a good reason to fight someone.

She had only fought Liora once, and had lost miserably. Liora didn't have any empathy for her opponent, even though the fights were in class, and she had known her opponents for much of her life. Liora fought to win.

Skye would back down, which always got her poor marks. In mock fights, assassins were supposed to recognize that their lives were often on the line, just like their targets' lives were. Skye couldn't make that mental leap. She wasn't sure if she could make it if her life really were in danger. So far, in all the years she had been working off her debt to the Guild, she hadn't had to find out.

Skye wove through the crowd, careful to keep someone

between herself and Liora. She wasn't sure why she felt it imperative that Liora didn't see her, but Skye trusted her gut. Her gut had gotten her into and out of serious situations before, often without harming anyone.

Something about Liora seemed off to her, but she wouldn't be able to describe what that something was.

Liora made her way to the central concourse of Krell, doing her best to remain out of sight just like Skye was. Skye had no idea whom Liora was trying to avoid, but she thought someone else might be around. Or maybe she was trying to avoid the surveillance cameras which everyplace—including Krell—had in abundance.

The difference between Krell and most other places was that Krell never released its footage to the authorities—any authorities. Krell sat in the NetherRealm, the neutral space between several jurisdictions, and resolutely refused to join any of them for any reason.

Liora headed to the very bar that Skye and Jack had frequented the night before. Only Liora ducked inside.

Skye wasn't sure how she could follow—Liora would recognize her after all. Then she saw where Liora sat, toward the back, facing the wall, obviously thinking more about going unseen and unrecognized than worrying about her own safety.

Odd. That went against training. But sometimes just acting on training alone allowed others to find Assassins Guild members. Maybe the improper position was more of Liora's cover.

Skye elbowed her way to the bar. She ordered that same lemon fizzy thing she had ordered the night before. Only this time, she sat at the very edge of the bar, just behind an obese man who seemed to be a regular here.

He had been in the very same spot nursing a different drink the night before.

Liora sat alone. Skye scanned the area including the concourse, looking for another familiar face. Through the open door, she saw one, but not one she expected.

She saw Jack.

He didn't look inside the bar. Instead, he headed away from it, his movements furtive and odd. Her heart pounded. She both wanted him to look in her direction and she didn't want him to. Her cheeks flushed.

She felt like a vulnerable teenager—or what she thought a vulnerable teenager must have felt like, because she had never been one. All those crushes, all those sleepless nights thinking about attractions and the opposite sex—she left all of that to girls like Liora. Skye had had secret crushes, but she had never acted on them and had always ignored them.

In some ways, she continued to do that now. She didn't want to see Jack again. The night before, that marvelous night, had to become a memory. She couldn't lose focus or she would make mistakes.

And mistakes would cost too much—either she would lose her life or she would lose her freedom, at least for another few years. She worried about that more than dying; she'd either be imprisoned, or demoted within the Guild and forced to stay there.

Jack had stopped just outside the Starcatcher. He looked a little lost. Was he searching for her?

She took a deep breath and made herself look away from him. What he thought no longer mattered. She was done with him. She had to be.

She focused on Liora. A beer sat in front of her,

untouched. Then a man put his hand on her back in a familiar way as he sat across from her. He grinned as if he knew her—and he must have, because Liora hadn't jumped when he touched her. Nor had she reacted in any other way.

He was slight with scruffy brown hair, and a jacket that he kept pulled around him. Among the shady characters who made their way around Krell, he looked shadier than usual. Or maybe Skye just thought that because he was with Liora.

Skye hoped Liora would continue to disregard protocol. Because if she did, then Skye could find out what was happening. She had an enhancement that allowed her to focus her hearing the way she could focus her vision. But the Assassins Guild had jammers that blocked such equipment.

Apparently Liora wasn't using her jammer, because her voice became stronger as Skye focused on it.

"You're late," Liora said to the man.

He shrugged. "I didn't think you cared."

"My time is precious," she said.

Skye frowned. She'd never heard an assassin have a conversation like this, but then, maybe Liora was playing a role to get close to this guy. Although why she would need role-playing was beyond Skye. If this guy was the target, he'd be pretty easy to take out.

Maybe he was supposed to lead her to the target.

"There are things about this job that make it difficult," Liora said.

Skye twirled the straw in her fizzy drink, keeping her head down, but listening closely. She had no idea what was going on, but she didn't like it.

"You are the third in line," Liora said. "I'll reserve your time, but there's a good chance that we won't need your services at all."

"I find it ironic that you're even talking to me," the guy said.

"If you don't want the work—"

"Oh, it's interesting," he said. "I'm all in. My team is all in. Just let us know when you need us."

"*If* we need you," Liora said. "Give me an account to send the information. I'd rather not discuss the rest of this in person."

The man chuckled. "And here I thought sending it would be dicier."

"No one will know who the job came from except you," Liora said. "And the payment will go through so many accounts that even the best accountant couldn't track it."

Skye felt cold. What was going on? She wanted to turn around and just ask, but knew better. In fact, she really had to make sure Liora didn't see her at all, because there was something very, very wrong here.

"It's not my neck," the guy said. "Everyone already thinks I'm a criminal. But you, you're Assassins Guild. You have light and right on your side."

"Or I will when this is done," Liora said. "I'll send everything to you."

"I'll be waiting with bated breath," he said.

"Whatever that means."

A movement caught Skye's eye, and she bowed her head. Liora was leaving the table. Skye leaned forward just a little so she could see around the obese man.

Liora didn't look back. She headed out of the bar as if nothing had happened.

Skye resisted the urge to glance at the guy Liora had met. Skye already had a good image of him, and would track down who he was when she had a private net connection. She didn't want to try looking up anything in a place this public.

She sat for just a moment, wondering if she should follow Liora. Skye had other work she needed to do—an entire list of people she should be vetting for the Guild—but lately a lot of strange behavior had surfaced while she worked other jobs, behavior involving the Guild, behavior she didn't understand.

And because she didn't understand it, she investigated. Unlike so many of her colleagues, she didn't care if something happened to the Guild. In fact, she rather hoped it would.

That way, she could get out sooner.

Or maybe, just maybe, the right information might free her. And maybe Liora would lead her to that information, whatever the hell it was.

Chapter 8

JACK STOOD OUTSIDE THE SMALL FENCE THAT ENCLOSED the Starcatcher's open-air section. He felt shaken. He didn't usually feel shaken. Tired, yes, or maybe even unsettled, but shaken was new. Or old.

He hadn't felt shaken since he was twelve. A horrible young couple had promised him they would adopt him, and then turned around and adopted another boy in Tranquility House. That boy, the staff had told Jack, was better behaved, smarter, and just plain nicer.

Jack hadn't talked to anyone for days. He felt like his entire world had fallen apart.

And, oddly, he had felt like that since he left Skye.

That coldness in her eyes as he got dressed reminded him of the couple. They had seemed so loving at first, and then they had rejected him.

He knew he was reacting out of an old, old place, and Skye hadn't rejected him at all. She had told him, right from the start, what she expected—and he had agreed to that expectation.

The fact that the entire incident had disturbed him was about him, not her. And about his damn heart.

He hadn't realized how very vulnerable it was.

He scanned the open-air section of Starcatcher for Rikki Bastogne. She had called this meeting and he had suggested the place, much as she hated it.

She had been his only friend in the early years of

Tranquility House. In fact, she was the one who suggested he stop waiting for someone to parent him, and to take care of himself. She had even told him to pick his own last name.

He was glad he would see her today. But it seemed she hadn't arrived yet. Most of the tables were full, but she wasn't at any of them.

Neither was Skye, not that he expected to see her again. If she followed her plan, she was probably gone already. His heart ached at the thought.

He had no idea how to find her again, or how she would feel if he did.

He wondered if she had thought the night as special as he had or if she had just led him on.

Not that it mattered. It was one night. He had to remember that, and be grateful for that much. If he hadn't had last night, he would never have known how spectacular lovemaking could feel.

He took a table near the concourse, and ordered his favorite burger from the robotic server that floated near him. He also got a special soda this time and he would drink it. All of it.

Hell, he might even treat himself to a beer later.

Given the year he'd had so far, he deserved it.

Out of the corner of his eye, he thought he saw Skye. But when he turned, he realized he was looking at a woman who had the same body shape and wedge-cut dark hair. Other than that, she looked nothing like Skye. Her face was hardened, her mouth downturned into a perpetual scowl.

She was a woman he didn't want to cross, one of the many people on Krell he hoped he would never see again.

The burger arrived. He took a bite, and then saw Rikki make her way down the concourse. Her hair was red instead of its usual rich brown, and she looked a little too thin. Something had shaken her up.

He felt a momentary sense of disappointment. All morning he had been looking forward to confiding in her. But he didn't think he'd have a chance now.

He hadn't seen Rikki look this upset since he'd met her. When she first arrived at Tranquility House she had been through such a traumatic experience, she hadn't talked for weeks. It wasn't until that night those horrible potential adoptive parents had rejected him that she had said anything, and then it had been to give him advice.

The least he could do was listen to her. After all, she had contacted him. She clearly didn't need to hear his problems right now.

She grinned when she saw him, then stopped next to the table. She picked up a spoon and rubbed some dirt off it.

"I can't believe you're eating here," she said as she picked up a napkin and wiped off a chair. Then she spread another napkin on the chair itself.

He said, "I can't believe you're going to sit on that. I think they wash the napkins less than they wash the chairs."

She started and for a minute, he thought she was going to shove the chair away. Instead, she turned just a little green.

"Then I'm just going to stand," she said.

He grinned. He had missed her. She had been his best friend forever, and she still was, no matter what was going on. Their relationship was purely platonic and would always be that way. He thought of her as his sister, not as the beautiful woman she had become.

"Hover," he said, his mouth full. "You're just going to hover."

She rolled her eyes. "Whatever. You could be a gentleman and give me your jacket to sit on."

"My jacket has been staying in this hellhole for the past three days, waiting for her ladyship to arrive." As if that had been all he was doing here. He was still investigating, even though he had enough evidence against the Rovers to... what? That was what he hadn't yet figured out.

She muttered something, then gave up and sat down.

They bantered for a few more minutes because that was their routine—that was how they felt comfortable. Then they'd get to the important stuff.

Still, as Rikki bitched about the restaurant and the food, he smiled at her. He had missed her. And he didn't realize how much he needed a conversation with an old friend until right now.

Chapter 9

SKYE STEPPED OUT OF THE BAR. SHE HAD A FEW errands to run: she needed to reserve her room again and then she needed to find some kind of private place to check the scruffy guy's image. Her stomach was a bit queasy from the lemon fizzy thing, or maybe it was the lack of sleep, or maybe the strangeness she had just witnessed.

Liora had taken off down the concourse a few minutes ago, but Skye didn't want to follow her. Now that she knew Liora was here, she could actually track her, using the Guild system. Generally assassins on the job kept their Guild tracker off or on low, but Liora wasn't acting like she was on any job at all. So Skye had checked as she stepped out, and saw that Liora hadn't been thinking about her tracker. The folks at the Guild on Kordita couldn't track her at the moment, but any assassin within a five-hour radius probably could.

She scanned the concourse for the scruffy guy. He had gone in the opposite direction from the one Liora had taken. Skye could see his back as he made his way through the crowd. He was heading the same way she had to go if she was going to renew that reservation.

She sighed. At least that would give her an opportunity to study him.

Then, because she couldn't help it, she glanced at the Starcatcher. She wanted to lie to herself, to pretend that she wasn't looking for Jack, that she was actually thinking of a greasy burger to settle her stomach.

But lying wasn't going to work. If only she were already free of the Guild. If only her life were her own. She would go to him, and say, *Forget what I told you about a single night. Let's acknowledge that we're in space. There is no such thing as day and night, and we can make sure our single night lasts for weeks.*

She smiled at the thought. Maybe if she saw him again, after she got out. Maybe she would track him, like she tracked so many other people. Maybe she would "accidentally" show up wherever he was, and proposition him all over again.

The very thought reminded her of that spark in his eye when he realized she had propositioned him, a spark that she saw later when he touched her bare skin for the first time.

The memory aroused parts of her that she thought too tired to respond. Then she shook her head at herself.

And in doing so, she caught a glimpse of Jack sitting in the crowded open-air section of the Starcatcher.

She did need lunch. She could do some of her work from the open-air section of the Starcatcher. She could take Jack's hand and see if he wanted to change his mind—one more real night only—and then, she could collect a few more memories.

After all, she had so very few good ones from the rest of her life, who would blame her if she stored up one or two more?

She took a few steps across the concourse and froze as a buxom redhead talked to Jack. He laughed, and so did she. Then she wiped off a nearby chair with a napkin.

He was clearly inviting the woman—who was drop-dead gorgeous—to sit with him.

Drop-dead gorgeous and in fantastic shape, the kind women got without enhancements, with a lot of physical work. Rather like Skye.

Only unlike Skye, this woman had other unenhanced parts that seemed to come as standard issue for attracting men—the large breasts, the narrow waist, the stunning face. And she looked so comfortable with Jack.

If Skye had to guess—and she rarely had to guess, that internal sense of hers was right so often—she would say that the relationship between these two had something to do with work, and a whole lot more.

They seemed so comfortable with each other.

Skye watched, mesmerized. She should have moved away, stepped out of view, paid attention to her surroundings. But she couldn't.

The woman sat down, ordered, and then her smile faded. She seemed upset. And that upset seemed to bother Jack.

Not only had they been close once, they still were.

Skye had to concentrate to breathe. She had to remind herself that she had set the rules. A one-time thing. A man who clearly told her he didn't do that ever. He had been so shy, so uncertain, that she had found it a turn-on.

She had thought him less experienced, not *in*experienced, just not quite as comfortable as she was. But what if he had actually had a girlfriend? A wife? A partner? Someone who let him go off with other women because it was hard to maintain a relationship out here, but someone to whom he felt a loyalty.

He had said he didn't, but men lied when they were

being propositioned. And she had already told him it was a one-night thing. Maybe he thought the relationship was none of Skye's business.

Maybe his uncertainty had nothing to do with his experience, and everything to do with this woman. Maybe, despite an openness (that, granted, Skye was just assuming was there), maybe he felt like he had cheated on the lovely redhead.

Maybe that was why the redhead seemed close to tears.

He reached across the table and put his hand over hers. Then she slipped her fingers through his.

The gesture had a lot of tenderness, on both sides.

The tenderness made Skye's heart hurt.

She wasn't jealous. She had nothing to be jealous of. She had no relationship with this man. Just a great night, one she would always treasure.

Or maybe she was jealous, but not of the other woman's relationship with Jack. Maybe she was just jealous because no one in her entire life had treated her with such tenderness, in a restaurant, in the middle of a conversation.

Or anywhere. No one had touched her out of love, not even her parents, who, if she told herself the truth, had abandoned her when she was ten, which was how she ended up on the Guild's doorstep. Not because they had brought her there, but because the man they had left her with finally gave up on them ever returning, and dumped her on the Guild.

She always took responsibility for that. When that "uncle" had dropped her at the Guild, she had not researched where her parents had disappeared to. She hadn't tracked them down for the very first time. Before that, she always had. Before that, she'd catch up with them, and then they'd find a creative way to dump her again.

She blamed herself for the Guild because she just didn't want to trace her parents all over the universe again.

She'd been following people for her entire life, spying on them and tracking them, and she was getting tired.

Just like she was tired of thc fact that no one had ever touched her the way that Jack touched the redhead.

Jack hadn't even touched her that way. Not last night. His touch had been gentle, yes, but it had had purpose, and that purpose had been brought him as much gratification as it brought her.

This touch with redhead seemed like something he did for comfort, something that was selfless.

Skye blinked. She had something in her eye. She ran a finger over her lashes, found moisture. Odd. She usually thought it too dry on Krell.

But it was a sign. She needed to put Jack in her past. She had Liora to worry about and a few other jobs to finish.

First, however, she needed a room. And it wouldn't be the one she shared with Jack. She couldn't think about him any longer. She'd get something small and unobtrusive.

And if there was a God, she would never ever come back.

Chapter 10

Skye made her way to Upscale Reservations. It was a hole-in-the-wall, given to past guests who had paid a lot of money on Krell. Too many of Krell's customers specialized in identification theft, so Krell used all sorts of methods to ensure that each "guest" was the one she was supposed to be.

The higher up Skye went on their guest list, the more in-person hoops she had to jump through. She always thought it strange that Krell allowed her through, because she had never once stayed here under her real name.

Still, the name she used made the folks who ran Krell sit up and take notice—primarily because she had been a regular guest for four years.

She opened the door and stepped into an antechamber. To her surprise, the scruffy guy stood off to one side, talking with two other men. They wore similar clothing to the scruffy guy, and had the same scrawny power. They moved away when they saw her, standing outside of normal ear range.

Fortunately, she didn't have normal ears.

She moved toward the main door, but made it seem as if she had a few other things to prepare before she entered. Then she focused her hearing on the scruffy guy. With luck, he would tell her what job he was doing for Liora.

Instead, Skye heard a name she hadn't expected.

"...yes, Jack Hunter," the scruffy guy was saying. "At the Starcatcher."

"He's probably working for someone else now," one of the other men said.

"It doesn't matter who he's working for," the scruffy guy said. "He's still our problem."

Skye's mouth went dry. How many conversations like this had she overheard over the years? None had made her heart rate increase like this one was.

She had to work hard to continue to feign disinterest. She pulled a small reservation tablet from the stand near her. She fiddled with the tablet as she listened.

"You know he won't do anything," the other man said. "He's a good guy."

"That's our problem," the scruffy guy said. "He doesn't think we are any longer."

A light went on near the door. It meant that the reservation room beyond was empty. Skye moved slightly to block that light from the men. She wanted to listen to this conversation for another minute.

"So?" one of the men said. "He's not going to be a problem. He's just an investigator."

"He's talking to Rikki Bastogne right now," the scruffy guy said. "He may be an investigator, but she's not."

"She left long ago," the third man said.

"To go freelance," the scruffy guy said.

"You think she's going to come after us?" the second man said.

"You want to wait to find out?" the scruffy guy said.

Skye frowned. Rikki Bastogne. Why did that name sound familiar? She would have to check it as well—and not just because Jack seemed to know her well.

"She can't take on all of us by herself," the second man said.

"Probably not," the scruffy guy said. "But she can go after some of us one at a time."

"He's just afraid she'll come after him," the third guy said to the second.

"I am not," the scruffy guy snapped. "Just get rid of Hunter. He's a problem."

"Get rid of?" the second guy said. "Are you serious? I'm not killing one of us."

"He's not one of us, don't you get that?" the scruffy guy said.

"He is to me," the second guy said, then pivoted and left.

"You going with him?" the scruffy guy asked.

"Naw. I figure there's money in this. You gonna pay me to take out Hunter?" the third man asked.

"Only if you manage it here," the scruffy guy said. "Otherwise, I'm bringing in real experience."

Skye's breath caught. She pressed her hand on the door frame and let herself inside the empty room. She wanted to flee Upscale Reservations and warn Jack, but she didn't dare—not from the antechamber, anyway.

If she registered again with the hotel part of Krell, she could leave from the back.

She forgot her resolve to get a new room. It would take too long. Instead, she went to the desk. A woman appeared. She was a hologram. Apparently the day was too slow to bring in a real person.

Skye asked to extend her reservation, noting with satisfaction that her voice remained calm as she did so. She had no idea what Jack was into, and she didn't really care.

She liked him. And that was enough. She would warn him about these men.

And Liora.

She wondered what Liora's involvement was. Had the Guild sent her? If so, why would she hire someone else to take out Jack? Liora was an assassin. She could easily kill someone. Liora could have killed Jack as she walked past the open-air part of the Starcatcher, and probably not have gotten caught. She was that good.

Skye didn't know what was going on, but she would figure it out.

She would warn Jack, find out what he knew, and get him out of here.

After that, he was on his own.

Chapter 11

Jack picked up the napkin that Rikki had knocked off her chair when she left. She had hurried away, anxious to leave Krell. Not that he blamed her. She hated it here. She usually worked jobs where she was more comfortable—her last was on a cruise ship.

And that had gotten her into the worst mess of her life.

He crumpled the napkin in his right hand and stared at the remains of the burger on his plate. Having two of those gut-busters in less than twenty-four hours wasn't good for him. He probably should have had the special soda and nothing else.

He sighed. Rikki had left him shaken. She rarely got upset. Never, really, not since they were children.

She had met a man on that cruise, an assassin with the Assassins Guild, and had fallen for him. She swore she hadn't, but Jack knew Rikki.

For the first time in her life, she was in love.

And if what she told Jack was true, she had fallen for the worst man she could possibly have found.

He set the napkin down and smoothed it out. She had asked him for his help. He wanted to do more than vet the guy.

Jack wanted to punch him. Just for upsetting Rikki.

Jack would find out everything he could about the man, even if it put him at odds with the Assassins Guild. He was already at odds with the Rovers. What would it matter if he offended the other large group of assassins in this sector?

He smiled without humor and started to stand, when a hand caught his left shoulder and forced him back down. He started to worm away, but the grip got tighter.

"Don't move," said a familiar voice he thought he would never hear again. "Pretend like you're happy to see me."

That wasn't hard. He was. He had to exercise great control over his face to keep from grinning like an idiot.

Skye stood next to him.

He turned, grabbed her by the waist, lifted her, and stood up all at the same time. He brought her close, hugging her like she was a long-lost girlfriend.

He had thought she was lost, just not that long ago.

Her body remained stiff for one half second, then she wrapped herself around him, burying her face in his neck, like she had done the night before.

When she had been naked.

He was instantly aroused and he knew she could feel it.

But to his surprise, she didn't look at him and grin. Instead, she wrapped one hand around his head, holding it in place.

"I just overheard something," she said. "I don't know what it is, but there's a man on this station who wants to kill you. He'll get paid if he does it here and soon."

She spoke so softly no one else could have heard it.

And he couldn't lean back to see her face. So he kissed the spot behind her ear instead, then whispered, "How could you know this?"

"I overheard it," she said. "You have a ship?"

"Yeah," he said, his heart sinking. Was this some kind of scam?

"Let's go there. It'll be safe."

"Not if someone is after me," he whispered.

"I want to show you an image of who is," she said. "I have no idea who he is."

Jack's heart rate had increased and not just because he held Skye. "Show me now."

"I can't," she said. "He might track the information."

"I have a jammer," Jack said.

This time, she rocked back and looked him in the face. Normal people did not carry jammers. Normal people had no reason to shut off any access to the various nets and webs and information flow that constantly swirled around them.

His gaze met hers. Her surprise seemed genuine. Or maybe she was just a good actress. Maybe she had known who he was all along.

"All right," she said. "Is the jammer portable?"

"Yeah," he said softly.

"Well, then," she said with a smile. "I still have my room."

That sentence should have made him happy. It didn't. For all he knew, Skye was trying to isolate him. It was an Assassins Guild trick—pretend to fall for someone, get him alone, and then kill him.

But if Skye was using that trick, why hadn't she killed him the night before?

He only had a second or two to decide if he could trust her.

He took a deep breath and forced himself to smile. "Well," he said. "Let's go back to your room. After all, I fit there."

Her smile seemed genuine. "Yes," she said softly. "You do."

Chapter 12

Jack followed Skye to her room, deliberately hanging back just a bit. He had left his jammer on. He had two internal links, which was probably two more than he should have had. Most assassins and most Rovers had none.

Internal links meant that someone could receive instant communication. It also meant that someone could be tracked easily.

Unless he had a jammer.

Jack had lied to Skye. He had three jammers, one internal as an enhancement, and two that he carried with him. He had had only the external one on when he sat down with Rikki. As he made his way to Skye's room, he turned on the internal jammer.

His heart pounded. He had no idea what she was about, but he had decided to trust her.

Even so, it felt odd.

She unlocked the door and pushed it open. The room looked no different than it had when he left it, except that dishes sat on one of the tables. Apparently, Skye had ordered some room service breakfast.

He worked hard at not looking at that couch. It was too short for him, but he had liked it anyway—or at least, he had liked how they had used it.

Skye did not seem interested in using it at the moment.

In fact, she had moved far away from him, as if

she were afraid he was going to jump her when the door closed.

"Still have your jammer on?" she asked.

He nodded.

She pulled out a tablet, then poked at it. He hadn't seen many tablets outside the Guild. And Rikki had a few. Assassins seemed to prefer disposable communications methods to links attached to their bodies.

His heart rate increased.

Was Skye an assassin? Had she fooled him after all? He had heard about the Black Widow assassin, a woman who toyed with her prey before she killed them. She slept with them, and sometimes got deeply involved with them, then murdered them, and moved on.

It couldn't be Skye. He would know, wouldn't he? He was an information guy.

But then, he really hadn't felt like he was in danger around her until just a few minutes ago.

He would know an assassin, right? Rikki had been one for years, and there was a part of her that was just a bit colder than the average person. Colder than he was, certainly. And she had always been that way. She could shut down part of herself, do something difficult for the good of others—or so she said—and then move on without it having an obvious effect on her.

He both admired that trait and feared it. He had certainly used it, growing up. Rikki had often defended him physically, even though he was always the bigger of the two of them.

He wished Rikki had links; he wished he could contact her now.

Skye handed the tablet to him. "You know him?"

Jack held her gaze for a long moment. He realized that he hadn't played this right; he wasn't acting surprised that someone was trying to kill him.

Of course, he wasn't surprised. Not after all he'd done. But he had never told Skye who he was, never said what he did, never explained anything about himself.

And the average person (there that stupid phrase was again) was never afraid of being assassinated. Or killed. Or robbed, for that matter.

But then, the average person rarely showed up on Krell.

It was too late to hide his initial reaction. And she seemed genuinely worried. A small frown line had formed between her eyes, and her mouth was thin. He wanted to kiss the frown away, but held back.

Instead, he took the tablet and looked down.

His breath caught. The image on the tablet belonged to Filip Heller, the nominal—maybe the actual—head of the Rovers. He was sitting in a familiar setting—Jack recognized the wall behind him—but he couldn't place it. Somewhere on Krell, obviously.

Heller had grown his hair out, and he had just enough of a beard to look like he hadn't shaved in a few days.

It was one of those deliberately bad disguises that the Rovers sometimes used when they were on a job. They wanted to be recognized by their client, but not by the target.

Jack had always thought that strange, but then, most Rovers weren't well-known among the general population. Hell, most assassins weren't.

"This is the man who's after me?" he asked, still looking down. He felt disconcerted. He had known he offended the Rovers, had known they might even try something drastic, but he hadn't expected Heller to do it.

"He sent two men after you," she said softly.

Jack looked up, his hand still wrapped around the tablet. She hadn't moved. She seemed to know this was a delicate moment for him.

"One of them declined the job," she said. "The other one has until you leave Krell to finish it."

Jack nodded. If Heller was hiring people, then more than one assassin would come after him.

Rikki wasn't affiliated with the Rovers—she hadn't been for years—so she wouldn't know anything about this. And given the turmoil in her own life, Jack couldn't ask her for help.

He was frightened. And that realization startled him.

He hoped the fear didn't show on his face.

"Who is that?" Skye asked.

She seemed genuinely interested, genuinely concerned. And he had never felt so alone or vulnerable in his life.

Of course, he had learned through countless investigations that when a man was alone and vulnerable, someone would always come around to take advantage of him.

But there was no point in lying about Heller's identity. She had his image, and Filip Heller was in countless databases, as a wanted felon in a variety of cultures.

"Where did you overhear this?" he asked, hoping she would take the misdirection.

She opened her mouth, then closed it, and sighed. She extended her hand for the tablet.

"You don't believe me?" she asked.

"Oh, I do," he said.

"You just don't know if you can trust me."

A small thread of relief ran through him. Just that tiny bit of understanding made him feel better. He really was vulnerable. He braced himself. She was going to cite their night together as a basis for trust.

"I can understand that," she said. "I haven't told you who I am or what I do."

She got that, at least. For all he knew, she was the Rover. He felt stupid now for failing to check.

A man deserved one night off, didn't he? One night worth enjoying?

He still clutched the tablet. "Thank you for the warning," he said. "I appreciate it."

He needed a plan, and he wasn't sure how to make it. Or where to make one. His ship was now compromised. He couldn't stay on Krell either. And taking a transport seemed too risky.

He wasn't used to thinking like this. He had been an investigator forever. He had gone somewhere, found information, and then he had left. Yes, people remembered him—how could they not, he was so tall!—but they never saw him as a threat, because he hadn't been a threat. Not to them.

He glanced at the door.

"You're going back out there?" she asked, and her voice was filled with concern.

"Yeah," he said. Maybe he could risk getting on his ship. Maybe he could get away.

"These men," she said, "they know what they're doing, don't they?"

"Yeah," he said.

"And you don't even carry a weapon," she said.

It had been a point of pride for him. He had been affiliated with the Rovers, but he hadn't been *of* the Rovers. He had been different, not a killer. Someone who prevented them from killing the wrong people, he used to say.

Until Heller took over. And then Heller would correct him: *You're just making sure we're taking out the right people*.

Even then, a few years ago, that sentence had bothered Jack. "Taking out" was not the way he wanted to think about the Rovers. And "the right people" meant that the people Rovers killed were legitimate targets.

Over time, there seemed to be fewer legitimate targets. Just people who deserved to die—according to the Rover who killed them.

"You have to trust someone," Skye said.

He let out an involuntary laugh. "And you think it should be you."

"We have that man in common," she said, and it was Jack's turn to frown in confusion.

"I thought you didn't know who he was," Jack said.

"I don't," she said. "But it seems he's here to do more than one job. And I want to find out what the other job is."

Job. People in his profession used that phrase for an assassination. It was a job. Nothing more, nothing less.

He felt his heart sink. So she was an assassin after all.

"You want to hook up with a man who's being targeted?" Jack asked.

"Apparently, you forgot," she said with a smile. "We've already hooked up."

"I'll never forget that." Jack didn't smile. He didn't

feel like smiling at all. "But I think it would be better if we followed your original plan."

"Because you've got a killer after you," she said.

He nodded.

"Did you do something worth dying for?" she asked, and the question seemed to have a deep meaning for her. That frown had grown deeper.

"Clearly this man believes so," Jack said, shaking the tablet.

She sighed. "You have no good options, you know."

"Believe me, I know," he said.

"I'm the best you've got," she said.

"I'm not sure why you're trying so hard to convince me," he said.

She nodded once in obvious surprise. "You know, I'm not sure either."

And that comment, more than anything else, calmed him just a bit more. If she were trying to con him, she should have continued to push. Instead, she admitted a weakness.

"Give me the tablet," she said, reaching for it.

He still didn't let go.

"You know I'm going to figure out who this man is the moment you walk out my door," she said. "So let me figure it out now. Let's see what we can do."

Jack sighed. She was his best choice.

Hell, she was his only realistic choice.

He handed her the tablet, and took a step back, closer to the door. He liked the illusion of escape, even if he was heading into a more dangerous place.

She took the tablet from him, gave him a quick smile, then bent over it.

He should just tell her. But he didn't want to. Better she find out for herself. He would see the change on her face as she reconsidered her offer. And then he could leave.

"Oh," she said softly. "This makes no sense at all."

And neither did her response. It wasn't one he would have predicted. He didn't move for the door—not yet. Instead, he waited—although for what, he had absolutely no idea.

Chapter 13

A Rover? Why would a member of the Assassins Guild hire a Rover?

It hadn't taken long to get the information on that image at all, just a fraction of a second after Skye had activated the tablet's search with the touch of a finger. She had done it as she got the tablet back from Jack.

Jack.

She looked up at him. His expression hadn't changed, but his eyes were so different from last night. They reflected a fear, a surprise, and a resolve that she hadn't noticed ever before.

How had that conversation gone? She reviewed it mentally:

The second guy, the one who refused to go after Jack, had said, *Are you serious? I'm not killing one of us*.

Then Filip Heller had said, *He's not one of us, don't you get that?*

But the other guy defended Jack. *He is to me*, the other guy had said.

Skye wasn't sure what that meant.

Jack's mouth was open just a little. She wanted to kiss it, just to calm him. But she couldn't do that.

He looked ready to bolt.

Assassins didn't feel fear, did they? She never saw actual fear among her colleagues. At least, not when lives were on the line, not even when their own lives were on the line.

She had always heard that Rovers were worse than assassins from the Guild. Rovers were tougher, harder, nastier. Rovers had no sense of right or wrong.

She had gotten none of that from Jack, and she was the person with the gut she had trusted since childhood. That sense was never wrong. She had pitched that sense to the Guild so that she could spy for them to pay off her debts to them, and the notoriously skeptical Guild had agreed with her.

So what had gone wrong here?

One of us. That phrase kept reverberating through her mind.

He had known that this Heller was with the Rovers, and he hadn't wanted to tell her. He had deliberately avoided her direct question.

And now Jack's eyes filled with just a touch of sadness. A Rover and an assassin from the Guild meet in a bar. It sounded like the beginning of a bad joke. That's what she thought about Liora and Heller.

But she could be thinking it about herself and Jack. Except that Skye wasn't an assassin.

It felt like her world, already topsy-turvy from the night before, had just fallen on its side.

"This makes no sense," she said, and realized she had said it again. She had spoken out loud when she first discovered who Heller was.

"That he's a Rover?" Jack asked softly. "Or that I'm affiliated with them?"

He still hovered near the door. He would run out there if she said anything wrong. Maybe, since she had already misjudged him, her assumption that he couldn't take care of himself was wrong. But she still had that feeling so strongly that she didn't want him to go.

Or maybe she was so blinded by the attraction between them that she wasn't trusting her gut.

"Both, actually," she said.

He didn't move. "It doesn't frighten you that I might be a Rover."

Amazing that he saw that so clearly. She didn't think she was usually easy to read. But then, she wasn't acting like a frightened person. She wasn't sure she knew how.

"It surprises me," she said. "You don't seem like the type."

His smile was thin. "What type is that?"

"The kind who kills for a living," she said, wondering what kind of answer he had expected from her.

"People who kill for a living usually aren't obvious about it," he said. "Most folks can't recognize them. That's why assassins are so good at what they do."

"I suppose," she said flatly. She had always recognized them before. Maybe not as actual assassins, but she could see the tendency. She couldn't see it in him.

"Who are you, really?" he asked.

She took a deep breath. This was the moment of truth. She didn't even know how to lie to him. How could she lie away her reaction? This room? Why she was here? How could she convince him that she was an average person when she clearly was not?

"I investigate people for a living," she said.

He started, as if the answer surprised him deeply.

"I usually can tell what a person is, even if I don't know who he is," she said. "Everything about this is surprising me."

"Even Heller?" Jack asked.

"No," she said. "I knew what he was. I just didn't know who he worked for."

"You were surprised he was a Rover," Jack said. "You thought he was from the Assassins Guild?"

When he asked it so plainly, she saw that the assumption made no sense. If Heller had been from the Guild, she would have known him, right?

She hadn't thought that through. Although she might not have known him if he had been a wash-out or a relatively new recruit.

Except that he hadn't looked new.

"You haven't answered me," Jack said. "Who are you?"

He was relying on her. And honestly, she wanted to help him. She couldn't remember the last time she wanted to help anyone.

Maybe it was selfish. Maybe she wanted to think about his rangy six-foot-six frame hunching its way through the sector. Maybe she wanted the possibility of seeing him again, even if she knew realistically that it would never ever happen.

He wouldn't be able to save himself. Even if he was a Rover. An unarmed Rover. Which was just plain strange.

She had investigated his body closely last night. He didn't have the muscles for a man who killed barehanded. And he didn't have the enhancements that some in the Guild used to make their own bodies into weapons.

He should have been armed. That detail bothered her.

A lot.

If she was going to help him, she would have to reveal a lot about herself just to get him off Krell.

"My official name is Skylight Jones." It felt strange to hear herself say that. Had she ever said that to anyone outside of the Guild? She wasn't sure. Not since she had become an adult, anyway. She couldn't call herself a spy. That was too much. She was going to hedge just a little. "I'm an investigator for the Assassins Guild."

He let out a small laugh. Then he shook his head, and laughed again. His gaze didn't meet hers. His laugh grew, until it sounded almost panicked.

"God damn," he said after he managed to collect himself. "What are the odds?"

His reaction was strange.

"The odds?" she asked.

Instead of answering directly, he said, "I didn't lie to you about my name. I'm Jack Hunter. And, until recently, I was an investigator for the Rovers."

Chapter 14

At first, Skye thought he was joking with her. Unlike the Guild, which had rules and regulations, the Rovers didn't. They weren't a real organization, not one with bylaws and meetings. They didn't even have a real headquarters.

She had investigated a number of Rovers, especially lately, and they didn't even seem to have a code of ethics like some groups that skirted the edge of the law did.

Jack didn't belong to the Rovers, not in the way that she had initially thought. It did explain, at least, why he didn't have a weapon, why one man would say *he's one of us* and another man would deny it.

"You can look me up on your little tablet," Jack said, "although it's risky, considering. A tablet that can overcome one of my jammers is powerful indeed, although why you would overcome a jammer to use a public system is beyond me."

She set the tablet on a nearby table. She would talk to him first.

"The tablet has its own database," she said. "I wasn't on any system at all."

He nodded, still looking a bit shocked. She glanced at the tablet, wondering if she should look him up.

Then she realized she no longer trusted him. Not after he claimed he did the same job for the Rovers that she claimed to do for the Guild.

She had misread him. She thought he was a straightforward guy, one who wouldn't lie to her. But he had. And if he worked for the Rovers, he'd been lying to her all along.

Of course, he had laughed when she told him. Was that a laugh of surprise, a laugh of recognition, or the laugh of a man who had just uncovered something he could use?

"I didn't think Rovers had investigators," she said.

"Rovers are subject to laws of the sector like anyone else." He sounded tired. "They're licensed assassins, just not through the Guild. And if they kill someone and get arrested for doing so, they have to show that they have a client who authorized the work and that the work was authorized for a reason that would get the target convicted in at least six cultures on five worlds."

The Guild rarely parsed the rules like that. Instead, the Guild explained to its potential assassins that they had to go after targets who were bad people—mass murderers, serial killers, child rapists—people who had somehow slipped through the existing legal system. People who couldn't be stopped by any other means.

When someone looked at the various rules as coldly as the Rovers seemed to, there was a lot more leeway. A person who stole high-end items could get convicted on most worlds, but by Assassins Guild rules didn't justify an assassination. The Rovers got their difficult reputation partly because they were willing to assassinate someone who committed what the Guild called lesser offenses, someone who had managed to escape (or would escape) conventional justice.

The Guild always denounced the Rovers for their loose interpretation of the rules of paid assassination.

Only, technically, the Rovers rarely violated those rules.

Until lately. She had gotten a lot of hints of actual murder for hire. Murder, not assassination. The Guild defined murder as a death that came out of emotion, not logic, one that was based on betrayal or a personal crime against one human being, not crimes against humanity.

Skye had never entirely understood those distinctions before, and had ridiculed the Guild privately for them. Yet she was standing here, judging a man she was attracted to because he worked for an organization that bent (maybe broke) rules that she had mocked.

"Still," she said, "I didn't think the Rovers cared whether or not they violated treaties or interstellar laws. I thought they took money and did the job."

His cheeks flushed. The color was darker than it had been in the throes of passion, almost as if it matched his mood.

"Still," he said using the same tone that she had just used, "they would need an investigator to help them find the target."

She had offended him. She wasn't exactly sure how, but she had. Apparently, he was sensitive to the accusation that he lacked a moral code.

She didn't dare tell him that she believed most of the Guild members lacked one too, which was why they used the Guild's codes to substitute for their own moral compass.

She had actually said that to Director Ammons once. The director had glared at Skye, but hadn't corrected her, which made Skye believe even more that she was onto something.

"It doesn't matter whether you believe me or not," he

said. "I have to get out of here. I trust that you won't say anything to your Guild counterparts about me?"

She wasn't sure why that mattered. If he left this room, he would probably die.

"And I thank you for the warning," he said. He reached for the door.

"Wait," she said. "I want to help you get off Krell safely."

"Why would you want to do that?" he asked tiredly. "You don't believe me, and even if you did, you think I'm ethically challenged. You Guild people are exceptionally judgmental for people who kill other people for a living."

She supposed she deserved that. Still, she couldn't help being defensive.

"I've never killed anyone,' she said.

He raised his head. "Then how can you be part of the Assassins Guild? Are you a student?"

He seemed to know a lot about Guild customs.

"I'm unusual," she said. "I didn't test well on the assassin's part of the study. I'm very good at investigation."

"So am I. And yet here I am, rather surprised that I'm a target." He sighed. "Right now, I don't need investigators. I'm better off with an assassin. But barring that, I need a smuggler. I need a good way off Krell, and I don't think there is one."

The word "smuggler" made her smile. "You underestimate me, my friend," she said.

"I'm sure I do," he said tiredly, "but that really doesn't matter at the moment."

"It does matter," she said. "Do you know how I got my name?"

"I didn't even know what your name was until five minutes ago," he said.

"Well, let me tell you a story," she said. "And then we'll figure out a way to get you off Krell for good."

Chapter 15

JACK WASN'T IN THE MOOD FOR A STORY. HE CERTAINLY wasn't in the mood for a story as strange as the one Skye told him.

Her parents had been smugglers or pirates or, she said, "Just plain thieves with fancy credentials." Her entire childhood had been a continual series of escapes from bad situations, usually caused by her parents. They were constantly on the run from this person, that community, or some government. They avoided all forms of law enforcement.

They named her "Skylight" because of their closest call. They'd been trapped in a building on some planet (she never found out which one) and it had a skylight forty feet up. Somehow they had managed to climb the walls and go through that skylight without tripping any alarms.

They'd thought they were going to die, and they didn't. Then they discovered that Skye's mother was pregnant, and they retired from their crooked life.

"That lasted until I was born. I was always being grabbed and pulled out of some place I had just settled." Then Skye's face clouded. "Until they figured I was old enough to stay behind."

He wanted to find out about that, he really did. But not right now. His heart was pounding hard, because he felt that, with each passing moment, he would lose his own life.

"So," she said, "let me get you out of here."

What choice did he have, really? He was an investigator, a spy, an information guy. The kind of person who lurked in the shadows, observed too much, and sent those observations back to whomever had paid for them.

He'd never once had to escape from anything. Sure, he had to slip out of a room when a subject noticed that Jack was staring too hard, and yes, he'd had to dump some net accounts because a subject's security systems had identified him, but he had never ever had to run away from some place. If he got confronted, he'd laugh and make up a story—he was good at that—and no one had a second thought about him.

Except maybe that the tall guy was a bad choice for a spy, so obviously he couldn't be one. He was too memorable.

"What do you propose to do?" he asked. "I'm very recognizable, and they'll be guarding my ship. Someone will remember if I get on a transport."

"Yes, they will," Skye said. "Do you have money?"

There it was. That was what this was all about. She was shaking him down. Heller hadn't caught up to him after all. She was trying to get Jack to pay for her extravagant lifestyle.

"No," he said so flatly that she looked at him, eyebrows raised.

"I don't need it," she said. "I just thought you might feel odd if I paid for everything."

He was about to tell her that he would not give her anything, not for any reason, when he realized what she had said.

"Pay for everything?" he repeated lamely. "And then I'd pay you back?"

That would be the scam.

She shook her head. "The Guild covers all of my expenses, no matter how extravagant. They know I'm tailing high-end targets, so the Guild expects me to have a huge expense account. They pay me a base expense amount every month, whether I bill them or not. I have more money than I know what to do with."

He frowned, trying to wrap his brain around that. He had clearly joined the wrong organization. Not that he'd had a choice. He hadn't gone near the Assassins Guild, afraid that they'd turn him into a killer.

He had just floated along in his life. Researching the Rovers, then deciding to leave them was in some ways, the first time he had ever done anything for himself.

And he had felt off balance the entire time he did it.

Still felt off balance.

Of course, Skye wasn't helping. She had surprised him on such a deep level, he wasn't thinking clearly. Not that he had thought clearly about her last night either.

"You'd fund our escape?" he asked.

"It'll be the most excitement I've had in years." Then she grinned. "Except for last night, of course."

In spite of himself, he smiled at her. "I've never met anyone like you," he said.

"You said that yesterday," she said.

"And I had no idea just how right I was," he said.

Her grin faded. "I already have a plan. But you'll have to trust me. If someone was watching you, they saw us hook up, but they probably don't know you're in this room. You'll have to wait here while I set up our escape. I would understand if you don't want to do that, but you're so recognizable that it'll be harder if you come with me on the initial rendezvous."

He clenched his hands into fists, then made himself release them finger by finger. He knew she was right about being recognized. He also knew that she was right that he would have to trust her.

She had been the one to tell him about the threat. She had been the one to show him this room. The money still bothered him, primarily because her offer was so unusual.

"I need the image back," he said.

She frowned at him, not understanding what he was going to do. Good. That meant she wouldn't have time to prepare for it.

She handed him the tablet.

"Are there other images of Heller on here?" he asked.

"I took a few other shots," she said.

He poked at the flat screen until he found one of the other images. Then he recognized the place. It was the interior of the bar where he and Skye had been the night before.

But he had no idea how long that interior had looked like that. He would wager it had probably looked like that as long as he was alive. She could have taken this months, even years ago. Or doctored the image.

This was where his investigative skills came in, however. He knew how to find out if something was doctored or old. He tapped on the flat screen, looked at the image, then examined it in great detail. Then, he glanced at the other images the same way.

They were from this morning.

And one of them had the back of a woman who

looked like Skye on it. He moved through the images until he caught the side of the woman's face. Not Skye. That woman he had seen earlier, the one who had the same general body type.

"Who's that?" he asked, showing Skye the image.

She hesitated for just a moment. Then she said, "Her name is Liora Olliver. She's an assassin with the Guild."

"She's the one who is supposed to kill me?" he asked.

"She hired Heller this morning. That's what I thought was strange. Why would a Guild assassin hire a Rover to do a job?"

"Do you think that has anything to do with targeting me?" he asked.

"No," Skye said. "They were talking about a different kind of plan. Liora said that Heller might not even be used on it. She hadn't even given him all of the information yet."

No wonder Skye had called that strange. A Guild member should never hire a Rover.

It was intriguing, but not his business at the moment.

Jack handed the tablet back to Skye. He had confirmed what he could. Now he had to decide if he was going to trust her completely.

"I'll give you half an hour," he said. "And then I'm leaving the room."

"That works," she said, pushed past him, and let herself out.

Chapter 16

Skye needed less than thirty minutes. She slipped back into the corridor near the room with ten minutes to spare.

The corridor was empty, which relieved her. She was worried that someone had figured out who she was and had followed her. She also worried that they had found Jack alone and had hurt him.

She didn't want to think that anyone had killed him, not in that room, not after the night they'd had. She wanted that room to remain the way it was, locked in her memory as a place of pleasure, not as a place of death.

Her heart pounded. She had never felt like this on her own escapes. Not that she'd really run for her life as an adult. She'd slipped in and out of various high-end buildings, lots of space yachts, and more than her share of cabins on various cruise lines. She'd always worried a bit about being caught, but never worried that someone would kill her.

Plus, no one would ever figure out why she'd been in a room because she never stole anything—except information, of course. She figured that down the road, she would get caught and then she would tell them that she had the wrong room, that somehow her passcode had worked or the door was open or something along those lines.

And she knew that whoever caught her would think

the moment strange, but would believe her because she had no record and nothing would disappear.

This felt different, though. It wasn't her life or her liberty at stake.

It was Jack's.

And she actually cared about that.

The caring had made her act differently, although she had tried hard not to. She had paid off employees so that she could get into the well-guarded section of the dock bay, one for the high-end visitors. The employees had had a price already set, which led her to believe that she wasn't the first to ever do this.

Of course, on Krell, she probably wasn't.

She scouted the ships herself, even though one of the employees had pointed her to the ships he believed were the most, in his words, "accessible." She wondered if he got a fee when someone was caught or if he expected a finder's fee for whatever was inside.

She had just thanked him and continued the search on her own. Certain models of space yachts were more secure than others. Plus, she had learned, over the years, that some models were easy to break into but hard to fly. She'd never stolen a space yacht. Scratch that—she hadn't stolen one since she left her parents. (She'd made a daring escape at eight, and her parents had used her to communicate with various space ports, posing as a child who had somehow managed to fly a ship in trouble.)

But she had gotten into a lot of yachts, and because she collected information, she had looked at their navigation systems just to see which ones would be easiest to breach.

She found at least two here. She didn't look at them

too closely—she was afraid that employee would notice, and report it to someone—but she mentally marked where they were.

Then she left conspicuously, saying her thank-yous to all the employees whose coffers she'd fattened.

She wasn't planning to bring Jack through the front door of the bay. She'd been to Krell often enough to learn the back passages. If the employees caught her, so be it. She had already paid them and she was willing to pay them more.

But she would do this one delicately, and delicately meant smuggling Jack out without anyone seeing his tall, lanky frame.

She wasn't even going to suggest that he change his hair color or his clothing. That body of his (which she had enjoyed so much) would give him away every time.

She swallowed hard, then slipped into the corridor. She had kept an eye out for tails. The fact that she hadn't seen any didn't mean that she wasn't being followed. Even though she had borrowed one of Jack's jammers, she knew that some equipment was so sophisticated she wouldn't be able to fool it. She hoped no one had tried to track her with anything like that.

Her heart started pounding as she got close to the room. She was afraid he had lied to her, afraid that he had left just after she had.

She had the frightened feeling that if he had done that, he would have died quickly.

She hoped he had trusted her long enough to remain safe.

When she reached the room, she opened the door with a palm scan. At first she didn't see him. She had expected him to be somewhere nearby and he wasn't.

Her breath shortened, and she had to will herself not to panic, not to make things up. She didn't say his name. She didn't say anything. She just let the door close behind her, and hoped for the best.

He peered around the bedroom door, worry lines creasing his forehead. Then those lines vanished. He smiled, just a little, and then ducked under the door frame.

Apparently he had been worried she wouldn't return.

"You're early," he said.

"It took less time than I thought," she said. "This next will be the hard part."

She still wasn't used to looking up at anyone, and she was looking up at him. She had watched him duck under that door frame, and she worried that he might have the same trouble in the back corridors.

"I don't think we can hide you," she said. "You're too tall."

He nodded. "That's one thing enhancements can't change. However, jammers can hide me if you tell me our route."

"Jamming the security feeds will be suspicious," she said.

"That's not what I'm going to do," he said. He walked over to the wall screen that she hadn't touched. "I can get into Krell's systems and change my signature on the security equipment."

"Someone will find it," Skye said.

He looked at her over his shoulder, then he grinned. "Yeah, someone will. If someone looks. The problem for Heller is that I was the only one on his team who could do things like this. The Rovers aren't the Assassins Guild. They don't have enough money to hire redundant employees."

"Don't Rovers get paid for their jobs?" she asked, rather than telling him that the Guild didn't have anyone quite like her either. He might never understand that. She wasn't sure the Guild did.

"Sure they do," he said, "but they get the money directly and then pay the Rovers if they remember. When the job comes through the Rovers, the Rovers keep half of the up-front fee and let the assassin take the rest."

"Sounds inefficient," she said.

"Inefficient, impossible to enforce, and ripe for theft," he said. "I always made sure I got paid up front."

She shook her head. She couldn't imagine working like that. It had to be stressful. Her salary and bonuses went to paying off her debts. But she could live off her expense account. If she decided to stay with the Guild after all her debts were paid off, she would make a small fortune.

All the time he spoke to her, he worked the screen. She shifted from foot to foot, not used to waiting for someone else. She had a plan. They needed to execute it, before Heller's man got to the employees at the dock. If Heller's man paid them more than Skye had—hell, if Heller's man paid them less and then promised them a lot more with the capture and/or notification—then she and Jack were screwed.

"Is he smart enough to look at the security feed?" she asked.

"Never underestimate a Rover," Jack said, still working.

"I meant—"

"I know what you meant. You folks at the Guild follow rules and rarely do anything that hasn't been approved by someone somewhere. Rovers have to think on their feet. Of course, he would look at the security feed. He probably knows I'm in this room."

Her breath caught. "Then we have to get out of here now."

Jack pressed his entire hand on the screen, then turned around and grinned at her. "Okay," he said. "Let's go."

Chapter 17

Skye gave Jack an odd look, then raised her eyebrows just a little as if to say, *What the hell*. Then she opened the door, looked both ways, and waited for him.

He had shut off all but his personal jammer. He hadn't told her about that. She would probably protest. She would want him to jam as much as possible.

But then she also didn't know that as far as the Krell security feeds were concerned, she would be walking through the station with a five-foot-five, clean-cut, blond man. Jack hadn't used that disguise before, at least not around Heller, so no one would be looking for it.

And he trusted Krell security to be so lax that when he did show up at the docking ring, they'd not even double check the feeds like most well-run places did. They'd think the six-foot-six black-haired guy belonged there.

The words "Krell" and "security" really didn't belong together. It was more like Krell monitoring so that someone else's security could use the feed after some crime happened. Or if some criminal wanted to track someone. Or whatever anyone paid for the monitoring feed.

Still, as Jack stepped into the empty corridor, his heart was in his throat. He had told Skye not to underestimate the Rovers. He had to be careful that he didn't either.

At least he knew most of their tricks. He knew where to look for them.

Skye was already halfway down the corridor. She

stopped, opened her hands in another *What the hell?* gesture. Only this one was a question, and an irritated one. *Hurry up. Stop dawdling. You are afraid of being killed, right?*

He could almost hear her say all of those things. He appreciated her silence, though. He didn't need to answer her, which was a good thing. He hadn't had a voice print to work with, so he hadn't been able to modify his voice.

It was hard to track someone in a space station by the way that they spoke, but he'd done it in the past. He didn't know if Heller had ever done it, but Jack would wager that other Rovers had.

And he had no idea which other Rovers were actually after him.

Skye had stopped in front of a wall panel. It looked no different from any other part of the wall. As he got close, she brushed the side of the panel with her hand, and the panel opened.

The back corridors. Every station had them, and they were usually easy to find.

In a place like Krell, they were predictably filthy and predictably unguarded.

He took a deep breath of the somewhat fresh air in the corridor, then followed Skye into the back passage. She could stand upright with inches to spare. He had to crouch in a way that actually twinged his back.

Normally, he wouldn't walk through this at all. If he didn't lean over far enough, his head would brush against a ceiling that probably hadn't been cleaned since the station was built.

And then there was the smell. He couldn't quite separate all of the odors out, but he recognized rancid grease right away. The fact that the back passageway smelled this bad meant that the environmental systems in here were worse than they were outside of the passageway, or that they had given up a long time ago.

He wanted to ask Skye how far they had to go, but he didn't dare talk.

She fit easily between the walls and under that ceiling, and she didn't seem bothered by the smell. Although he couldn't quite tell what she was feeling, since he only saw her back.

He found himself watching her perfect little bottom, which was too much of a distraction for him. He couldn't think about touching that bottom, being near that bottom, not right now, not when he was hunched over and walking on a squishy floor that he had trouble keeping his balance on.

He had to keep his eye out for anything unusual, a scraped-off area, other fairly fresh footprints, *something*, and he was having trouble concentrating on any of it.

So much for the fear-for-your-life thing focusing him. It focused him on Skye, and nothing else.

Still, he worked to maintain his concentration as she led him through tunnel after tunnel. He mentally repeated the directions they turned, and kept track of how far they walked. He had an enhancement that would also do that, but he didn't want to activate it.

He had learned long ago that people could be tracked through the oddest enhancements, because most people never shut theirs off. That was why he had so few of them, and rarely used them.

Finally, Skye turned into a wider corridor. She looked over her shoulder (he envied that movement; he couldn't do the same thing without scraping his head on a gushy wall), and put a finger to her lips.

As if he needed to be told to be quiet.

Then she stepped forward, one hand behind her in a stop and wait gesture. He wanted to stop and wait in a place where he could stand upright, or at least stand up a bit more. He wasn't sure where that place was, but he knew this wasn't it.

She left his line of sight for a brief moment, then came back and gestured him forward.

He stepped into an open area where he could stand more or less upright. He had to tilt his head sideways to keep from brushing the ceiling, but at least the ceiling here wasn't covered in goo. He suspected that this part of the tunnels smelled better, but he couldn't do more than suspect because the previous tunnels had ruined his nose for at least the next few hours.

He grimaced at the thought of that smell dogging him for the rest of the day. Dogging him, hell. *He* probably smelled like that after the walk through the tunnels.

Skye moved so close to him that he could kiss her. She didn't seem interested, though. Instead, she brushed off his sleeves and gestured him to move his head closer.

He didn't groan, but his back silently protested. He had to get close to that weird position he had been in just a moment ago.

"We're about to go into the docking ring," she whispered. "You let me talk, and don't disagree with me or volunteer anything, no matter what I say."

He wanted to say, *What kind of amateur do you think I am?* But he knew better than to speak up. She had no real idea who he was, and if she was from the Guild like she said, she thought him a dangerous and difficult amateur just because of his association with the Rovers.

So he nodded. She patted his arms, getting some more junk off them (he must have brushed against those horrible walls after all), then turned around.

He stood upright (more or less) and couldn't suppress his sigh of relief.

She took his hand, pulling him forward, then opened the panel. At that moment, he silently cursed himself.

He should go out there first. A Rover could be waiting, one she didn't know, and they would both die.

But Jack hadn't thought of it until now.

And he hoped now wasn't too late.

Chapter 18

THE EMPLOYEE LUNCHROOM BEHIND THE DOCKING ring was empty. Still, Skye stepped into it gingerly, hoping no one hid nearby.

The lunchroom had been tacked on later, probably placed in what had been designed as a guard station. The ceiling was as high as the ceiling in the ring, which was to say, higher than the interior of Krell, and she knew that Jack would appreciate that.

One large, very clean table stood in the middle of the floor, which was also startlingly clean, startling not just because they were on Krell, but because Skye had never seen a clean employees-only lunchroom, not even in the Guild.

The blinking red lines were the only thing that moved in the room besides her. She stepped out of the panel and let out a sigh of relief.

She had paid off one of the docking ring employees to clear this room, but paying off someone didn't mean they'd do what she asked. Hell, he might not have done what she asked—the room might be empty at all times except whenever lunch was—but she didn't care.

She had gotten Jack this far.

Now came the tricky part.

She pulled him forward.

He stepped out of the panel, looked up, and then stood upright with such a sigh of relief that she felt for him. Then he brushed off the top of his head, as if he had touched that horrible ceiling in the passageways. He did have some black streaks on the side of his face.

She probably did too, which made her shudder. Those passageways had been nasty.

She inclined her head toward a nearby sink. Jack looked at her with gratitude, then cautiously made his way over there. She followed. They needed to clean off as best they could and quickly.

Jack finished up, then stepped aside so she could rinse off as well. That hadn't cleaned up the smell. But she headed toward the door, hoping he remembered her admonition.

It slid silently sideways instead of opening outward. Three employees stood near their stations, theoretically monitoring any ship that wanted to land on Krell. Automation didn't work here; there were too many variables, most of them with shady reputations.

The employee that Skye had talked with, a man still so young that his enhancements couldn't cope with all of his bad skin, winked at her. She winked back.

Then she slipped right toward the part of the ring where the high-end space yachts got stored. Most of them had security too tight for her to breach, but two models built for speed rather than comfort didn't. Apparently a lot of the comfort items on a space yacht slowed it down, or at least ruined the sleeker designs that enhanced swiftness.

She could feel Jack behind her. He was going to have to duck again as they walked into the ring. This part had been upgraded most recently. The walls actually gleamed here, and the ring itself, while still plain, had a bounce to it that suggested custom-made materials.

The ships she wanted were farther down the ring, in their own hangers. She made it to the first. Fortunately, it was also her first choice, primarily because it was newer, and because a cursory search didn't show any affiliations with known crime rings. She'd learned that one from her parents as well.

She slipped into the airlock and beckoned Jack to follow. The ships docked half in and half out of the ring. When they wanted to leave, they unclamped and backed out before they took off.

This allowed someone to flee even if no employees were working and even if someone else tried to shut down the automated docking system.

Jack slipped in with her. The space was narrow, partly because the nose of the ship pushed up in here as well. Earlier, it had taken her a minute to find the door. It blended into the ship's blackness with no obvious lines around it.

His body pressed against hers, but he remained hunched. Still, he grinned.

None of the airlocks had security cameras, and apparently he knew that because he said, "You know how to get into this thing?"

Those were the first words he'd spoken in nearly an hour. But instead of answering him, she tapped the side of the ship. The round door opened inward, leading them directly into the cockpit.

"That's not very efficient." Jack pushed past her and stepped in first, almost as if he thought he could protect her from someone inside.

"Actually, I think it's really efficient," she said as she followed him. "We're in the cockpit and ready to go."

The cockpit was large. It took up a third of the ship. That was the other way she knew this ship was built for speed. Another third was cargo, and the remaining third were bedrooms, the kitchen, a bathroom, and oddly, some kind of guarded space which could probably be used to hold prisoners.

She didn't want to think about that. This ship was probably used for smuggling illegal items, and that space meant some of those items might not be things but people.

At least, that was what she told herself to feel better about all of this.

"Strap yourself in," she said. "We're getting out of here fast and I have no idea how good the environmental controls are."

Mostly, she was worried about the gravity. Some ship owners had the ships set to zero-G after takeoff. She didn't have the time to find the specific gravity controls before they left.

She had to get the ship to follow her commands, and that would take a few minutes. It was a relatively simple procedure that many yacht owners knew nothing about. With the help of that employee, she'd registered herself as an emergency repair engineer on Krell. Now she uploaded that code into the ship's systems.

Theoretically, the ship would contact Krell's automated docking bay system and find her.

Not that it mattered. Even if the Rovers who were after Jack figured out he'd left by ship, they wouldn't know which ship for some time.

At least that was what she hoped.

She strapped herself into the pilot's seat, and clicked on the controls, and prayed her plan would work.

Chapter 19

JACK WATCHED SKYE'S NIMBLE FINGERS DANCE ALONG the navigation board. He couldn't tell what she was doing, but piloting a ship had never been his strong suit. The ship he was leaving behind here had simple controls, designed for idiots with minimal piloting experience.

He had flown a lot, but he didn't care about mastering the skill, so he just set everything to automatic and hoped that nothing would break down.

Usually he used flight time to research the latest possible client or target for the Rovers. Or lately, to research some of the things the Rovers had been into.

He would miss his ship. He'd had it for years. Maybe, when this was all over, he could come back for it.

Fortunately, Skye seemed to know what she was doing. She frowned in concentration, and she bit her lower lip ever so slightly as she worked. He liked that quirk.

He liked everything about her.

Then the ship lurched backward. Ships weren't supposed to lurch.

"Ooops," Skye muttered.

Jack gave her a sharp glance, but Skye wasn't looking at him. She was staring at a holographic screen that had just appeared in front of her, showing the docking ring and the ships on it in three dimensions.

It took a moment for Jack to find their ship, a sleek

model the shape of a pilsner glass. It was slowly separating from the dock.

Now he couldn't feel the movement of the ship, which was how it should be. He gripped the seat's arms, feeling the smooth leatherlike fabric beneath his fingers, and kept his gaze on that 3-D representation of the ship moving away from Krell.

So far, he saw no other ships leaving, but that didn't mean anything. All someone had to do was contact a ship nearby, and he'd get followed.

"Where are we going?" he asked. "Centaar?"

Centaar was the nearest planet, not too far out of the NetherRealm where Krell was. Centaar's main city, Oyal, had its own laws, most of which ignored laws from other regions.

If Jack and Skye arrived in a stolen ship, no one from Oyal would care.

"I figure they'd look for us there first," she said. "I'm thinking we head to the Brezev Sector, and see what we can find there."

"The Brezev Sector?" he said. "That's not part of any affiliated group."

"Yeah," she said. "Filled with criminals, pirates, roving bands of mischief makers. You know, like the Rovers."

"Not even Rovers go there," he said. She shrugged. He felt his heart sink. "You're serious."

"I am," she said. "It's not as dangerous as it's made out to be."

"And you know that how?" he asked.

She grinned at him. "I grew up there."

Just the fact that she came from the Brezev Sector made him rethink everything she had told him. Even after she had left to find this ship, he hadn't looked up anything about her. He felt it wasn't necessary. He had gone with his instincts, something he rarely did.

What a perfect setup. He had given her his name the night before. Then, after he left in the morning, she had checked up on him. Maybe she had already known that Heller was on Krell. Either way, maybe she made up a story about Heller trying to kill him, and then she had moved forward with a kidnapping plan.

But she had to know that there was no one to ransom him.

Although Heller might pay to get Jack back, just so that Heller could kill him.

She glanced at Jack. Her smile faded as she saw the look on his face.

She said, "I'm exaggerating. I sort-of lived in the Brezev Sector. Until I was ten. My parents always fled back to the Brezev Sector when they felt like they'd gotten into too much trouble."

"The people who named you Skylight to honor one of their escapes." He couldn't help letting his sarcasm through.

"Yes," she said.

"I'll wager you haven't been back since," he said, hoping he was right.

"You'd lose," she said. "I've gone in and out countless times, researching targets."

He didn't get the sense she told him this to calm him down. And yet, it had that effect. He was wildly out of his element, and trusting a woman he hadn't researched.

He hadn't realized until now just how much he relied on information. Not information someone had told him, but information he found himself.

It gave him security.

Apparently, it also kept him from making things up. That kidnapping thing had to be unrealistic. After researching him—and if she were kidnapping him, she would have researched him—she would have known that he had no resources. Just a savings account, a ship, and his brain.

Which he had apparently shut off the moment he met Skye.

She was saying, "You'd be surprised how many criminals use the Brezev Sector as home base."

He focused back on the moment. He wasn't surprised about criminals and the Brezev Sector. Criminals liked places like the Brezev Sector and Krell because those places gave them cover.

"You realize we're criminals at the moment," she said in that same conversational tone. "We don't own this ship."

He'd been trying hard not to think about that. He figured they would deal with it wherever they ended up.

"What are you going to do with the ship?" he asked. "When we get to the Brezev Sector, that is."

"Sell it," she said. "Then get us another ship."

Or maybe I'll just take a transport, he thought, then discarded the idea. Who knew what kinds of pickpockets, thieves, and generally bad types populated those transports.

Of course, there had to be good people in the Brezev Sector. He'd just never heard of any.

"And then what?" he asked.

"I don't know," she said. "We're playing this by ear."

"Yeah," he said, not sure how he felt about it all. "I guess we are."

Chapter 20

Jack sounded mournful, as if he were already regretting this trip. He had trusted Skye on everything, from the threat to the escape. Now she was taking him on a stolen ship to a place that harbored known criminals. She supposed she could understand why he worried.

She might have, in his shoes.

Although she couldn't imagine being in his position. She would never have worked for the Rovers in the first place. They made the Guild seem like heroes.

She turned on all of the proximity alarms, setting them to scout for ships at the farthest reach of the sensors. Then she hit the holographic navigation screen, setting it so that the walls of the cockpit disappeared, and it looked like the cockpit floated in space.

The ship's automatic pilot had a setting called "Escape" built right in. She glanced at the onboard manual and saw that it would take an unusual flight path at the highest possible speeds to get to the destination.

She programmed that into the navigation panel and turned the setting on. The ship acknowledged her, then took over. It was better to have a computer randomly set their route than her. Humans could never do true random, always picking a pattern.

"No one followed us," she said.

Jack was looking at the star-lined space around them. "You're sure?"

"The ship's sure," she said. "That's good enough for me."

"Then can I get out of this harness?" he asked.

She smiled at him. She would love to get him out of the harness, and all his clothes. She'd always wanted to make love in space. This would be the next best thing.

"Before you get out of the harness, let me check one thing first," she said.

She let herself out of her own seat and crossed to his. She sat on his lap and eased her hands around his face, kissing him. He tasted good. She had wanted to do that all day.

But he broke off the kiss and peered around her shoulder. "I don't think this is a good idea."

His body was clearly interested, but his prodigious brain was obviously not allowing him to focus.

She could get him to focus.

"You don't think what is a good idea?" she asked.

"Um… this. Now." He was shy. She loved that about him.

"I think it's a great idea," she said. "What else are we going to do? Worry?"

He nodded, his hands still at his side. "Someone has to worry. I'd like to find out what's going on."

"We can find that out easier in the Brezev Sector, where no one will be searching for us," she said. "God knows how they'd look. They might even track data usage. And if we stay off the grid, then what will we discover? Only what's in this ship's database."

His gaze flicked away from the screens to her. Two spots of color rose on his cheeks. "And our tablets," he said. "We can combine information."

She wiggled her eyebrows at him. "We can combine other things as well."

He smiled. The smile seemed reluctant. "Skye, I'm still uncomfortable—"

"With what?" she asked. "Me? The stolen ship? The circumstances? Of course you are. But they are what they are. And if it's me that you're not comfortable with, send your mind back to last evening. We didn't know each other at all then, and we managed to have a good time."

His smile grew, and this time it reached his eyes. He shook his head just a little.

She was getting to him.

"Besides," she said, "I've always wanted to have sex in space, and I could never figure out how to do it in a space suit. Want to try it here? I could shut off the gravity."

"I'm not good at anything in zero-G," he said, his voice thicker than it had been a moment before.

"Well," she said, "you're good in Earth Normal gravity. We've already tested that."

She dipped her head and kissed him again. This time his hands came out and caught her waist. He participated fully in the kiss, his mouth open. He tasted her as if she were a favorite dish he hadn't had for a long time.

She felt like she hadn't tasted him in forever. Maybe that was because she had already given up on ever seeing him again after they separated. Or maybe she was just addicted to him.

Whatever it was didn't matter. She had never ever been attracted to anyone like she was attracted to him.

She wedged her knee against the end of the harness,

so he couldn't let himself out of it. He didn't seem to notice. His hands spread across her back, leaning her in closer, his arousal straining against his pants. She shifted slightly, then, without breaking the kiss, opened his shirt and pulled it out of his waistband.

His hands slipped under her shirt, reaching up, and finding her breasts. They'd never been very sensitive, yet somehow his touch made desire run through her. It was as if he knew every button to push to make her respond in ways she had never responded to anyone else.

She didn't think she could get more aroused, and yet she was. She wanted him now.

She leaned back just a little, undid his pants, and grabbed him. He was large and warm and ready.

So was she.

"Let me loose," he said, his mouth against hers.

"Not yet," she said.

She rose on her knees, undid her own pants, then stepped off him for just a moment as she kicked her pants away. She left her shirt on—she was in too much of a hurry to take it off—and then she lowered herself on him.

Slowly.

He strained upward, but the harness held him in place. She only sank onto the tip of his penis, moving up and down, feeling him at the edges of her, little ripples of pleasure shooting through her.

"Skye..."

She didn't want him to beg, but she wanted him past ready.

"Skye, if you continue this, I can't..."

He couldn't finish a sentence, that's what he couldn't

do. That was okay. She doubted she could even communicate. His hands remained on her breasts, but squeezed tighter as he became more and more aroused.

She lowered just a bit farther down, taking him halfway, and did the same thing. Up, down, feeling him inside her then at the edges, those ripples continuing.

"Skye, dammit…"

She focused on him, on her, on fractions of an inch, and the differences that made. In, out, forward, back, just a little, as she found new ways to torture them both.

"Skye, really… I… ah, hell."

He grabbed her hips and pushed them downward. She felt him slide all the way into her, and it was so magical that her entire body erupted. She tilted her head back, feeling the orgasm pulse through her.

Hers had nearly ended when she felt his surge into her, and she joined him again.

Then she leaned forward, spent and damp and breathless.

"My God," she said. "I didn't even look at the scenery."

"You're disappointed," he said against her shoulder.

"Hell, no," she said. "I just figure we're going to need to try this again."

"Only if you let me out of this chair," he said.

She smiled, even though he couldn't see it.

"My pleasure," she said.

Chapter 21

Repeating the marathon session from the night before simply wasn't possible. Their bodies wouldn't cooperate. Skye knew of assassins who had gotten enhancements so that the pleasure could continue over days, but she didn't have one, and judging from the look on Jack's face, he didn't have one either.

He was sprawled on the floor of the cockpit, his clothes gone. Somewhere along the way, he or she or both of them had removed her shirt as well. She was curled alongside him, facing him, the stars and blackness of space around them like a hug.

She loved that.

They had managed one more round, slower, not nearly as electric as that moment in the chair, but pleasurable just the same.

She had no idea how long they'd lost themselves in each other. It felt like days.

It had probably been an hour or less.

She didn't want to move, but she knew she had to. She sat up slowly, her hair falling across her face. She had no idea that a wedge haircut could get messy, but this one had.

She ran her fingers through it.

"Don't," Jack muttered.

"Don't what?" she asked.

"Do that," he said. "It makes your breasts move, and

shows how lovely the line of your neck is, and damned if that's not getting a response."

She looked down. His penis was growing again.

"I'm going to have to stand up," she said. "I'm not responsible for your response."

"Oh, yes, you are. I've never been like this." Then he blinked. "Except, you know, puberty and adolescence. But that was different. I could think the word 'breast' and I'd need tissues."

She chuckled. "Now you just have to look at one."

"At yours," he corrected. "And your neck, your back, your waist... ah, hell."

He was hard. She stroked him, and he twitched. Hard and sensitive.

"I think we both need a rest," she said.

"No kidding," he said.

"But not on the cockpit floor," she said.

"You are unkind." He sat up, looked at his penis as if it weren't part of him, and grinned. "Well, at least part of me has energy."

She kissed her index finger, then touched the tip of it to his tip. It bobbed toward her in response. She laughed.

"It looks ready," she said.

"Its owner needs either rest or nourishment or both," he said.

"You own it?" she asked.

He grinned. "Well, I'm certainly not renting it."

She laughed too, feeling better than she had in weeks, maybe years. When had she last been this happy? Had she ever been? She had no idea.

She stood up, and he moaned. "You're killing me here," he said.

It would kill her too if she continued using his body the way she wanted to. She had sore muscles and her knees ached. She couldn't quite remember what she had done, and then she recalled that movement up and down while he was still in the chair.

Apparently, she had used thigh muscles she hadn't used in years—maybe ever. And then there were the bruises on her knees.

She carried her clothes over one arm. "I'm going to see what kind of shower this place has," she said.

He was sitting up, but one leg was raised, hiding that eager penis. He ran a hand through his hair as well, and it only served to make the strands stick up more.

"Not food?" he asked.

She glanced at the navigation map. They weren't far from the Brezev System.

"Food eventually. But first, I think we need to be ready in case something happens," she said.

"Something did happen. I got hit with your energy-sapping enthusiasm ray."

She laughed again. "I mean something else," she said, letting herself be serious. "We're not too far away from the system boundaries. We're going to have to be on guard."

"For what?" he asked.

"For anything," she said, and left the cockpit.

Chapter 22

Skye sure knew how to kill a mood. Of course, she knew how to start one too.

Jack smiled, then levered himself off the cockpit floor. He felt less wobbly than he had after last night, but he still felt like he'd lost more energy than he thought possible.

He braced one hand on his chair, noted that the harness had fallen to the side, and that there was an unidentifiable stain in the center of the seat. Or maybe it was identifiable.

He didn't want to figure out what, exactly, it was. He pressed one of the cleaning controls on the chair's side, and hoped that the nanocleaners were up for the job.

In the meantime, he searched for his clothes. Somehow they had gotten strewn all over the cockpit. His shirt had slid against the wall, and looked like it was now bunched up against some of the planets in the Brezev Sector.

Skye was right; they were close.

He hoped she came back soon because he was not only unequipped to fly this thing, but he also had no idea where they were going.

He stood for a moment, naked in a field of stars. At least that was what it felt like. He hadn't really paid attention to the scenery, outside of his focus on Skye, no matter what she said about this being like making love in space.

Although she had said *having sex*. He let out a small

sigh. It felt more profound that simple sex to him. He wondered if it had to her.

She leaned in the door, her hair shiny and her face a bit ruddy. "The best sonic shower I've ever had," she said. "It's yours now. I'm going to rustle up some food."

He wanted to kiss her again, but she had already vanished. He felt the last of the arousal leave his body. He did need the shower. He also needed rest, but he doubted he would get any.

He took his shirt away from the screen and thought he saw some movement there that he hadn't expected. He squinted, trying to see if the movement was just reflective of their travels or if it was something else.

It could be anything else. Asteroids, ships going in different directions, moons, or just a trick of the light.

Still, it might've been something.

So he walked over to the navigation center. It was in a language he had never seen before, with symbols he didn't recognize. He couldn't pilot this thing even if he wanted to.

He glanced at that part of the screen again, but didn't see anything unusual.

Still, that moment left him unsettled. Skye had been right earlier: they needed to distract themselves so they wouldn't worry.

But the distraction had gone to the other part of the ship, searching for food. He needed to figure out what he was going to do in the Brezev System.

He had let Skye take the lead so far, and he was grateful. But it was his life on the line, and he needed to figure out how to protect himself.

He grabbed his clothes and walked out of the cockpit.

The narrow corridor was tall enough for him to stand upright. A door to his left opened into what had to be the master suite. It was done as sparely as the rest of the ship, although the bed's thick mattress beckoned. That bed was probably large enough to fit him.

He couldn't think about that. Instead, he went through another door and found the shower, which was the size of the airlock. Here he would have to crouch, and he hoped that the shower would get all the pertinent parts.

He dropped his clothes outside the shower door. It finally hit him that he had left everything on Krell, from his ship to his clothing to the only possessions that meant anything to him.

He always traveled light, but not this light. He didn't even have his weapon. And if he accessed his accounts, the Rovers would probably find him.

He was going to have to move money in Brezev, and quickly. Then he would have to thread it through half a dozen accounts, and flee to somewhere else all at the same time.

He leaned his head against the cool shower door. He was probably going to end up one of those people who spent his entire life on the run.

That thought destroyed any good mood he'd already had. Sure, he used to travel a lot when he worked for the Rovers, but he had built himself a home not far from Rikki's on Unbey. He rarely used it, but he liked knowing it was there.

The problem was that the Rovers knew too.

He had gone from being a silent collector of information to one of those guys whose life was forfeit because he knew too much.

And he wasn't really sure how he had gotten here in the first place.

Chapter 23

SKYE'S FIRST INDICATION THAT SHE MIGHT HAVE chosen the wrong ship came in the kitchen. It was well stocked. And by well stocked, she meant stocked by a ship that someone used not just for short hops, but for long ones. Plus most of the food here was extremely fresh, the kind of fresh that went for a premium on a place like Krell.

Someone had planned to take this ship soon.

She took advantage of the fresh apples and oranges, probably grown in Krell's own hydroponics lab, and created a salad with fresh greens as well. Then she mixed it with a dressing she'd had on Krell, and added bread baked so recently that it still smelled like it had just finished cooking.

She put two bottled waters against her arm, and carried everything back into the cockpit.

Jack hadn't arrived yet. She could probably check on him in that shower, but that might lead to more delays.

Then she grinned. *Might* was the wrong word. It *would* lead to more delays.

And right now, she couldn't afford the distraction.

The navigation console had two food trays built in so that the pilot and copilot could eat here without worrying about spills. She hit the button that made the trays extend to their full length, set the salad on them, and then got to work on the ship itself.

She had looked at the registry before stealing the ship, but she well knew that a registry meant nothing. She'd forged dozens of them. She needed to do more than search through the registry to figure out whose ship she had stolen.

The ship's name was *Rapido*, which seemed both an obvious reference and a placeholder name to her. It suggested little about the owner. That owner would have no way of knowing Skye was taking *Rapido* toward the Brezev Sector, but eventually, he (or she) would find out. Information traveled quickly. And if the ship's owner was someone known for taking revenge, then Skye would have to dump this ship as quickly as possible.

She was deep into her research when she felt Jack enter the room. She could always tell when someone was around, but her body never went into a pleasurable alert like this. Her skin tingled, and she hadn't even looked at him.

"There's a lot of fresh food," she said. "I made us salads, but if you want something else—"

"That's fine," he said and returned to his copilot chair. He smelled faintly of the shower's built-in soap and something she had come to recognize as Jack.

She didn't look directly at him. The fact that he sat so close took too much of her attention already.

"The food made you nervous, huh?" he asked.

She stopped and looked at him. His face was freshly scrubbed and he had gotten rid of some of the stubble that had started to grow. He had combed his hair. He looked like a man on a mission, not like a man who had spent a good part of the afternoon on the cockpit floor.

"How do you know?" she asked.

"You haven't touched it." He took his plate. "Besides, food this fresh would have freaked me out."

"Would have?" she asked.

"Does," he said. "It does freak me out. But I'm too hungry to care."

Then he nodded at her plate.

"Eat something," he said.

She wasn't sure if he was waiting for her to take a bite before he did, but it wouldn't surprise her. Anyone who had lived among assassins knew that it was better to let the person who prepared the food take the first bite.

Of course, if he were truly paranoid, he would switch plates with her.

She picked up her fork and ate some apple. It crunched. Jack smiled and started to eat as well.

She felt oddly relieved that he hadn't tried to switch plates. In her circles, that was a mark of trust.

"Whose ship is this?" he asked.

"That was what I was just trying to figure out," she said. "There are layers and layers and layers here."

He nodded. "Let me help."

"I can—"

"I know," he said, "but this is my specialty, just like it's yours. With both of us doing the work, we might learn something."

"Yeah," she said. "Something we don't want to know."

Chapter 24

The ship's owner had more aliases than most Rovers. Jack didn't like that at all. Someone with that many aliases had something to hide. He quit working on tracking the man before Skye did, just because somewhere along the way he realized that a guy like this wouldn't keep his true identity anywhere on this ship, especially not in his own database.

Skye paused to finish the extremely good salad she had prepared for them. Jack couldn't remember the last time he'd had anything that healthy, nutritious, or fresh. He'd just kept treating himself to gut-busting meals like the burgers on Krell, and he knew that eventually that would catch up to him.

Skye looked at him sideways. Apparently he had done something to attract her attention.

"What?" she asked as she chewed the last of her bread. He even liked that. She burped like a freighter pilot and ate like a soldier. Manners were clearly not her strong suit.

"We're not going to find him here," Jack said.

"I know," she said. "But I may have screwed us royally by taking this ship."

He grinned. "No, you screwed us royally on that chair, and we enjoyed it."

She chuckled.

"However," he said, "we do need a plan. Someone

will recognize this ship, so we need to go to a place that will look the other way."

He didn't know a lot of places in the Brezev Sector. He had a hunch the ones he knew about were the ones everyone knew about. He never trusted places like that, because that meant they expected their potential clientele to be idiots.

"Most shipyards in the Brezev Sector take hot ships," she said. "But most of those shipyards are indebted to existing big players, folks we might not even know about. They don't advertise."

"I know," Jack said. He didn't know much about exchanging hot ships, except that he knew how to track someone who had stolen a ship. He knew how easily some places gave up that information as well, although he'd never tried in the Brezev Sector.

Most people in the Brezev Sector considered the Rovers to be too law-abiding because the Rovers made sure their assassins were licensed and they worked on jobs that were sanctioned.

Or they had until Heller came on board.

Jack shuddered.

"What?" Skye asked. She was picking at her salad now.

"Nothing," he said.

"Do you want to do something else? Because I'm not sure how long we can use this ship."

"I know," he said. "I realized in the shower that I need to figure out what I'm doing."

"If you play it right," she said, "you can just stay out here. I doubt anyone could find you."

He had considered that already. It would be easy

enough to disappear. He could vanish entirely and no one would find him.

Until they needed to—and even then he might be able to stay one step ahead of whoever wanted to catch him.

The problems went deeper than that. He'd have to give up his friendships. Most of his life was built on connections. That was how he got information. Of course, he knew that most of those people gave up the information easily, but that didn't make them any less valuable to him.

And he'd have to abandon Rikki. She was his only family. He couldn't just leave her behind with no word.

Especially not now. She was involved with a man she didn't really know, and he was messing with her head.

She had asked Jack to find out about him, and Jack would. In fact, he would ask Skye about him at some point.

Just not right now.

Jack had other pressing matters on his mind.

"I know no one could find me," he said after a moment. "At least, I know it intellectually."

"It's a big universe," she said, and she wasn't being fatuous like most people when they mentioned how large the universe was. He could tell. She was trying to be helpful.

He glanced over at her and smiled. "I know that too. I could start a new life."

She was watching him closely, as if what he said next mattered to her.

He almost said, *I'll start a new life if you come with me*.

But he didn't. Not because of her. God knows, life with Skye would be interesting, and if they cooled on each other sexually, they could move on, no strings.

Although even that thought disturbed him.

He didn't examine why. At least not yet. Ever since yesterday, he had been responding to people, not taking action on his own.

He needed to do things for himself first.

"But you don't want a new life? You're not willing to start one?" She sounded almost defensive, and he wasn't sure why that was. Did she want him to start a new life? If so, why?

"Would you?" he asked, realizing that he was just asking his question sideways.

"Start a new life if I were in your shoes? Absolutely," she said.

He shook his head. He hadn't been asking that question. "Would you start a new life now? Would you just walk away from everything you know?"

"You realize that's why most people get assassinated, don't you?" she asked without answering him. In fact, she hadn't even looked at him. "They don't run when they should."

She picked up the last slice of apple from her plate, but she didn't eat. She stared at it like something was written on it.

"That's a fake statistic," he said. "Most of the people I find have been on the run for years. They lose track, they need to find their families again, they relax, and I locate them. Ninety percent of what I did for the Rovers was finding people who had theoretically vanished."

"Then they didn't do it right," she said.

He sighed. He used to think that too. "Most of them had. Some never had contact with their past again. We all leave traces, Skye. Sometimes the traces are really simple ones. We've left a lot of DNA in this ship, and no matter how thoroughly we clean it, we won't get it all."

He half thought she'd smile at the comment about DNA, but she didn't. Instead she set that slice of apple back on her plate.

"You're afraid they'll find you," she said. "They probably won't, particularly if what you say about the Rovers is true. If you were their go-to guy and you're gone, then who would search?"

He had wondered that himself. It would take a long time for someone else to learn his job—not that they could. They'd have to already know how to do it, because there was no one in the Rovers or affiliated with them who knew how to get information the way that Jack did.

"I want this settled," he said. "I don't want to spend my entire life on the run. I don't want to worry that if I relax for one moment, someone will find me and assassinate me. I mean, imagine if I have a family or something. You know these assassins. They'll take out an entire neighborhood to get one guy."

She made a sound of astonishment. "You're kidding, right?"

"I wish I were." That was another thing that had disgusted him about the Rovers. At first, Jack thought he could stop the killing of innocents by better research. He could even give some assassins real-time information.

But so many of them didn't want to hear from him at all, and so many of them didn't care who they hurt in the process of earning their money.

Sure, governments could prosecute for collateral damage, but so many of the governments either hired

Rovers or members of the Assassins Guild that they often did nothing at all. And when they did do something, it was usually in the form of levying a small fine, something any well-paid assassin could easily afford.

"Well," Skye said primly. He hadn't thought she was capable of prim. "No one in the Guild would level a neighborhood to get one target."

He swiveled in his chair. Her naïveté was breathtaking.

"Really?" he said. "Because I know of several cases in which that happened, and those were Guild cases."

"I'm sure whoever did it was sanctioned or kicked out of the Guild." Skye still sounded prim, although there was a small frown in the middle of her forehead.

"No, they haven't," Jack said. "Most of the folks I know about still work for the Guild. In fact, some of them have risen pretty high in the Guild infrastructure."

She took a deep breath. "That's seen as punishment. The Guild has a lot of rules, a code, really, and anyone who violates it—"

"Gets kicked out, demoted, or can no longer act as an assassin." He leaned back, having a sudden thought. "Were you demoted?"

She laughed, then frowned when she realized he wasn't laughing with her. "You're serious."

"Yes," he said.

"No," she said. "I never became an assassin in the first place. I didn't lie to you about that."

Now he had offended her and he hadn't meant to. She was helping him for no reason he could understand.

"I'm sorry," he said, and meant it. He had worked alone too long. He really had no idea how to deal with other people on more than a casual basis.

He didn't say anything else. He finished his meal instead. Then he picked up both plates and headed to the kitchen.

He really did need to make some decisions, and he needed to make them alone.

Chapter 25

Skye remained motionless in her chair. Jack had offended her.

He had offended her about the Guild.

She found that very strange.

She would have said she hadn't felt enough loyalty to the Guild to be offended. After all, they had essentially tricked her just to get her services.

Yes, they had taken her in as a ten-year-old, but then they had had her sign a legal document at fourteen, the earliest age they could, telling her that they would cover her room, board, and schooling, which she could work off long after she graduated.

She had always thought she could work off that schooling as a chef or a teacher or one of the support staff at the Guild. And then, when the Guild put her into assassin's training, she balked. She had said she didn't want to be an assassin.

And they told her she had signed up for it.

She went through everything, and failed much of it, because she wasn't suited to it. Her case had gone all the way to the top of the Guild. Director Ammons made a deal with her, so that she would spy for them instead of kill for them. Skye was stuck with it, until her massive debt was paid off.

She always said she hated them for that.

And yet she had just defended them to Jack.

Did she actually care about the Guild?

She stood up. He had left, clearly troubled. His apology had sounded heartfelt. Poor man. He had a lot to deal with right now. Including her.

And including their rival organizations.

Or rather, his former organization.

What had he done for them to want him dead? What did he know?

Maybe he should share that with her, and then they'd be able to solve this all together.

He had to know something that would threaten the Rovers' very existence. Right? Or was this Heller guy just acting alone?

Something moved in the spacescape in the back corner of the room. It took her half a minute to remember that they were in the cockpit of a ship. She had been so focused on Jack, on the past, that she had lost track of where she was.

She went back to the navigation panel, and tapped it, magnifying the image a thousand times of whatever she had seen.

Ships. She saw ships.

And they seemed to be heading toward *Rapido*.

She hit the ship-wide communications array.

"Jack, I need you here now," she said.

Then she poured over the route that *Rapido* had set. It was random, like she had programmed. Then she went deeper into the navigational system and found something she had missed earlier: This ship had a program that allowed it to bypass "dangerous" systems. The program was customized, meaning that whoever owned *Rapido* had designed the dangerous systems route to stay away from places where he was in danger, whatever that meant.

She was afraid she knew what it meant.

"What?" Jack ducked under the door.

"Look." She showed him the ships. The navigation panel showed that they were even closer than they had been.

Then she explained about the dangerous route program.

"Crap." Jack sank into his chair. "So what we know about this guy gets worse with each passing moment. He took an expensive ship built for speed to Krell, which isn't the most savory place in the universe. He has more aliases than a Rover with a death wish, and he has places he needs to avoid. We, of course, flew right into one of them."

Somehow she felt that as a personal affront, although she knew that Jack didn't mean it that way. "If I'd known we had to activate the escape system and the dangerous route program at the same time, and compare them, I would have," she said.

"You didn't," he said. "But you'd think they'd be linked somehow so that they would activate at the same time."

"You would think that...." She frowned. "Unless he sometimes had to do business on these places."

Jack let out a small laugh. "Of course he did. Under an alias."

"Or two. Or three."

"Well, shit," Jack said, and he wasn't looking at her. He was looking at those ships which had gotten so much closer that they no longer fit in the magnified viewing screen. "Obviously, there's a lot more here that we should have known."

"We were trying to find out..."

He put a hand on hers, sending a jolt of electricity through her. "We didn't. I'm not blaming you."

She knew that. She wasn't sure why she was so defensive, and then she realized what was going on.

She felt like she had made a mistake. She hadn't investigated clearly enough. She had focused in the wrong direction.

She had thought about getting Jack away from those Rovers and she had thought about stealing a ship so that no one on Krell would catch them, thinking they'd dump the ship as soon as possible. That was why she hadn't worried about who owned the ship.

She figured the owner would come after the two of them and never find them.

But she hadn't done her due diligence. She hadn't figured out who she was stealing from.

And, granted, the last time she had done anything this elaborate, she'd had her parents as backup. They had probably done due diligence together or maybe, knowing them, they hadn't cared.

"How do you make this thing smaller?" Jack asked, looking at the screen magnification. She appreciated the fact that he did not sound panicked. She might have sounded panicked in his shoes.

She tapped on the navigation board. The ships now fit into the raised-up screen, but they kept moving forward.

"I can't read this language or I'd help you here," Jack said. "If you show me what to do..."

She glanced at him in surprise. Languages were a major part of Guild training. But of course, he'd had no formal training, and he probably used translation devices when he researched.

"I don't have the time at the moment," she said. She needed to do something else first. She needed to find out what *Rapido*'s defensive capabilities were. She knew in general, but now she needed to know in specific.

"If you get hurt," he said, "I can't run this thing. At least show me the automatic pilot."

She tapped the screen. "I just set the language in the autopilot to Standard so that you can read the instructions. If you need the automatic pilot, you give it one of the aliases and then tell it to engage."

He looked at her sideways. "What's more important than showing me?"

"Figuring out what the hell weapons systems we have."

"There are a dozen ships out there," he said. "Weapons aren't going to help us. At least two of those ships are military issue."

She glanced up. He was right. The ships out front were standard space yachts, but they were being followed by two military ships.

"Those military ships could be after the space yachts," she said.

"Or they could be after us," he said. "This thing have shields?"

"Good ones, if he kept factory issue," she said.

"Then let's get out of here," Jack said. "We're not going to use weapons. You told me this ship was built for speed, and we need to run."

He was right; she knew he was right. She just had to take action.

"We need to figure out where we're going," she said.

"Somewhere not on that danger map. We don't want to get caught like this again," he said. "And we need to go somewhere that will let us sell a hot ship without turning us over to the local authorities."

She felt a thread of irritation. "You don't ask for much, do you?"

"If I knew more about the sector, I'd help," he said. "But I'm a little constrained here. I don't know the language on this ship, I can't fly the damn thing, I don't know much about the Brezev Sector, and I really don't want to be blown to smithereens."

"Details, details," she said, and activated the screens. Then she studied the controls. "There is a maximum speed here, but I don't know how long this ship can sustain it."

"I really don't give a damn," he said. "Get us the hell out of here."

"Yes, sir," she said, and slapped her palm on the speed controls. The ship jerked, which shocked her, and then everything became ribbons of light.

Damn. If the speed indicator on the navigation board was correct, they were going faster than she thought possible.

She hoped the ship could sustain this speed.

She hoped to hell none of those space yachts could match the speed.

Because if they could, this ship wouldn't protect her and Jack for long.

Chapter 26

Skye wobbled as the ship hit its maximum speed, and Jack put out his hands to catch her. He really needed her now. He hadn't been kidding about that. He couldn't fly this thing, and he had no idea where the weapons were located even if he did figure out how to fly it.

Then there was the matter of a destination.

"Where're we going?" he asked. He wouldn't insult her by double checking that she had compared their new destination with that danger map. He hoped like hell she had.

"It's a place called Zaeen," she said. "I haven't been there since I was a child."

"Great," Jack said. He hadn't meant to sound sarcastic. He just couldn't help himself.

"It's the only place I could think of," she said.

Before he had wondered if she felt defensive. Now he knew she did. Defensiveness didn't suit her. Besides, she had nothing to be defensive about.

"You're saving my ass, you know that, right?" he said.

She shook her head, as if she didn't want to hear it. Her hands kept flying along the navigation board. "I feel like I'm the one who has been constantly putting it in jeopardy."

He stared her for a moment. "Anyone following us?"

"Not that I can tell," she said, still looking at the screens. "Nothing's showing up on any of the sensors."

"And unless someone greets us when we reach our destination, we're home safe," he said. "There's no way they can know where we're going, right?"

"Oh, hell," she said. "There's always a way. You know that. They can tap into our comm system, and they could view the navigation, and—"

"I suppose," he said. "But you know how hard that is, and I do as well. Besides, it's nearly impossible when you weren't planning for it, at least from that distance."

She raised her head and looked at him. "You're a 'glass-is-always-half-full' kinda guy, aren't you?"

He laughed. Rikki had accused him of that. Being too optimistic had hurt him in the past, particularly when someone talked of adopting him as a child. But he always felt he was better off believing the best of people rather than the worst.

"Do you really see yourself as a 'glass-half-empty woman'?" he asked her.

"Oh, I don't know," she said, glancing at the navigation. "I'm not sure there's anything in the glass at all."

He wanted to take her in his arms, and for the first time, the feeling wasn't sexual. He wanted to comfort her. No one should be as pessimistic and sad as she was. Not for any reason.

"So, Miss Empty Glass, are we in the clear?" he asked, trying to keep the tone light.

"For the next hour or two," she said.

"Okay," he said. "Then sit down. You're making me nervous."

She glanced at herself, then chuckled. "I'm just making you stand."

"That too," he said. "You know, someday, I'm going

to build myself a custom ship, one with plenty of room, so I don't spend my entire life hunched."

"You could spend your entire life planetside," she said. "Then you have an actual sky above you and you wouldn't have to worry about banging your head."

He gave her a wolfish grin. "I like having a Skye above me, and I rather enjoy banging."

She looked at him sideways, her luscious mouth upturned just a bit. "Focus," she said. "We'll need all the energy we can get to survive going to Zaeen."

"I'm not familiar with it," he said.

"I haven't been there in nearly two decades," she said. "But I've been checking it out—"

"In your copious spare time, as you research me, this ship, and the criminal who owns the ship," Jack said.

That upturn became a smile. He liked it when she smiled. It made her dark eyes light up.

"No," she said. "Before I met you, I'd been researching Zaeen."

"Why?" he asked.

"Because," she said. "It was the last place I ever saw my parents."

He let that sink in. He would have thought the last place she ever saw her parents was Kordita, where the Assassins Guild was. Someone had to drop her off there.

"And you were a child," he said.

She nodded, her chin set. He recognized that look too. It was a common one among the children in Tranquility House, particularly among those kids who believed that their parents would come back for them.

Of course, the idiot parents never did.

Jack sighed. Sometimes he could be a glass-half-empty

kinda guy, particularly when it came to parenting. Humans had been around for millennia, and a large portion of the human race never seemed to master parenting at all.

You'd think there'd be some kind of rule book or something, and first in it would be, *Put the needs of the child above your own*.

But then, that would be too difficult for most of these bastards.

"That surprise you?" she asked.

"Nothing surprises me." He was lying. He had just surprised himself. He should have mentioned his own childhood, the fact that he couldn't even remember his own parents and he had no idea why they dropped him at Tranquility House. Even though he'd tried to research it, he never found a trace of them.

It would have helped if he had known his real name.

Or theirs.

"They gave me to a so-called uncle who was supposed to take me to Kordita to wait for them. My father thought he could work with the Guild, or so he said. He figured they needed thieves. My uncle kept me for half a year before just giving me to the Guild."

She said it all matter-of-factly, but Jack could tell it hurt.

"Did you ever figure out what happened?" he asked.

She looked at him, her face bleak. He recognized that expression too. Kids often got it too young, when they knew that the people they cared about the most never cared about them.

"To my parents?" she asked.

He nodded.

"Exactly what happened every time before when they dumped me. They figured they found a sucker who could take the kid, and they'd be able to live kid-free and unencumbered for the rest of their days." She shrugged, as if trying to pretend that it didn't hurt. "Guess they finally accomplished that."

He wasn't sure he could ever encounter those people. They'd tried to abandon their daughter more than once? He'd heard of parents like that from the kids at Tranquility House but he had always accepted it as part of those kids' lives. He had been young and hadn't thought about the kind of pain it caused.

Clearly, for Skye, the pain remained, much as she pretended otherwise.

And then things at the Guild hadn't worked out either. No wonder she liked working alone. He would have too in her situation.

He felt a brief moment of amusement. He liked working alone as well, for similar reasons.

He hoped that amusement hadn't shown on his face, because it had been directed at himself, not at her.

"And this so-called uncle," he said. "He didn't…"

"Want me?" Skye said. "Of course not. I'm the proverbial unwanted kid. Or I was."

The present tense was telling as well. She still saw herself as that abandoned child.

Well, he saw himself the same way. Maybe that was why they had such a deep connection.

"I was actually going to ask if he hurt you," Jack asked.

"By dumping me off?" She turned toward Jack with such surprise that he could feel it as if it were his own. "I felt no attachment to him."

"No," Jack said gently. "Sometimes 'uncle' is a euphemism for a man who has expectations of a certain kind of sexual—"

"Ew," she said. "No. *No*."

She shook her head as if trying to get an image out of her brain.

"No," she said a third time. "I won't say he was a good man, because he was a friend of my parents and he did similar things to make money, but he actually tried to do right by me. Leaving me at the Guild was smart on his part, since my father said they'd eventually show up."

Then her mouth flattened. She ran a hand over her face.

"But," she said, "if no one had ever opened that gate for me, I would have been completely alone. He walked off before they took me in."

So the so-called uncle wasn't a good man after all. Just a better man than Skye's father. But Jack didn't make the commentary. It wasn't his to judge.

She looked at the navigation panel in front of her. "I never really thought I'd go back to Zaeen."

Yet she'd been investigating it. Jack almost didn't ask about it, but he was ever curious, and he couldn't quite restrain himself.

"Even though you'd been researching it," he said.

She lowered her head, laughed once—an odd almost reluctant sound—and then leaned back in her chair.

"I could tell you a partial truth," she said. "I could tell you I've been checking up on them for years."

"Seeing if they came back to Zaeen?"

"Yeah," she said.

"Had they?"

She shook her head. "Not using any identification

that I could find," she said. "Doesn't mean they don't have aliases I don't know."

He nodded. He understood that.

"Why is that a partial truth?" he asked.

"Because—" She glanced at him, her expression speculative. He could almost sense her trying to figure out just how much of her own life she wanted to trust him with. "Because I'm going to be done with the Guild in a couple of years, and then I want to find them."

"And do what?" he asked.

"That's the thing," she said. "I don't know, exactly. Show them what they missed? See if they even think about me? Get them arrested? The one thing I know I can't do is kill them. I'm not that person."

"Although you're still that angry," he said.

"Probably, deep down," she said. "Yeah. I am."

He nodded. "Me too," he said. "Not at your parents, but at my own."

Chapter 27

The story Jack told her seemed pretty simple on the surface: his parents had abandoned him into some kind of government-controlled child care, and had never come back for him. Jack told it simply as if it were nothing more than a fact of life, but Skye could hear the pain underneath it all.

She recognized it. She had felt it herself, and she hoped she had kept it mostly hidden.

Although she was a bit shaky after telling him about her parents. She'd told dozens of people that story over the years, although never all in one piece, and never quite as clearly. Usually someone with authority would ask, and she'd tell them only what they needed to know. Then they'd need more and she'd tell them that.

Finally, they'd have the entire sorry tale, although most of the time they wouldn't recognize that she'd told them everything. They'd forget parts or confuse her with someone else or ask her all over again.

Jack was the only person who had heard it all at once, and he was certainly the only person who had ever asked her if her so-called uncle had used her for his sexual pleasure. Jack hadn't asked it salaciously either. He'd been concerned for her.

She wondered what he'd seen in that child-care place. Probably more than she ever wanted to think about.

Someone had dumped Jack as well, although she

wasn't sure it was his parents. The fact that he had no idea who he was and couldn't figure it out disturbed her. It sounded like there had been some trauma back there, trauma locked in his brain. Trauma no one had tried to figure out.

She made herself focus on him. She owed him that for listening to her.

"You've tried to find them?" she asked.

"Yeah." He sat perfectly still in the copilot's chair, maybe the first time she'd seen him sitting that motionless. "The ultimate hunter. I started out by breaking into the files at Tranquility House. I hired a few investigators to look for me, and discovered I was better at searching than they were."

"You did a DNA match?" she asked.

He didn't seem insulted by the obvious question. "When I could afford it," he said. "And nothing. Not even a blocked category. It's like I started to exist at eight and had no history before that."

She twisted a little in her chair. "You don't think someone was trying to hide you?"

"The secret prince syndrome?" He laughed. "Every kid at Tranquility House believed he was royalty that someone had hidden. It's part of being abandoned, I think. Only Rikki didn't."

"Rikki?" Skye asked. "Who's he?"

"She," Jack said. "She's my oldest friend. She knew who her parents were. They'd died rather horribly, and she had nowhere else to go."

He was silent for a moment. He seemed to be contemplating something.

"Speaking of," he said. "Do you know an assassin

named Mikael Yurinovich Orlinski or, I guess, Misha? He's with the Guild."

Skye stiffened. Why would Jack want to know about an assassin with the Guild? What did it matter to him?

"Why? What's he got to do with you?" Her tone sounded a little sharp, even to her.

"Not with me," Jack said. "Rikki. She wanted me to check on him."

That seemed odd to Skye. She was about to say so when Jack added, "I used to be Rikki's go-to guy for information. This one's important to her. It's personal."

It got stranger. Skye shifted in her seat. She wasn't used to talking about the Guild or its members with anyone from outside the Guild.

"Personal?" she asked. "Wouldn't you think assassination is always personal?"

Jack laughed, which surprised her. "Rikki's an assassin too. She trained with the Rovers, but she left long before I did. She met this Orlinski on a job and she's worried about something. I guess he—God, I don't know how much I can say without breaking confidence."

"He's not poaching from her," Skye said. "He never would."

She'd known Misha for years. He was probably the most stand-up person she'd met in the Guild.

"That's not it." Jack sighed. "I guess he's interested in Rikki, and she seems to be interested in return."

Misha? Skye rocked back in her seat in surprise. Really? She'd've thought him a eunuch, if it weren't for a rather ugly breakup he'd had with Liora Olliver.

The very thought of her made Skye wince. She hadn't considered anything about Liora since it became clear that the Rovers were after Jack. She'd left Liora on that station with Heller.

"Do you know Liora Olliver?" she asked Jack.

"No, why? Should I?"

She shook her head.

"Does she have something to do with this Orlinski?"

"Not anymore," Skye said. "Except that they're both part of the Guild."

She'd have to tell Jack about Liora at some point. Just not now.

"Here's what I know about Misha," Skye said. "He's one of the best men in the Guild. He never breaks rules. He goes out of his way to minimize collateral damage, sometimes abandoning jobs to keep innocents safe. He's quick, he's good, and he's probably the most honest man I know."

Although she wanted to consider Jack the most honest man she knew. But she hadn't spent enough time with him. She wasn't sure of him. Not yet, anyway.

But her gut said he was reliable. Maybe more reliable than Misha.

"I'll be honest, though," Skye said. "I can't imagine him falling for someone outside of the Guild. He's all-Guild all the way."

"You sound like you don't approve," Jack said.

She shrugged. "They haven't exactly treated me well."

Then the ship lurched again, and stars formed around them. Visible stars.

Skye couldn't talk any longer. She needed to look for threats and wayward ships.

She leaned over the navigation board, putting in information, and making sure she hadn't missed any warnings.

Jack didn't say anything as she worked. He just watched her, then got up and peered at the various screens, as if he could see something.

"Where's Zaeen?" he asked.

"About fifteen minutes out," she said, a little startled that they were this close.

"What port are we stopping at?" he asked.

"I don't think we're stopping at a port," she said. "This ship is too much trouble."

"Meaning what?" he asked.

"Meaning that if we land her, one of those other ships will find us. I don't want to risk that, do you?"

"What do you propose?" he asked.

"We'll set the automatic pilot and let her go on her way."

"And then what are we going to do?" he asked.

"There are lifepods," she said. "I think we'll take the largest of them."

"You're kidding, right?" he asked.

She grinned at him. "You'll find that I don't joke about life and death matters."

"Someone's following us again, aren't they?" he asked.

"I'm not sure," she said.

"If they are, then getting into a lifepod is stupid. They'll catch us."

"No, they won't," she said. "You can change sensor indicators."

"Not on a lifepod where I don't even know the language," he said.

"Then talk me through the way you usually do it," she said. "I'm sure I can make it work."

"I'm glad one of us is," he muttered. "I really am."

Chapter 28

THE LIFEPOD WAS AMAZINGLY BIG, CONSIDERING THE size of the spaceship they were vacating. But "amazingly big" and actually big enough for Jack were two different things. He had to hunch his shoulders, bend his knees, and squeeze in sideways just to get through the hatch. Then he had to crawl to move to the controls.

He felt ridiculous. It didn't help that Skye had to duck to get inside as well, and bend over to walk to the controls. He still took the stupidity of the design personally.

The thing was decked out like some kind of tent. A fabric floor with tons of padding underneath, matching fabric walls and ceiling, made Jack wonder what else this pod got used for besides a possible escape from the parent vessel. Jack had a hunch, but he wasn't going to say anything to Skye.

A few hours ago, he might have told her, but a few hours ago, they weren't being stalked by ships whose crew thought they were someone else.

He inched his way to the control panel. Skye sealed off the main door, then hit release.

She had set the main vessel's autopilot to engage the moment this pod left. Jack had no idea how she'd done that, but he was glad she had.

She made her way over to him, her movements closer to walking than his had been. Still, she looked odd as she slowly eased toward him. And, dammit, he found even those odd movements sexy—the way that she touched things, that frown on her face as she worked to keep her footing, the way she dropped down beside him with a sense of relief.

She tapped on the navigation screen, hit a few glowing lights, and transformed the entire thing into Standard. Suddenly he could read and identify everything.

"Why couldn't you do that on the ship?" he asked.

"I tried. It didn't exist in the ship proper," she said. "But apparently someone forgot to fix it in the lifepods."

It only took him a few seconds to change the sensor indicators. The job here was actually easier than the one he had done on Krell.

"Got it," he said.

"Good," she said. "Those ships are too close."

She flattened her palm against a gigantic red image that was clear in any language: that was the thing that separated the pod from the ship.

Then she scooted him over just a bit, her hip touching his, her leg warm. He glanced at her, hoping to catch her with just a small grin or something. All he wanted was a kiss. Just one, because she was so close and because they had made it this far.

But she had turned on the navigation controls. She was pointing the pod directly at a gigantic space station. He assumed that was probably Zaeen. Most places to buy spaceships, particularly hot ones, weren't on any planet, but orbited around them.

He watched the pod's image on the internal screen. The pod drifted toward the station. Behind them, the ship itself lurched and he tilted his head.

He had hated that when he'd been on board. He

thought it truly strange that it happened now, when the ship was supposed to be hitting its autopilot.

Besides, even as the ship lurched, he shouldn't have seen it. Hell, he shouldn't have felt it on the ship itself. The attitude controls should have taken care of the problem.

"Skye," he said as he finally realized what was going on, "we need some speed here."

"What?" she asked, still frowning over the controls.

The ship still hadn't left the area, although it seemed to be trying. It moved forward, then back, then forward again, each time bobbing up and down as if it were a bottle in a bucket of water.

"Just do it," he said.

She tapped the screen and the pod zoomed forward.

She leaned back. "With that, we should be in Zaeen in—"

But she never finished the sentence, because the pod's shields went from Standard to Hardened, and a voice told them in bad Standard to strap in. Not that Jack could find any straps.

Not that he looked.

He was staring at the images of what was going on around them. The ship behind them exploded into a bright white light, making his eyes ache even though the screens adjusted for the glare.

"Go, go, go," he said to Skye.

"Don't tell me again," she said.

"Any way to cloak this thing?" he asked.

"It's a damn lifepod. Of course there isn't," she said.

He should have changed the specs to invisible. The pod was now moving so fast that he couldn't mess with anything. Besides, when shields hardened, all available energy went there and not to any other system.

Debris shadowed them, some of it as large as the pod itself. The screen was so filled with debris, in fact, that he couldn't see the ships they'd been fleeing from.

"You still have navigation control?" he asked.

"I sure as hell hope so." Skye was doing all kinds of things to that board that he didn't entirely understand.

"We don't want those ships to see us," he said.

"No shit," she said.

"I mean," he said, "use some of that debris to hide us."

She glanced at him, her eyes wild. He couldn't tell if she thought his idea brilliant or the stupidest thing she had ever heard. But she leaned over the console again, and the image on the screen changed.

He couldn't even see the pod any longer—and the screen was supposed to show the pod above all else.

He hoped to hell that was how it worked for those other ships. He didn't want the folks flying them to catch up to the pod.

"How far out are we?" he asked.

"Too far," Skye said. "This debris could shred us. These shields are cheap-ass things."

"You'd think in a ship that expensive—"

"Yeah, you would," she said. "But it didn't. So I need to focus."

He agreed with that. She did. He would watch the area around them, not that he could do any good. He would have to trust her.

Just like he'd been trusting her all along.

Chapter 29

Skye had the pod's controls on manual because the automatic controls sucked. She dodged all kinds of debris with hands-on flying, while keeping the speed of the pod as high as she could get it.

For a moment, she'd been tempted to slow the pod and let the debris go around her. The debris had a lot of momentum. It would go past her relatively quickly, or so she thought until she realized just how much debris there was.

Those ships had been too far out to destroy the ship she'd been on that thoroughly.

She hit a scan on the navigation board. There had to be someone else hiding around here, someone big and mean, someone who might come after them on Zaeen.

"What're you doing?" Jack asked.

He was looking at the scan.

"Someone destroyed that ship," she said.

"Yes, they did," he said, "but they aren't here."

He sounded certain. She didn't have time for certainty, particularly misplaced certainty.

"I'm not sure we should go to Zaeen," she said, "but I don't see any way around it. I don't think this pod will actually fly anywhere else."

She couldn't look at Jack because she was still doing hands-on flying, up and over one bit of debris, followed by a lateral move to dodge yet another, followed by a dip to avoid a third. Sometimes she had to do all three things at once, and that made her job exceedingly complicated. She—

"We don't have to go anywhere else," he said.

She didn't want to argue with him right now. She needed to focus. Things were still coming at them at an incredible rate of speed. If she were on a normal ship, the ship would help her, but this was a damn pod with minimal everything, from controls to shields to—

"No one shot at us," he said.

"The ship exploded," she said.

"Yes, it did," he said. "Because it was set up that way."

That caught her attention. She had to look at him. He was watching the screen.

"Careful," he said, "that bit of something..."

She saw it, and knew she couldn't look away at all anymore. She had to keep flying this thing or the pod would get damaged.

Or worse.

"I don't understand," she said. "The ship blew. Someone had to do that. I checked the systems. They were fine."

"They were," Jack said, "because you couldn't access parts of the system."

More debris—a lateral move, a flip, a sideways direction. She glanced at the screen. Some of this dodging took them away from Zaeen. She had to wrestle the pod back on course.

Somewhere, she'd lost the piece of debris she'd been hiding behind. But she didn't see the ships anymore.

Maybe they'd left when they realized they'd destroyed the ship.

"You can't know that," Skye said when she got a chance.

"That lurch," he said. "Ships don't lurch."

"Something needed fixing, that's true," she said, "but it was probably the attitude controls. When they need repair, that sometimes causes a lurch."

She didn't want to explain anything to him right now, but the conversation did keep her from panicking. She was a good pilot, but nowhere near as good as she needed to be for this. She knew dozens of pilots who were better, hundreds even. And here she was, dodging even more junk.

Pieces had started to hit the shield. Small pieces, tiny pieces in fact, but they were making a difference, hurting the integrity of the shield. The shield should have held up better.

Of course she had no idea how good a lifepod's shields could be. You'd think that lifepod shields would be *better* than those inside a ship because lifepods usually had to escape from somewhere.

Hell, you'd think that a lifepod on a ship as expensive as that one would have been spectacular, not a piece of junk like this—

"Oh, shit," she said, finally understanding what Jack was telling her. "You mean the idiot who owned the ship did this?"

"Yeah," Jack said. "I do."

She wanted to bang her head against the console, but had no time. Whoever owned that damn ship didn't care if it got stolen. That was why it was so easy to break into.

But he was one of those bastards who got revenge

on anyone who took anything from him. So he had designed the ship to get away from wherever it was before exploding.

That first lurch as the ship left Krell? That had probably been the fail-safe kicking in. The other lurches had been as the system set.

"It shouldn't have let us into the lifepod," she said.

"If there had been no lifepod, we would have known something was up," Jack said.

"I didn't check for lifepods when I was stealing ships." She wrestled the pod back on course. The shield had lost twenty percent of its effectiveness. She could either take it off Hardened and down a degree or she could hope nothing would go through the weaker part of the shield.

"I meant when we were trying to leave the ship. I don't think he figured we'd abandon the ship. I think that—"

"When the autopilot engaged at that fast speed," she said. "We would have done that if we were relaxed."

"Exactly," he said. "And relaxing, leaving the cockpit, resting—"

"We wouldn't have seen anything set." She swore again, then dodged some debris twice the size of the pod.

She finally saw an opening, and if she were in a real ship, she would have zoomed toward it. But there was no zooming in this stupid pod. Just moving forward and praying.

She hated praying.

"What the hell was this guy hiding?" Skye asked.

"I don't think he was hiding anything," Jack said. "I think this entire system existed in case the ship got stolen, and then he'd write it off. I think we could have dug for weeks and never figured out who he was."

"Not that we would have had weeks," Skye said. "We hadn't even been on that ship six hours."

"Exactly," Jack said. "But we got six hours farther away from him when the ship exploded."

She shook her head at it all, but part of her admired the guy's brilliance. She had never thought of anything like that. She wouldn't do it if she had thought of it.

That was why she wasn't an assassin. Assassins were trained to think like that.

Then she felt cold.

"This couldn't be one of your Rover buddy's ships, could it?"

"No," Jack said. "No one in the Rovers has all of these skills."

"But you've been gone from the group," Skye said. "You might not know who joined it."

She threaded the pod through some more debris, going beneath it.

"I keep track." Something in Jack's voice made her want to look at him. But she couldn't.

They were almost out of the debris field.

She went even lower. Ahead of the pod, bits of debris dipped below the pod as they continued on the various trajectories the explosion had sent them on. But pod itself was clear.

Finally.

She sat back and let out a large sigh of relief.

"We're safe?" Jack asked.

"For the moment," she said. "I can't promise what will happen in Zaeen."

"At least we're going to get there," he said.

She leaned back toward the console. She still had some red tape, regulations, and lying to do.

"We're not there yet," she said. "So let's not be overly optimistic."

"I don't see why I shouldn't be," Jack said. "Just today, I dodged an assassin or two, didn't die in an explosion, and spent some lovely time with a beautiful woman. I think I can afford to be optimistic."

Skye smiled in spite of herself.

"I told you," she said. "A glass-half-full kinda guy."

And in spite of herself, she liked that.

Chapter 30

Apparently, everyone on Zaeen had seen the ship explode. It had happened so close that Zaeen had to suspend ship traffic and turn on its own shields. A few of the automatic lasers had destroyed the largest bits of debris just to keep them from damaging the station itself.

If station was the right word. Jack had never seen any place like this megalopolis. He'd been on big space resorts in the past, but they had a lot of private areas and one central purpose, usually some kind of relaxation for the rich and powerful, with a small section reserved for other travelers who had to stop but couldn't afford the main part of the resort.

Zaeen was like five gigantic cities mixed with three resorts and seven shopping centers, none of it geared exclusively toward the filthy rich. Most of it seemed made for the middle-of-the-road traveler who needed time away from his horrible life or for the residents of Zaeen themselves, the people who actually worked on this place, and needed to house, feed, and clothe their families.

The landing area wasn't a bay or a dock. It was a full-fledged port. And it took Skye a bit of negotiation to get someone to allow them entry. She had to prove that they wouldn't be indigent.

Apparently, Zaeen would have turned them away,

even if they arrived on the lifepod after that large explosion, if they couldn't pay for their own way on the station.

Jack thought he'd seen it all, but even so that seemed remarkably cold to him. He felt outrage but didn't express it. He didn't want Zaeen to turn them away.

After they got clearance to enter, they got off the pod with the shirts on their back, and were forced into some truly rigid (and stinky) decontamination chambers, after which they had to buy new clothing, because their clothing was deemed contaminated, even though it wasn't. The way Jack knew that it was all rigged was that Skye had to pay for the clothing *before* they got off the lifepod. She was promised a refund if their clothing wasn't contaminated.

Jack wanted to call it all a scam, but he didn't dare. He needed to be grateful. He was alive, he hadn't been blown up by the ship they stole or murdered by his former colleagues.

And as he had said to Skye not an hour before, he had spent more than twenty-four hours in the company of one of the most beautiful women he had ever seen.

Hell, if he were honest with himself, she *was* the most beautiful woman he had ever seen. And he wanted to see her again.

After he got out of decontamination—well, after he got through the large retail center attached to the decontamination unit—he went to the "Reuniting Antechamber" as the section was called, hoping Skye had waited for him.

Part of him worried that she hadn't, that she got some kind of payment for bringing hapless people like him to this place. Granted, he might not have gotten that idea if it weren't for some warning brochures that he watched while going through the somewhat rude decontamination process. Apparently, a lot of people got dragged here with the promise of riches or jobs, only to discover that they simply fodder for the gigantic economic machine that was Zaeen.

The Reuniting Antechamber was as small as the retail center was large. It was a white room with a high ceiling (thank heavens) and bench seats in small groupings. Two other people sat on the benches as far away from each other as they could get.

Jack sat near the door, figuring he would give Skye an hour or two before leaving the Chamber.

Then he would have to figure out what to do next. If he accessed his funds, he would alert the Rovers to his presence. That was the bad news. The good news was that most Rovers never came to the Brezev Sector; there just wasn't enough work here for outsiders. Everything got handled in Sector, or so he always thought.

Or maybe it didn't get handled at all.

He'd been sitting only five minutes when Skye stumbled in. She was wearing form-fitting black pants stuffed into shiny boots and a black top that left little to the imagination.

Not that he needed his imagination to know what was under her clothes. Just his memory.

The memory made him stand, since remaining seated would have shown his reaction to the memory to everyone else in the room. He tugged on his pants—not form fitting (except at the moment) but black just like Skye's.

She grinned at him. "I hadn't planned to dress like twins."

"I don't think anyone would mistake us for twins," he said softly, then kissed her.

She wrapped her arms around his neck and pulled him down farther. There was relief in that kiss and passion, and a whole lot of promise.

He couldn't break it off.

She had to.

"I was going to say that the clothing might make them think us a performing troop," she said, her cheeks flushed, "but I don't think I could perform in public."

Jack's cheeks heated. He couldn't either.

He slipped his arm around her shoulder, then led her to the exit. The other people in the room watched them as if they were nothing more than some kind of video display.

Still, he was happy to get out of there.

"I don't think we should stay here long since our arrival was pretty dramatic," he said softly as he pulled her close.

She put her arm around his waist, and that warmed him. He hadn't expected it. He wished he were just a bit shorter so that she could rest her head against his shoulder while they were walking.

"I don't think anyone will notice our arrival," she said.

"They already have," he said. At least one person mentioned it to him in Decontamination.

"All of Zaeen noticed it," she said, "but that's not going to last."

She sounded certain. He wasn't sure how she could be.

"You seem pretty confident for a glass-always-empty woman," he said.

She chuckled. "You have no idea how big this place is."

"I thought you haven't been here in years," he said.

"I haven't. But it was big then."

He didn't say what he was thinking. Places that seemed large to children weren't always large to adults. He knew that better than most. He'd been a pretty scrawny kid. By the time he hit his growth, everything from his past looked small.

He smiled at the thought, then felt a moment of worry for Rikki. He needed to get out of his own predicament so that he could find out information for her.

"You don't believe me, do you?" Skye asked.

He didn't answer that, partly because he didn't, and partly because she sounded amused.

Why would she sound amused?

Then the doors to the restricted area opened, and a cacophony hit him. Sound first—voices, music, laughter, all vying for attention, getting louder and louder as each moment went by.

But sight hit second, mostly in colors—red, green, blue, yellow—he couldn't process it all because it was so bright. The lighting was higher than lighting he'd seen anywhere else.

Then the smells, everything from frying food to perfumes to the sour stench of human sweat.

Skye's arm pushed at his back. "Come on," she said.

She had to be almost shouting but he barely heard her.

And he hadn't realized until that moment that he had stopped.

She pointed up, and his gaze followed her finger. The ceiling was high.

He let out a small breath of surprise. Ceilings were never high in space stations. Never.

But that explained the echoey noise, the overwhelmed feeling, the sense that he was about to enter a new world.

"Most of these people had no idea that anything happened outside the station," Skye said.

"I guess not," he said, but he couldn't even hear himself.

Her grip around him tightened as if she sensed his nervousness. He hadn't been this overwhelmed since the first time he left the Tranquility House.

"Do you know where we're going?" he asked louder.

"Not yet," she said, "but I will."

He read her lips as much as he understood what she was saying.

They moved through the door and into the crowd. He felt a little dizzy, but he always did in crowds this large. He could see the tops of their heads, and that made the crowd seem more like a single entity rather than a bunch of human beings. The heads became a unit, like water through a conduit, with other conduits coming into it, changing some of the flow. He could see everything as a unit, but individuals were hard to see at all.

"Must be nice for you," Skye said. "You can see over everyone."

And she couldn't. He hadn't realized that. To her, it probably looked like the worst kind of obstacle course.

"Tell me where you need us to go and I'll get us there," he said.

He needed a purpose to get through this crowd, and leading them forward would give him that purpose.

"The maps I looked at on the ship showed that there was an entire section devoted to spaceship sales not too far from here."

Of course it would be near the port. That way people could see the ships.

He scanned over the sea of heads, noting that his eyes

had grown used to the brighter lights. The music sounded tinnier in here, maybe because he caught echoes of so many different strains.

He could see signs, but he couldn't read them even though they appeared to be in Standard. They were too low, eye-level for people like Skye.

Then he saw a ship in the distance. It seemed to be made of yellow light, and it floated over the crowd. He saw some hands pointing upward. Alongside the ship was a banner, also in the shape of a ship, informing anyone who wanted something like that to go to Pavilion Fifty-three.

Fifty-three pavilions. He suspected where they stood was considered a pavilion. His stomach clenched. He was starting to get a sense of scale here, and it was unbelievably huge.

All of Krell could fit into this pavilion or whatever the hell it was. And there were fifty-two more of them?

No wonder Skye had been confident that no one would care about them.

Hardly anyone was looking up at him, no one commented on their appearance, and as they made their way through the crowd, they had to shove just like everyone else.

He was glad he didn't have a bag or his usual equipment with him, just the chips with information embedded in his hand. His default was to shut all of that off, so no one could lift information as he passed.

Good thing, too, because he hadn't even thought of pickpockets until now.

He kept a tight grip on Skye, their bodies glued at the sides. Even so, she nearly lost hold of him once or twice as people continually banged into her.

He steered her toward that ship, and she didn't seem to care. She seemed relieved that he knew where he was going.

He only knew what he could see, and he could see just a bit more than she could.

They used their bodies almost as a battering ram to get through the crowd. People of all shapes and sizes passed them, some slamming into them, some carefully avoiding them.

He could see dozens of businesses, but could barely read the signs. Most of the signs, he realized after a few minutes, were on the ground, in bright lights, with arrows or maps leading to the storefront.

"I'll get us to the ship area," he said to Skye, "but you might have some luck getting us to the right store."

He nodded at the floor in front of them. Her mouth opened a bit—she hadn't noticed that—and then she nodded.

They had become a strange team, him looking up and her looking down.

It took nearly fifteen minutes to cross this part of the Pavilion. They finally got close to that floating ship which, Jack realized, was *huge*. It towered over him and would have crossed the entire width of the concourse on Krell. Here, it nearly vanished amongst the choices.

What kind of money maintained a place like this?

As soon as he asked himself the question, he realized he didn't want to know.

Skye's fingers dug into his side, pulling him to the left. He glanced down at her.

"Over there," she said.

He looked toward the thing she nodded at. Rows and

rows and rows of storefronts, all advertising ships at cheap prices.

"Crap," he said. "How do we know where to go?"

"We guess," she said, and pulled him forward.

Chapter 31

IT FELT LIKE SLOGGING THROUGH A SPACE WALK IN the bulkiest space suit ever invented.

Skye had not expected so many people here on Zaeen. If she were honest with herself, despite what she said to Jack, she hadn't expected the place to be so big.

She had been doing her research, of course, but knowing that a place was the size of a small planet and actually *going* to that small planet were two different things. Zaeen had grown tremendously since she'd last been here. This kind of growth would have been unprecedented in any sector outside of the Brezev Sector.

Regulations barely existed here, and what ones did exist could be bribed away.

That thought was one she chose not to share with Jack. Despite his "glass-half-full" thing, he seemed like a bit of a worrier, and anyone with a brain would worry about the fact that Zaeen did not regulate anything.

Parts of the station could fall off at any time.

For all she knew, parts had.

She had initially toyed with the idea of buying Jack his own ship and getting him out of here. She didn't want to be separated from him which, she knew, was more the lust and loneliness talking than anything else. She had helped him a great deal, and if he would take her money (with the promise of paying her back; she already knew him well enough to know he wouldn't want anything else), then they could go their separate ways.

She had initially planned to stay here to find some trace of her mother.

But the whole Rover thing was bothering her, as was the involvement of Liora Olliver. Something was up, and Skye wasn't sure she could spend time here without losing what little lead she had.

She also knew that her reaction to all of this might simply be a rationalization so that she could stay with Jack.

She didn't want to examine that.

There had to be fifty shops purporting to sell spaceships ahead of her. If she logged into Zaeen's network this close to the shops, she would find positive information on all of them, with the most positive on the shop that could afford the most advertising.

She should have researched ships before abandoning theirs.

As if she had had time.

She knew what she wanted, though, so she pulled Jack toward a kiosk that had lots of information on it.

"Is that wise?" he said when he saw what she was about to do.

"You have links that can access the public networks?" she asked. "Because I have nothing internal."

He smiled at her. "Me, either. And if I did, I certainly wouldn't do so here."

He was right: credit rip-offs, identity theft, tracer software, everything she worried about and more would come into a person's internal links through the Zaeen network.

If she had initially wondered where the money came from to run this place, she wondered no longer. Just ripping off the careless would bring in millions. Maybe tens of millions.

And since Zaeen was in the Brezev Sector, there was no recourse for the average citizen who suffered a catastrophic financial loss.

The kiosk stood a foot higher than she did, and blocked her view of that part of the Pavilion. She didn't like that, but she saw no way around it.

She plugged in information on fast ships with some weaponry and great shields. She also needed a ship with a registration that was valid in several sectors so that no one would arrest them for flying an unregistered ship in the wrong sector. A valid registration wouldn't guarantee that the ship wasn't stolen, but it would make the theft harder to prove.

Not that she cared. She didn't plan to use the ship long and she knew that Jack was smart enough to understand how dangerous buying a ship in this area actually was.

She also needed a ship that was fly-ready. She couldn't wait weeks for the ship to be delivered and/or repaired.

Only five shops met all her needs, and only one was close by. Its information displayed in purple. All she had to do was follow the purple arrows, and she would get there.

"Got it," she said.

Jack kept his back to the search, protecting her, making sure no one else got close enough to see what she was doing. It was probably a futile effort—some bot somewhere probably tracked all of the information displayed in the kiosk—but she appreciated the gesture anyway.

She tapped his back. He turned and encircled her with his arm. She liked that more than she wanted to admit.

She put her arm around his waist like she had before, and they walked toward the shop she had chosen.

It wasn't the biggest, the brightest, or the loudest shop in this ship-oriented part of the Pavilion. That distinction belonged to the store that had floated the ship above them. Tethers of yellow light connected that ship to the outside of the store.

Instead, she led Jack to the store down a narrow passageway from that one. The exterior had purple lighting, but strangely, it was tasteful. It blended with the shiny black door. Only a small purple ship, glowing in the center of that door, advertised what the shop sold.

"Nice," Jack said, and she could actually hear him without lip-reading. The noise factor in this part of the passageway was down significantly.

It made her relax just a bit. She wondered if that was intention of the shop owners, then decided it didn't matter.

When she pushed open the door to the shop, a light flared in the back. The shop itself was silent, startlingly so. Tiny replicas of ships sat on top of displays. More images of ships floated across the walls. The map of the interior of *One of Our Best Models* covered the floor. A star field covered the ceiling, and she had a hunch it hid all kinds of surveillance equipment.

The most startling thing of all, though, was that Jack could stand upright. He didn't even have to duck as he went through the door, although he did. Force of habit, she assumed.

His gaze met hers. "I'm not comfortable with you paying—"

"We'll talk about it later," she said. She didn't add the word "again" because that wasn't fair. She would have been uncomfortable too. "Let's just get out of here. Then we can work out the details."

She knew how that would sound to anyone watching the surveillance, and she didn't care. She wasn't trying to hide the fact that they wanted out, and she wasn't all that interested in saving money.

"Let me handle the negotiation at least," he said.

She shook her head. She didn't want to waste time bickering over price. "It's just better if we get it done."

He looked like he was about to say something, when a wizened little man walked out of the back door.

"Welcome," he said in accented Standard. "Let me help you find the perfect ship."

Chapter 32

Jack felt jittery. Some of it was the lack of sound in the shop, but most of it came from Skye's determination to handle the entire ship purchase. She did it in a way that he never would have, fast without much negotiation.

In fact, most of the discussion she had with the wrinkled little man who ran the shop was about the type of ship, its specs and its registrations, not its pricing. She also asked some technical questions that Jack didn't understand because he wasn't a pilot.

He paced, looking at the images of the various ships, feeling out of his depth. He and Skye hadn't discussed what was coming next, and that made him uncomfortable too. She hadn't asked about the complexity of the automatic pilot. He started to, but she held up a hand, silencing him.

He let her. He was used to being with Rikki, who often took a commanding lead with things. But it made him even more uncomfortable.

Then Skye whipped out a payment chip, and walked to a payment kiosk with the little man. She didn't consult Jack at all—and that was when he decided the ship was hers, no matter what she said. She would help him get out of this place, he'd figure out where to go and what to do next, and then she could have the damn ship back.

No matter what it did, how easy it was to fly, or whose name she registered it in.

That thought made him walk over to the kiosk. Skye glanced at him, as if he didn't belong.

He had to ask the question without acting suspicious. "I was going to make sure you had all the information for the registration," he said.

"I do, thanks," she said as the little man added, "We always register in the name of the account where payment comes from."

Jack held back an *oh* of surprise, but just barely. He hadn't thought of that. Of course. Zaeen was in one of the most lawless sectors of the galaxy. No one wanted to admit who they were, no one wanted their account information on record anywhere, no one wanted to be traced. So businesses had to adapt.

It was like Krell times a million.

"All right then," he said, feeling stupid and useless. He walked back to the front of the shop.

He hadn't even seen what they purchased. What *she* purchased. He hoped it would work.

She came over to him and slipped her left hand through his arm. In her right hand, she held all kinds of chips and swipe meters.

"It's going to take two hours to prepare the ship," she said.

"I thought we were going to have one—"

"That's fast," she said softly. "They have to change parts of the registration, and I paid to have it fully stocked with food and water."

He wanted to ask her if she trusted the little man to do that, but apparently she had.

Then she leaned her head against him, as if they were some kind of loving couple.

"I'm hungry," she said. "Let's get lunch."

He had lost track. Was lunch the next meal? He had thought the next meal was dinner. He thought for a moment. It *was* dinner, but he didn't correct her, because she might have been trying to conform to local time. Here, on Zaeen, it might actually be midday. There was no way to tell without linking up to the network or simply asking someone, neither of which he wanted to do.

She eased him out the door. The noise returned, not nearly as egregious as it had been. Voices, music, all of it had become a blur to him. He didn't even try to pick out distinct sounds.

Instead of heading toward the overwhelming wall of noise, she turned away, going farther down the passageway.

The lack of people made him as uncomfortable as all of the people had in the center of the pavilion. He had to be honest with himself: he didn't like it here. It was too big, too noisy, and too unfamiliar.

Usually he researched a place to death before arriving in it. He hadn't researched anything before coming here. He was trusting Skye and trust did not come easy for him.

Small restaurants dotted the passageway, usually crammed up against the entrances to various ship shops. Most of the restaurants promised exotic meals, but one offered sandwiches. Skye was about to walk past it, when Jack pulled her toward it.

"Let's just stop," he said.

She glanced inside, then smiled at him. She agreed, apparently. She pushed the door open, and they stepped into the interior.

A waiting bot floated in front of them. Dozens of

patrons sat inside, eating everything from sandwiches to tortillas to some kind of egg dish. Jack's stomach growled. He wasn't sure how long he had been hungry, but he remembered his stomach making the same protest shortly after they arrived on Zaeen.

The bot was trying to decide which face it should float in front of—his or Skye's. It had apparently not been programmed for this kind of height disparity. It floated up to him, then down to her. As it hovered near her, she said, "Have you a private room?"

It showed her a menu with costs on it, suggesting a variety of private rooms—some large and a few very small.

She tapped the small one just as Jack was about to recommend the small one. He was thinking practically: he didn't want to have any space for a sexual moment; he needed time to focus on the future, not on Skye's lovely body. And she was too tempting for him to ignore in the right circumstance.

The bot threaded its way through the throng of patrons, and a narrow door opened. For a moment, Jack thought he might not be able to fit inside. Then he realized he could do so if he ducked and went in sideways.

Just when he was getting used to everything being at his height, the station threw something like this at him.

A table with two chairs pushed up against it filled most of the room. The walls were close. Jack wasn't sure he could sit, but the table apparently read his size and adjusted slightly inward, so that there was room for him and the wall. He hoped there would be room for his knees as well.

Skye closed the door and took the far chair. As she sat, a see-through menu rose before her.

Jack sighed and went to his chair, expecting to hit his knees against the extra part of the table. But he didn't. It was as if the entire table could mold itself to accommodate him without having to adjust its own mass. A menu rose in front of him as well, listing nearly six hundred items.

That overwhelmed him. He just pressed the word "sandwiches" and his choices narrowed by five hundred.

"I have a couple of questions for you," he said to Skye.

She tapped something on the screen and her menu disappeared. Apparently she had ordered.

He tapped the first sandwich that had ingredients he recognized, then his menu disappeared as well.

Her gaze met his. "We're lucky to get the ship in two hours," she said, anticipating one of his questions.

"We're getting it sight unseen," Jack said. "Aren't you worried about that?"

"Most places like this don't allow you to test drive," she said. "The theft rate would be too high. They don't have a police force to go after everyone who blows out of the port in a stolen ship."

Good point, and one he hadn't thought of. He rarely dealt in thefts before the fact, and even then, not thefts as small as the theft of a ship. The thieves he had always vetted for the Rovers had been the guys with vision, the ones who stole millions or billions and destroyed lives. Jack had never even investigated someone who stole one or two things, even if those one or two things were ship-sized.

"What about the food?" he asked. "Do you trust that it's not tainted?"

"Yes," she said. "We can test when we get on board,

but I think it'll be fine. It won't matter, though, if we aren't planning to be on the ship long."

He recognized the question in the form of a statement. What was happening next?

He wished he knew.

"We have choices," he said. "You don't have to travel with me if you don't want to. Traveling with me has clearly proven itself unsafe."

She smiled as if she'd thought of that. "How will you pilot your way back to the NetherRealm?"

"The ship should have an autopilot," he said. "Right? And then you can give me an account so that I can pay you back."

Her smile faded. "Is that what you want to do?"

"What I want and what's best are two different things," he said.

"What do you want?" she asked.

He wanted to find a room somewhere and spend the next week in it alone with her, having food delivered, and investigating all the things their bodies could do together. He wanted to turn back his entire relationship with the Rovers. He wanted to take back that last conversation he'd had with Heller.

He wanted a lot of things, but he couldn't have them.

"I want things to be easier for both of us," he said. "I'm getting in your way."

She raised her eyebrows, then smiled. "I can't deny that," she said. "I accompanied you here. But I'm not on any schedule."

"You're working, right?" he asked. He still didn't know a lot about her.

"Not here." Her face clouded.

"So you need to get back," he said.

"Yeah," she said. "But I've finished most of my pressing work. I'm tracking something else entirely, and I'm not sure if it's on a timeline."

He waited. He didn't want to ask her what that something was. He didn't want to pry.

Then she shrugged. "Let's figure out what you need first. I understand if you want to stay here."

"I *definitely* do not what to stay here," he said so quickly that he surprised himself. Zaeen was too crowded, too uncomfortable, too strange for him. And he thought he could get along anywhere.

"You go back to the NetherRealm and you have to contend with the Rovers," she said.

He nodded.

"Have you thought of what you'd do?" she asked.

"Maybe I should hire someone from the Assassins Guild to take out Heller," Jack said. He was mostly joking, but the joke didn't feel funny to him.

"Well, that would bring everything full circle," she said.

His breath caught. He looked up at her.

"It would?" he asked.

"Yeah," she said. "Remember that woman I saw Heller with?"

He let out a small breath. He had forgotten all about her. "The assassin from the Guild. Hiring a Rover."

"Yeah," Skye said. "It bothers me, and not just for the obvious reason."

"Looks like we have time," Jack said. "Tell me what this is all about."

Chapter 33

Their drinks rose out of a side pocket of the table, startling Skye. She glanced around the room, wishing she had a more sophisticated way to check for surveillance equipment. She would have to assume that their conversation was being recorded, but she would also have to assume that no one would care about it, that every conversation was recorded here on Zaeen. With that much information being stored somewhere, only bots could search through it, and if she avoided trigger words, then no one would ever hear this conversation.

Of course, she had no idea what the trigger words were, so she could only hope she would avoid them.

Jack grabbed the cups and handed her hers. He sipped his. He looked a bit nervous, as if something she had said unnerved him.

Although he'd been nervous since they arrived. Even before he loudly stated that he didn't want to stay here, she had the sense that he hated Zaeen.

She didn't feel much better about it.

"This morning," she said, then paused. "I think it was *this* morning. All of the travel has my time sense confused."

"Our morning," he said.

"When I saw one of the most proficient members of the Guild talking to Heller, I started worrying. She had to have a reason to hire someone like him." She decided to skip the word "assassin," figuring that might trigger something. She hoped Jack would be as cautious.

"Someone proficient?" he asked, and it took her a moment to understand. He had clearly taken her cue and was also avoiding trigger words. He sipped his beverage again. He seemed to have relaxed since she started into this.

She took a sip of her beverage too. She'd only asked for lemon-flavored water, and that was what she got. She was thirsty, and she hadn't even realized it until now.

At some point, both of them would have to stop and actually sleep. Not do anything else. Just sleep.

But the idea of being in a bed with Jack made her cheeks warm. She wondered if he could sense what she was thinking about. Probably not, since he seemed preoccupied with what she had just told him.

"She's one of the best," Skye said. "And here's the thing. She said that he was the third in line. She said there was a chance that they wouldn't need him, but they were reserving his time."

"For what?" Jack asked.

Skye shrugged. "She was going to send the information to an account, along with payment. She wasn't just reserving him. She was reserving a team."

"Oh, God," Jack said. He seemed to understand what that meant. "This may be tied to something I know, but we can't discuss it here."

Then he glanced around, somewhat pointedly. She got the message, even if she hadn't had it before.

"However, I can ask a few questions," he said. "Is this woman someone you're investigating?"

"No," Skye said. "But there've been some unusual

things coming out of the Guild, and they don't entirely make sense. I'm worried, and that's what I was going to investigate."

"Worried how?" Jack asked.

"The Guild's all about rules and regulations. I think there's a rogue element, not following those regulations."

"You want to stop that?" Jack asked.

She smiled. She had told him enough to make that question relevant.

Then food popped up from that same part of the table. Her sandwich stood six inches high and had more food stacked around it. It smelled of ham and cheese and fresh bread.

Jack's was identical, except that it had chicken and different vegetables. Otherwise, there was the same kind of bread and just as much unnecessary food.

"We could have split something," Skye said.

"And still had enough to feed an army," Jack said. But he reached over, grabbed his plate, and slid it to him. As he did, silverware and napkins popped up near him.

She grabbed her own food and slid it toward her. After just a few hours, Jack was clearly beginning to figure her out.

That should bother her more than it did.

"Initially, I started tracking this rogue group because I thought maybe I should join them," she said. "I was looking at a variety of possibilities. I figured that if I could find someone else who broke the rules, I might get permission to break more of them. Then I realized that it was more pervasive than that, so I thought I could use these people as an excuse to get me out of the Guild."

Jack hadn't picked up his sandwich yet. He was

watching her intently. She couldn't remember the last time she'd been the subject of such regard from someone.

She picked up a baby carrot, which looked fresher than any she'd seen in a while.

"The more I investigated, the more furtive it all seemed," she said. "And not in a good way. These people were up to something, but what, I couldn't tell. It bothered me. After all, my job is to investigate things, and I started investigating my own people, and I found things that disturbed me."

"But things you could use if you wanted to," Jack said.

She shook her head. "It was more than that," she said. "It was… scary, on some level. I only got bits and pieces, but what I got didn't seem right."

"Right for what?" he asked.

"Right for… decency?" Her voice went up at the end. She wasn't even sure herself. She had hated the Guild for so long that she knew her feelings about the Guild weren't always a great guide.

"You found it hard to believe that the Guild broke the rules?" he asked, sounding like he didn't find it hard at all.

"It wasn't that the Guild broke the rules," she said, "although that was part of it. No one trained by the Guild broke the Guild's rules, not without punishment."

"Provided they got caught," Jack said.

She switched the carrot to the other hand. "Yeah. And I haven't reported them yet, because I want to know what they're up to. But each time I find something, I discover something else."

Jack wrapped his long fingers around his sandwich. Skye realized that one of the reasons she hadn't picked up hers was because it was so thick. She set the carrot down and grabbed her knife and fork instead.

"Heller," Jack said, "and his people only do one kind of job."

She so appreciated Jack's caution. She understood what he meant. Heller and the Rovers were assassins, nothing else.

"I know," she said.

"So why would someone from the Guild need Heller and what does it mean, as a backup?" Jack took a bite of the sandwich. Parts fell all over the plate. That didn't seem to bother him.

"I have a theory." She pressed down on the bread. The interior of the sandwich squished out. He was making a mess. It didn't matter if she did.

But she wouldn't be able to talk and eat at the same time.

"One of the Guild's directors got murdered a while ago," Skye said. "Someone in-house did it, and everyone said that person was crazy. But what if that's not true? What if it was supposed to happen? I mean, everyone in the Guild must submit to constant medical testing, both physical and psychological. I can't imagine how someone's craziness got through the tests."

"Yet all this behind-the-scenes suspicious stuff is going on," Jack said.

"But that's not crazy," Skye said. "I'm not sure it would come out in tests."

Jack nodded. "Have you investigated the director's death?"

"It happened before I was one of the investigators for the Guild," Skye said. "There's some kind of rift, and it's been around for a while. I just keep thinking that the only reason to hire an outside killer—"

"Is to hide the Guild conspiracy," Jack said.

She shuddered. She hadn't really thought about that word until now. *Conspiracy*. It was such a nasty term.

"But why?" she asked. "I mean, if you don't like the Guild, leave after your time period is up. Start a new organization or join Heller's organization. Or start your own company. There's no reason to destroy the Guild."

"Unless you hate it," Jack said.

He spoke quietly, calmly, as if hating the Guild were the most normal thing in the universe.

She felt cold. She hated the Guild, but she would never destroy it. And maybe hate was too strong a word. She hated parts of the Guild, the parts that trapped her, the parts that assumed she could be a killer. The parts that seemed arbitrary.

But she appreciated parts of it too. She respected a lot of her teachers—not the ones who taught assassination, but the ones who taught history and languages and survival skills. She loved the buildings and the gardens. She liked a lot of the people she had grown up with.

She wouldn't purposefully harm any of them.

But maybe that was because she wasn't an assassin. Maybe someone with assassin training and the same hatred for parts of the Guild would try to destroy it.

"I don't want to be the one to save the Guild," she said.

"Then ignore all of this," Jack said.

She shook her head. "That's the thing," she said. "I can't."

Chapter 34

Skye felt more unsettled than she had when she first touched Jack. Strange how his words unnerved him more than that instant connection had.

Perhaps his words unsettled her because they echoed what she had been thinking. He hit on the same analysis she'd been doing with herself before she saw Liora Olliver talking with Heller.

Skye hadn't had a lot of time to think about it afterwards. She'd been a bit relieved to focus on Jack.

She took a bite of her squished-down sandwich. The ham was real and so was the cheese. All the ingredients were better than any she'd had off-planet. This place amazed her.

Jack ate too. He seemed to understand her need to reflect.

He finished his sandwich quicker than she did. Then he pushed his plate away, with a lot of food left on it.

"Here's one piece of information you need to know," he said. "Heller does the pricier jobs himself. He only deploys a team when he's convinced that one person can't do the job."

"I figured." Skye didn't want to sound dismissive, but she understood how jobs worked. Even the Guild deployed a team when the job sounded too hard for one person.

She took another bite of her sandwich. The food was restorative. She felt less tired than she had.

Jack didn't seem disturbed by her terse response. He said, "Part of what he's trying to do is become the go-to squad for various governments. He told me once that every government needs an extra-legal organization to do its dirty work. He wants the—um—his people to be that."

Skye frowned. Everyone believed that the Rovers already did such jobs. Now she was paying attention.

Jack had just told her that the Rovers had once been different. It explained a lot. It explained how he could seem so honorable and yet work for them.

"You mean that's new?" she asked.

"Since Heller," Jack said. "And just in the last few years. Despite what everyone thinks, the organization wasn't bad. Not really. There were always bad guys affiliated with the group, but they didn't last long."

"If the group has no rules, how could that happen?" Skye asked.

Jack twirled his glass in his hands. "What I was told is that those guys had an inordinate number of accidents."

"That didn't bother you?" she asked. She felt a bit emotionally whiplashed. She thought she understood him, and then he would say something that surprised her, so she understood that, and then he would say something like this about the accidents.

That would bother her. The Guild reprimanded people: it didn't help them meet with "accidents."

"It didn't bother me at the time," Jack said. As he spoke, her heart sank. Had she read him wrong?

"I knew some of those bad guys. The 'accidents' were often quick, efficient, and better than they deserved."

She understood that. She had felt that way about a

lot of the people she investigated. Part of her was quite harsh: she believed some people just needed to leave the universe to improve it.

But she also felt really uncomfortable with assassination as the way to do it. She had said so back at the Guild. It played with dangerous things, and she had protested that. She had protested her part of that.

Death by hire, even if it was legal or nearly legal, crossed certain lines, lines she didn't like, lines she couldn't participate in.

She felt like a hypocrite sometimes, but she truly didn't know a better system. So she made sure that her lines remained firm.

By providing information, she made certain that the right people (or the worst people, in truth) got assassinated, while those with indeterminate guilt or no guilt went free.

She never asked what happened to them when the Guild refused the contract, however. Did those who wanted that person dead go to the Rovers? She didn't know the answer to that question, and she doubted Jack did either.

They would have to research it, and she wasn't sure she wanted to.

She had a hunch she might not like the answer.

"So what changed your mind about your group?" she asked, still avoiding the word *rovers*.

"Too many people who were innocent died," he said. "I did the research before the jobs, and Heller or someone accepted the job anyway, even if I recommended against it. Then I found out about this extra-legal thing. Here's the problem: if you work for a government, the government sets the agenda. The government might despise a group of people for their religion or the clothes they wear or the fact that they are peaceful dissidents. Neither group—yours or mine—should be involved in things like that."

His voice had lowered, yet it sounded even more passionate than it had earlier. He was gripping the glass so tightly that his knuckles had turned white.

This really upset him.

She let out a small breath. She understood that upset. She related to it, and it made Jack a good guy to her. It confirmed the sense she had.

He seemed shocked by the fact that the Rovers had instituted the change. She wasn't, but mostly because she had always thought the Rovers did things like that.

She had been more surprised that everything she had known about the Rovers in the past wasn't true.

"Forgive me for asking this," she said, "but you're telling me this is a change of policy?"

"Yes," he said with quiet force.

He moved the glass near the plate. She got the sense he had done that to avoid crushing the glass between his powerful hands. Then he grabbed the rest of the dishes and replaced them on that part of the table that had delivered them.

"I know what people believe," he said, "and it was never true. When I was part of it all, we let the rumors stand because it made us more unpredictable. It also brought in certain kinds of work that no one would approach the Guild with—not extra-legal work, but dicier jobs, the kind we specialized in. I would investigate, and if I said no, this wasn't our mission, this didn't fall into the kind of legal work that the governments in the sector looked away from or never prosecuted or even encouraged, then we didn't take the job. Back then, my group listened to me."

"And they don't now," she said.

"It's worse than that," Jack said. "It's not about my ego. I could handle it if it were. Now they take the jobs I recommend against, and they ignore the other jobs. They let you guys handle those."

His fingers tapped on the tabletop. As they did, the food dishes he had placed on the side disappeared.

He looked at the mechanism in shock, then leaned back in his chair, hands off the table.

"All of that changed under Heller," she said.

"Yes," Jack said with that quiet forcefulness. "It changed, and then it changed again. Now it's so bad that it doesn't matter who the contract goes out on. The death will happen if the contract exists."

His hands shook. He clasped them together, but the shaking continued.

Finally, he moved them off the table, apparently thinking she couldn't see how upset he was.

"It sounds like this was gradual," she said. "Why is he after you now?"

"Because I was stupid." He started to get up, then looked at the ceiling, and clearly thought the better of it. He obviously needed to fidget.

Skye waited. She had no idea what else she could do.

"I went to the entire group," Jack said. "Or what passed for the entire group. And I told them what I knew, how wrong it was, how many innocent people would be at risk, and you know what they did?"

She was afraid she did know, but she shook her head anyway.

"They laughed at me. They called me naïve. They said innocents get hurt all the time, and if it concerned me, I was in the wrong profession." He ran a hand through his hair. "I agreed with them, so I left. I figured that was the end of it. Then you tell me that Heller's after me."

She was frowning. She understood his confusion. It made no sense to her either.

"I figured that he thought you knew something he didn't want out."

Jack shook his head. He rocked in his chair for a moment, his expression hardening.

"I don't think so," he said. "I mean, how can I ruin their reputation? I can't. Everyone already thinks the worst of them."

"But you have another idea," she said.

"Yeah," he said. "I don't like it."

She waited again, knowing if she pushed he might not tell her. He rubbed a hand over his mouth.

"I think it's personal now. I questioned him in front of everyone, I exposed him, and now he wants me gone."

"He's that petty?" she asked.

"He's a little tyrant," Jack said. "He wants me dead to prove a point, to make an example. He wants to show that he can destroy me or anyone who gets in his way."

Skye's stomach twisted. "If that's the case you don't have a lot of choices."

"I know," Jack said. "Believe me, I know."

Chapter 35

Jack felt trapped in the small room. He wanted to leave, but he didn't want to head back to the crowds in Zaeen. He wanted to pace, but there wasn't room for him to stand up. He needed to move, and Skye wasn't even done eating yet.

Her point made the trapped feeling worse.

"You could just stay in the Brezev Sector," she said, picking at her food. "No one would come here. You could start over."

His sandwich sat heavily on his stomach. He could stay in the Brezev Sector or go somewhere else, but he was six-foot-six, for heaven's sake. He would be out of place, and people would notice him—if he stayed in space, which he loved.

Plus running would mean looking over his shoulder. It would also put Rikki at risk. When Heller had asked Jack what Rikki thought about the changes in the Rovers, Jack had said, *She has no idea what the hell you're doing and she doesn't care*.

He hadn't realized until just now that he had probably saved her life with that statement.

But if he ran away, he would put Rikki's life on the line. The Rovers would go after her, thinking she knew where Jack was. And then they would hurt her, or Heller would.

Not that she couldn't take care of herself. She could.

But he didn't want Rikki on the run as well because of something he did.

And he didn't want to lose her friendship. She was family. If he ran, he would have to apologize, tell her he was never coming back, leave her to fend for herself, and vanish.

What kind of man would do that? What kind of *person* would do that?

Skye was watching him. She had finished most of the sandwich. "If you don't disappear, you'll have to do something. They'll continue to come after you and there's nothing we can do to protect you."

He wasn't sure if the *we* was the Guild or if the *we* meant her and him. He didn't want to ask, either. He wouldn't put her in danger just because she was with him. Unlike the assassins, unlike Rikki, Skye couldn't fend off a trained killer any more than he could.

"I know," Jack said. "I have to come up with something else."

He deliberately avoided the *we* that she had used. But he did need some information from her.

"Would the Guild care that a Guild member has hired Heller?" he asked.

"Yes," Skye said. "Of course."

She was clearly thinking about it. She frowned, then slid her plate aside. "I had hoped to have all the information when I approached the Guild, but I could tell them that this is happening. They would do something about Heller."

"He doesn't rise to their standards for a target, though, does he?" Jack asked.

"It depends," she said. "If he has been hired to harm

someone important in the Guild, then yes, he would. It would be defensive. They would go after him and whoever else was plotting with him."

"We can't just speculate, though, can we?" Jack asked.

"I worry about the Guild doing the investigation," she said. "I don't know who is involved. After today, I think a lot more people are involved than I expected."

"You don't know who to trust," he said.

She nodded. "We have to bring facts to the people in charge."

Now was the time for him to ask about the word *we*. He wrapped his hands together. He felt nervous—he wasn't sure why he felt nervous. Maybe because he felt like a lot was at stake with her answer?

He wasn't sure.

"You mean you and me?" he asked.

"Well, yes," she said as if it were the most natural thing in the universe. "Your people are coming after you, some of my people are involved, there's all kinds of investigating to be done. Why wouldn't you and I do the work together?"

A thread of joy started through him. He ignored it. He couldn't be sidetracked by the idea of spending time with Skye, as enjoyable as he would find it.

Much as he desired it.

"They might catch us before we find out all of the information we need," Jack said. "It's dangerous."

She grinned. "I'd love to tell you that danger is my middle name, but you'd know different. Still, I think it's better for both of us if we go after this together. I mean, how are you going to let the Guild know if you figure out who is involved there?"

"I suppose," he said. He hadn't gotten that far mentally yet.

"And you know who to investigate from your side," she said. "We have a lot of stuff to do."

She sounded happy about it, as if a path made her more comfortable as well.

Still, he had one more question for her. "You spent all this time researching Zaeen. I can only assume it was to find your parents. Don't you want to stay here and do that research?"

"You hate it here," she said.

He didn't like that answer. "That's not a reason for you to leave."

Her grin faded. She did stand up, and he envied that. Still, she didn't have room to pace either. So she just grabbed the back of her chair and ran her hands across it.

"I've researched this place and them to death," she said. "I could stay here for a year and not figure out what happened."

"That's still not a reason for you to leave," he said.

"I know," she said. "I just… they left me, you know? And as a kid, I'd track them down and join up with them again, only to have them leave again. I started researching them, just like I had as a kid, and then I talked us into coming here, and I thought… I'm doing it again. I'm chasing them, and they don't want me."

Her voice didn't break when she said that last bit, but it sounded odd, strangled, as if she had trouble getting the words out.

"And that's if they're alive," she said. "If they're dead, then what have I gained?"

He wanted to get up and hold her. But she had

placed that chair—and the table itself—as a barrier between them.

"Knowledge," he said. "You would know what happened to them."

"Knowledge is overrated," she said.

He shook his head. "I've researched my history for more than twenty years and found nothing. I would love to have a name, an idea, a place to start with."

She stared at him. Then she said, her expression bleak, "I have knowledge. I know they had a pattern. They had no idea how hard it was to raise a child. They had no one to help them and no money. So they'd drop me with so-called friends. Over and over and over again. They were going to send me to the Guild anyway. Their last friend did. They never came for me, they never paid my fees at the Guild, they never even acknowledged me."

Her hands continued to run across the back of that chair. He understood the fidgeting. He had just done it as well. He wanted to take her hands and pull her toward him, but he couldn't move in this tiny room.

"They're the reason I'm trapped by the damn Guild," she said. "I could have gone to school there, and if they had just paid the stupid fees, I'd be free. But I'm still associated in ways I don't want to be because they abandoned me. So why am I chasing them?"

This time her voice did break. And this time, he couldn't stand it. He stood, hit his thighs on the table, and winced as pain threaded through him. He managed to get around it, and he shoved her chair aside. He pulled her in his arms.

He had expected a fight, but she didn't give him one. She buried her head in his shirt.

But she didn't cry. Her breathing didn't even change. He rubbed her back and after a few minutes, she relaxed against him.

How long had she carried that abandonment all by herself? When he talked with her about the Guild, she mentioned that she knew people, but she never mentioned friends.

He didn't have a lot of friends, but the ones he had he valued above all else.

Skye was being his friend. He needed to value that as well.

"Maybe you just want answers," he said. "Maybe you want to stop guessing about why they kept leaving you behind."

Her breath hitched. Then she stiffened, and stood, tilting her head upward so that she could look directly at him.

"Those answers can wait," she said. "They've already waited for most of my life. What's another year or two? Besides, if I help you and we solve whatever is going on with the Guild and Heller, then maybe I can get out of the last of my contract. I'll be free to pursue the investigations I want to pursue."

He smiled at her. "And I can help you."

He was about to add, *We'd make a good team*, when her expression closed down.

She moved away from him. "One thing at a time, Jack. One thing at a time."

Chapter 36

She didn't want to think about the future. She certainly didn't want to think about the future with Jack.

If he had asked her what was wrong, she would have answered him in less blunt terms. She would have said, *Let's survive this first*.

But he didn't ask, and she had the sneaky feeling that he knew what she was thinking. She didn't like that.

She didn't like it at all.

She had been alone her entire life. She wasn't about to change it.

That didn't stop her from wanting to help Jack. She would have done it even if it hadn't benefitted her, although she didn't tell him that. Let him think she was doing this out of self-interest. Both of their worlds were filled with self-interest, and he understood it.

Hell, she did too. It was, she once said to Guild Director Ammons, what made the universe tick.

The best way she could help Jack was to get them out of Zaeen safely. They needed to go to a system or an area where they could research everything without worries of getting caught.

They also needed a place that would allow them to talk freely about the Rovers and the Guild.

They needed to be alone.

It was impossible to be alone on Zaeen.

They left the restaurant and picked up supplies,

including clothing. Over Jack's protest, she bought a laser pistol as well. She had been trained to use one; it was time to have one with her.

They sped through the shopping, and didn't worry about prices. Or at least, she didn't. Jack occasionally made a few faces. He also complained about the fact that she hadn't negotiated the ship.

But she hadn't wanted to negotiate. She was pleased with the ship, which according to the registration was *Hawk*. She and Jack arrived at the port less than two hours after the purchase, and she watched the crew from the store load the last of the food on board.

The ship was huge, just like everything else on Zaeen. She wouldn't have thought it built for speed except that she saw the additions to the engines as she walked around the ship.

Jack walked with her, looking up as she looked down. She would have thought that he would like Zaeen, since it seemed to be the only space station in the universe that could accommodate a man as tall as he was. But he had hurried them through the stores, and then he had taken one store's offer of transport to the port without a second thought.

He wanted to leave immediately, but she wasn't going to let that happen without all of the safety checks she could think of. Since Jack didn't have any real piloting skills, she handled the actual examination of the practical things like engineering and the navigational systems.

She gave him the task of examining the communications systems, the nonship-related computer systems, and she also asked him to make sure that no one had placed tracking devices on the ship.

He had gladly taken that job. Although as she walked around the engineering area and looked at the cargo space, she also looked for tracking devices.

In one of her bolt holes, she had left a device that located tracking devices. She hadn't ever used it on a job, so she had decided it was too much baggage.

She wished she had it now.

It took three hours to examine the ship. When she returned to the cockpit, Jack was there, folded underneath one of the navigational desks, his body tilted so that he could reach upwards.

"Did you find something?" she asked.

Instead of sliding out, he extended his left hand. He turned it upward, and then opened his fingers. On his palm, she saw dozens of tiny chips.

"Trackers?" she asked.

"The obvious ones," he said, and slid out.

"You mean there were some that weren't obvious?" she asked.

"Most of them," he said. "I neutralized them. I don't suppose you found any."

"Just the ones I expected," she said. "The ones that were built in."

"What I found wasn't built in," he said. "They were added to the computer system. I also found some in the trays of food the catering service left."

"I expected that," she said.

"Me, too." He slid out. His cheek had a scrape on the left side, and a scratch on the right. He'd clearly wedged himself into some very tight places.

"You want to double check the engine room?" she asked.

"I wouldn't know what I was looking for," he said. "You might want to check for more of these things."

He held out that handful of chips toward him.

"If someone put those in the engine, the ship wouldn't run," she said. "I did check to make sure no one had tampered with it or with the controls. I reset everything to factory levels, then I customized it, and did it all again. I looked for add-ons and things missing. Nothing came up."

"We're not going to lurch when the ship leaves the port?" he asked with just the trace of a smile. This man was resilient, if he could smile about nearly dying just a few hours ago.

"Not if I can help it," she said.

"Did you check the living quarters?" he asked.

"I thought you were going to do that," she said, staring at those chips.

His smile grew. "I did. I meant, have you looked at them?"

"No," she said, feeling wary. "Why?"

"Five suites, and eight single cabins. We could take a crew out in this thing."

"It'll fly with just the two of us," she said.

He laughed. "You are determined to miss my point. This thing is amazing."

"Oh," she said with a bit of a smile. "It is."

"I think we should just take it somewhere we haven't been before, and try every one of the beds."

She laughed and blushed at the same time. "You thought of that?"

"You haven't?" he asked. Then he touched his forehead with the heel of his other hand as if he had forgotten something. "That's right. You haven't had the time to inspect the important stuff."

"Jack," she protested.

"I think bedrooms are important," he said. "Although I do have a fondness for cockpit floors."

Her cheeks grew hot. "We have to get out of here safely."

"Yes, we do," he said. "And then we're on no timetable but our own."

She hadn't thought of that. It made her breathless.

"We have research to do," she said primly.

"And I think we need some sleep," he said. "But then...."

She laughed again. "Then we'll check out some of the other beds."

"And maybe," he said, "the cockpit floor."

Chapter 37

THE THIRD BED THEY TRIED TURNED OUT TO BE JACK'S favorite. Not because it was the first bed he actually fit in, although it was, but because he learned something about Skye's body that made her coo.

He wasn't sure she was aware she had cooed. She probably would have told him that she "ooed," but she had made a sound that was uniquely her and something she probably didn't even know she could do.

Just the thought of that sound made him want to replicate it. He shifted slightly on the bed, so grateful that his feet didn't hang off the end and that he didn't have to worry about hitting his head on the low ceiling. The suite itself was magnificent, with built-in upholstered chairs, a table, and trim that looked like real wood.

He would have inspected all of it, if he weren't so interested in the woman beside him.

She had a hand behind her head, her eyes twinkling as she smiled up at him. "We're like teenagers," she said.

"And that's a problem how?" he asked. Then he frowned. "You're not saying that I am a bit too excitable?"

She laughed, and slid her hand down his flank. That simple soft gesture would have made him hard if he hadn't already been. She was like candy to him. Candy and alcohol and the best burgers in the universe, things he couldn't get enough of.

He'd never felt like this about a woman.

She slid her legs around his hips, then used her heels to guide him. Her hands played with his back, her mouth found his, and he was lost in sensation. Skin against skin, the tip of him pushing against her dampness, his tongue exploring the inside of her mouth as if he'd never explored it before.

But he had: her taste was familiar to him already, and the lower half of his body knew exactly where to go.

He slipped inside her slowly, rubbing against that spot that made her coo, and she did it again while her mouth was against his. He pulled her closer, her feet pushed him upward, and the rhythm started. He could barely control it, hitting that spot one more time.

She made a different sound of pleasure, a new one, and he slid all the way in. He buried himself in her, not moving, feeling her around him. She disentangled her mouth from his.

"Don't slow down," she said.

He smiled. "But slow drives you crazy."

"C'mon," she said. "Not slow."

But he ignored that. Slow made her even wetter, made her moan, made her tilt her head back so he could find that spot on her neck that made her grab him so hard he felt like he could fuse with her.

"Now," she said, her head back, his mouth on her neck. He felt the words as she spoke them. "Please."

The please got him. He moved in and out just a bit faster. Her hands grabbed his buttocks and pushed him deeper, and all idea of control left him. He started a rhythm that she matched, then she sped it up, he kept up, and her hands fell to the side of the bed. He'd obviously hit the rhythm she wanted, and that was the last coherent thought he'd had for some time, lost in her, the taste and smell of her, the feel of her against him, the thought of her—

And then he lost that last bit of control, pouring himself inside her. She matched his pulsing or maybe he just thought so because his orgasm was so powerful that he felt like he was turning himself inside out.

He collapsed on her, unable to support himself by his elbows. When he realized what he'd done—and he wasn't sure how long that was—he tried to push up, but she grabbed him again, those hands on his buttocks, which should have been (were, if he were honest) arousing, but he was exhausted too.

"We need sleep," he said.

"Okay," she said, and that was all he remembered for a very, very long time.

Chapter 38

He woke up hours later, still inside her—or as close as he could be without being aroused. Her hands touched on his hips, her head on his shoulder. He had rolled to one side at one point, but he still rested on her left thigh. Her leg had to be asleep, and one of her arms had to be asleep. He was probably crushing her and she hadn't yet noticed.

He tried to ease off her, but she moaned and flexed her hands, holding him. He waited a moment. She sighed, still asleep, and didn't move. He had to.

He needed to know if they were being followed. He needed to check a whole bunch of things. He wanted to stay in bed with her, but he also needed a shower, actual rest, some food, and a lot of information.

Jack continued to inch himself off her, managing to do so without waking her. She did clutch at him one more time, but her eyes never opened.

Her mouth was swollen and slightly bruised. Her hair was mussed. She had never looked so beautiful.

He finally managed to get out of bed, and staggered just a little. His legs were wobbly, his thigh sore from pressing against her. She sighed just a little, then shuddered visibly.

That was when he realized the room had a chill.

He grabbed the edge of the blanket and covered her, pausing for just a moment to look at her. Her nipples were hard, probably from the cold. Her breasts leaned toward the bed, confirming they had no enhancements at all. Her legs were long, considering her height (or lack of it), and her muscles weren't really visible; they just kept her trim.

He knew if he touched her again, he would wake her. He didn't want to do that, not yet. But it took as much control as it had when he had started to make love to her.

She was addicting.

He finally understood why some men chose to spend their lives with one particular woman. No other woman would ever measure up.

He tucked the blanket around her, then investigated the en suite bathroom. It wasn't as large as the bathroom in the captain's suite. He knew that from personal experience, since he'd made love to her there after they had tested that bed. But the shower was still large enough to handle him.

He took a quick, hot shower, then grabbed some clothes from the pile of clothing Skye had convinced him to buy as they were leaving Zaeen. He almost felt overdressed, primarily because he and Skye had had such a good time naked in this part of the ship.

As he passed through the suite, he glanced in. She was still in the same position, and still sleeping. She was probably as deep-down tired as he was. The sleep he had gotten felt good.

He went to the cockpit. Skye had shown him the basics of this navigation board. He knew how to run the autopilot. The ship was keyed to his voice, so he could do voice commands. And it was also keyed to his DNA so that he could shut the ship off from anyone except Skye.

He used the voice commands now, asking the ship to show him if they were being followed.

The ship didn't answer verbally. Instead it raised a holographic screen, which showed the ships that had followed them off Zaeen. Those ships flew off when it became clear that the *Hawk* was heading out of the Brezev sector.

Too many people were wanted elsewhere to leave the sector. And many others preferred easy pickin's, and figured that anyone who traveled between sectors probably had a lot more defenses than a thief would want to encounter.

He told the ship to keep monitoring, and then he moved to the workstation that he had isolated while Skye was checking the ship. After he had found the trackers, most of his work had been on this station.

It wasn't because he distrusted Skye, so much as he never trusted anyone. He needed a private place to work and research. Normally, he would have taken one of the cabins, and he probably would (after they had tried all the beds), but he also wanted a station here, since he needed to guard himself.

It felt odd to think about that. He always considered himself low-key, someone who didn't get noticed, someone not worth noticing. He figured no one would ever come after him for the information he had because no one would ever see him as a threat.

He figured wrong.

He and Skye had programmed the *Hawk* to leave the sector and head deeper into the NetherRealm. Krell was in the NetherRealm, but close to the junction of three sectors. He tweaked the ship's navigation program so that it would take the ship past an asteroid belt and into a part of the NetherRealm most traders, government agents, and thieves never entered.

He wanted privacy to research and time to figure out what was going on. Skye said she had no schedule, so she wouldn't mind.

Or so he hoped.

He set up his research area with passcodes and double access keys, as well as DNA and retinal scanning blocks. He also set the scanners to identify a handprint as the last access. The handprint had to come from him, and the hand had to not just be warm, but it had to have an obvious blood flow.

The last thing he wanted was for someone to sever his hand to get access. He'd learned from his assassin buddies that at least one personal entry code needed proof that the person accessing it was alive.

He settled in and started to work. Before he did anything on the possible conspiracy in the Guild or the ties between the Guild and Heller, he opened one extremely private file.

He needed to know everything there was on Skye, and he needed to know it now.

Chapter 39

SKYE WOKE UP DISORIENTED, UNCERTAIN HOW LONG she'd slept. She remembered clearly what she had done before she had fallen asleep, and that made her smile.

She rolled into the crumpled pillow that Jack had left, inhaled, and felt longing for him that startled her. She knew he had to be somewhere on the ship, but she already missed him.

And that frightened her.

She shouldn't miss anyone.

She'd prided herself on remaining solitary, on not needing anyone, on making sure no one needed her.

She thought about that as she took a shower—clearly the second shower in that particular bathroom in a very short period of time. The room still smelled of soap and Jack.

The thought of him brought up so many reactions in her. The memory of all that they'd done together aroused her, the thought of him holding her made her smile, and the way that she missed him even though he was nearby terrified her.

She dressed, then checked the internal computer system to see where he was. She told herself that she checked so that she wouldn't be surprised when she stumbled on him. Then, because she didn't believe that, she told herself she checked so that she would know what he was doing.

Finally, she admitted to herself that she just wanted to know where he was because it made her feel better.

She frowned. She knew where that emotion had come from. She used to check on whoever was watching her when she was a child because she didn't believe she could survive alone. Her parents had instilled that in her—that whoever was with her would leave, and she would have to fend for herself.

Now she knew she could fend for herself. In fact, she could survive better alone than with someone.

Only for the first time, she didn't want to be alone. She wanted to be with Jack.

She almost went to the cockpit to join him, but she stopped herself. She could use this time. She needed to use it, not just to research Liora, but to look up Jack.

Skye had trusted him so far. She had gone with her sense of him. She had looked for the small things, the easily accessible things, but she hadn't dug deep into the record.

She didn't know everything there was to know about Jack Hunter, and she needed to.

She couldn't just go on her gut. She had to know who he was, what he was, and what he might become.

But she also knew that her research would never tell her what she really needed to know. Was he trustworthy? Deep down trustworthy? Personal files on people, files scattered all over various sectors, never told you if a man abandoned his friends in time of need or if he stood by them through thick and thin.

Of course, any file on her wouldn't say that either. She had carefully avoided close friends.

She had made certain that no one got near her, no one needed her trust, no one relied on her.

If anyone looked her up, they would find the ultimate loner.

Jack had admitted to being a loner as well.

She ran a hand through her hair, knowing that her search would be futile.

She also knew that she had to do it. If something went wrong, she would forever regret not checking up on Jack—at least to the best of her abilities.

She left the suite they'd shared, gone back to the captain's suite, which had the most comfortable living area, and modified the secondary navigation access panel. She put all kinds of restrictions on it from DNA scanning to passcodes that she had stolen from other people's accounts to an emergency voice code.

No one could break into this navigation panel even if they wanted to.

Jack couldn't break into this navigation panel, even if he wanted to.

She closed her eyes for a brief moment before starting. Would he be offended that she didn't trust him? Or would he understand?

Should she even care about that?

She wasn't certain.

Then she opened her eyes. She couldn't change who she was, not for anyone.

So she went to work.

Chapter 40

After two hours of searching, Jack could find almost no information on Skye. He had expected that. It both thrilled and disappointed him. He saw the lack of information as a confirmation of much of what she'd told him, but he also realized he might never be able to verify what he'd learned about her in any real fashion.

It surprised him how much he needed to verify.

The last two days had shown him that a lack of information put him in jeopardy. He had known that before, and he had realized it again.

He stood up, stretched, and listened to his back crack. He could access old Guild files like he had done once before, and he still might do that. He wasn't sure what he'd be looking for about Skye—maybe confirmation that she had gone to school there. But he would be able to find out information about Misha for Rikki, and he could say that was what he was doing if Skye caught him.

He glanced at the navigation board and saw nothing out of the ordinary.

Then he realized what thought had gone through his head. *If Skye caught him*. As if he'd been doing something wrong.

He hadn't been. He'd been doing his job.

But was it wrong to investigate a lover? He didn't know. He'd never taken a lover before whom he had known so little about. He had never taken a lover whom he was attracted to first and foremost. Usually he'd like the information he'd learned about the woman more than the woman herself.

He'd never done it backward before.

And, thinking of Skye, he wondered if she was still asleep.

He clicked off the computer setup, reactivated all of the lockdowns so no one could break in, and left the cockpit. He went to that infamous third bed and saw the rumpled sheets, but no Skye. He peered in the bathroom, noted that it was different than he had left it.

Skye was up, somewhere. He could ask the shipboard computer where she was, but he decided to look for her.

He found her in the captain's cabin, hunched over one of the navigational accesses.

"Skye?" he asked.

She jumped, then looked at him guiltily. He wondered what she'd been doing, and resisted the urge to get close enough to check.

"You hungry?" he asked, because he could think of nothing else to say.

She nodded. She tapped the screen in front of her, then stood.

She wore one of the outfits she had bought on Zaeen. Their clothes shopping had been haphazard. Mostly they'd told the robot clerks to bring them clothing in their sizes and then bought it all. It was easier than making choices.

Still, the choices she had made emphasized how lithe her body was, and accented the blackness of her hair. The wedge cut was combed now, and she looked completely put together, not the wild woman he had discovered in all those beds.

She came over to him, slipping her arm through his. "Checking up on me, huh?" he asked.

She stiffened.

He smiled to himself. He'd been doing the same with her.

"Did you find much?" he asked.

"Not after you left Tranquility House," she said. "And nothing before that."

He nodded, then decided for full honesty. "I didn't find much on you either."

She glanced at him sideways, tilted her head back, revealing that lovely neck, and then laughed. "We're quite a pair."

"Yeah," he said. "We are."

Then, because he couldn't help it, he kissed her. She slipped her arms around his neck and kissed him back. They fell against the door frame.

"We really need to eat," she muttered against him.

"We do," he agreed as he lifted her and carried her to the bed. It wasn't his preferred bed, but it would do. "Later, okay?"

"Oh, yeah," she said as she opened his shirt. "Later is just fine."

Chapter 41

SKYE SPENT THE NEXT SEVERAL DAYS IN A SEX-INDUCED haze. That was the only way she could describe it to herself. She researched Liora Olliver and explored everything she could find about the Guild, but she did it between sessions in bed with Jack.

In bed, on the built-in couches, on the table in the kitchen, in the showers, on the cockpit floor—

He was endlessly inventive, and she was endlessly appreciative.

And she tried not to think about the implications of it all. That moment of terror after they had first fallen asleep together kept resurfacing. She wasn't made to be close to anyone.

But for the past several days, she pretended that she was.

When she wasn't spending time with Jack, she dug into Guild files. She found some connections with the Rovers that she hadn't known existed. Apparently, the Rovers called themselves that because they had "roved" away from the Guild.

In the early years of the Rovers, most of the assassins had been Guild trained. Either they had been banished from the Guild, or left after they had finished their apprenticeship. They all complained that they didn't like the Guild's tight rules, and they all claimed they preferred to be loners.

Some in the Guild believed that they liked receiving full payment for a job instead of paying a commission to the Guild.

But she had no way of knowing that.

Most of the early Rovers were dead or retired now. And none of them seemed to have a connection to Heller.

Only Liora Olliver had one, and the only way Skye knew about that was because of the meeting. Skye could find no other obvious connections.

Her research made her more and more uneasy, though, and she blamed some of her inability to assemble the pieces on a distraction named Jack Hunter.

She would wake up, often alone since he was more restless than she was, and think she needed to bring the ship into a port, so that they could go on their separate ways. They had helped each other, and they had taught each other about the two organizations.

But every time she either thought of leaving Jack on his own to face the Rovers who wanted to kill him or trying to convince him to take the ship and run, she remembered the conversation they'd already had about it, the look on his face as he said he couldn't do that, and the conviction in his voice.

What she believed now was that he might lie to her. He might actually tell her he was running away, just to keep her safe.

He would never vanish, not as long as the threat remained. And she couldn't leave him alone in more ways than one. Yes, she wanted him in her bed every chance she got. But she also knew he needed help so that he could survive this Rover threat.

Whatever that meant.

Still, she was enjoying these quiet days where no one interrupted them. She had never enjoyed any time more.

And she tried not to think about how much that worried her.

Chapter 42

THEY SPENT DAYS IN THE SAME PATTERN. MAKING love, researching, making sure they were alone. Jack thought it the most perfect two weeks of his life. He had never experienced anything like it before.

Skye didn't mind that he researched privately in the cockpit and he didn't mind that she did the same in the master suite. They often compared notes, and they helped each other as much as possible.

They set up one research area for joint research, and decided—together—to plunge into the Guild files. The joint area was in what would have been the entertainment room, had there been a crew to entertain.

But there wasn't. Just a few consoles, mostly to access parts of the cockpit if necessary, several gaming tables, and too many couches.

Jack and Skye tried out all of the couches. They even tested a couple of the gaming tables, and discovered only one that didn't hold their joint weight.

Skye had laughed as the table collapsed and they landed in a pile of plastic, felt, and chips. *At least we own the ship*, she had said. *No one's going to dock us for destroying it*.

Or ask us how we damaged it, Jack had said. He had laughed as well, even though the reminder that they owned the ship caught him. He had almost forgotten that she had paid for it.

Jack mostly let Skye dig into the Guild files, but he had some research to do on his own, and not just research about Skye. He did that when she wasn't around, and he did as little of it in the Guild files as possible.

What he had found confirmed what she told him: she had been left at their doorstep, she had been a scholarship student, she had flunked a lot of classes, and she then disappeared off everything except their student registries.

He didn't think she had tampered with any of that information, but he didn't know for certain.

So to make a comparison, he looked for Mikael Yurinovich Orlinski, the man that Rikki had asked him to research. Jack found a lot about Orlinski, things that unsettled him and would upset Rikki. Apparently Orlinski and Rikki had more of a history than Rikki remembered. Jack checked and double checked and triple checked.

Then he sighed, and waited a few days before contacting Rikki, just because he knew how much the information would bother her.

He used those few days to explore the Guild files under the guise of looking for more information on Orlinski, whom everyone seemed to call Misha.

The man was the straightest of straight arrows. He seemed to revel in rules, which was the opposite of Rikki. But that, and the earlier part of the history, made him sound like less of a problem than Rikki said he was.

The information also squared with everything Skye had said about Orlinski, that he was a good man so far as she knew, and she would trust him with her life.

In researching Orlinski, though, Jack found more about Liora Olliver, the woman who had hired Heller. And she didn't seem like such an upstanding citizen.

She'd gotten in trouble with the Guild from the beginning, and she seemed to like chaos.

When asked about her, Skye had said that she had never liked her, but she hadn't thought about her much until that day on Krell.

Jack finished what research he could. He still hadn't found everything he had been searching for, but he found enough to make him wary.

He knew he and Skye needed to do some more digging, but he also had one other thing he had to finish. He had promised he would contact Rikki as soon as he had information.

He had already waited a few extra days, mostly because he didn't want to have any contact traced back to his location. He could just make the contact, and take the risk that nothing would happen, or he could confide in Skye and take the risk that she might veto the contact altogether.

For the first time, he saw the downside of a team.

Still, he figured it wasn't fair to just contact Rikki without warning Skye.

He waited until they were doing some joint research in the entertainment room.

He swiveled his chair toward her. "Skye," he said, in his most serious voice.

She raised her head just a little. He recognized the movement. She was preoccupied.

"Skye, this is important."

She sighed and turned toward him. She wasn't wearing much—a tank top and some shorts that revealed her toned legs. Her feet were bare.

They had both taken to wearing as little as possible

because more often than not, the clothes just came off at the most unexpected times. (Then he smiled to himself. The clothes didn't *just come off*. They got removed, often in the heat of a very hot moment.)

"I'm following an unusual trail," she said. "Can we wait an hour?"

She must have recognized the look on his face and known what he was thinking about.

"Actually," he said, "I just need to talk with you for a minute."

She looked just a bit surprised. Then she blinked and frowned, clearly wrenching her mind away from whatever research she had been doing.

"Remember when I told you about Rikki?"

Skye nodded.

"I promised her that I'd let her know about your friend Orlinski as soon as I had information on him. I've had information for days, and it's bugging me—"

"Anything I should know?" Skye said.

"Just that he seems even more honorable than you made him out to be."

She smiled a little. "You sound disappointed."

Jack smiled at himself. "I might be. I don't like the idea of Rikki being involved with someone I don't know."

He didn't like the idea of Rikki being involved with anyone, truth be told. He knew there would never be anyone good enough for her, at least not in his opinion. No matter how straight up the guy was. Or how honorable.

"You're that close?" Skye asked.

He nodded. "She's family, remember?"

"I do," Skye said. "But you should remember that my experience of family isn't a good one."

His breath caught. He hadn't thought of it in those terms.

"I rely on her," he said by way of explanation. "She relies on me. We saved each other's lives more than once, first as kids and then as adults. We—"

"You don't have to justify the relationship," Skye said.

Was that what he was doing? Maybe. He wanted Skye to understand that his relationship with Rikki was different than his relationship with her. Different in a thousand ways.

Of course, he'd never really used the word *relationship* out loud with Skye. It was what they had, though. It wasn't just sexual. It was something more. Something he'd never experienced before.

Which was why he wanted her to understand how he felt about Rikki.

"I need to tell her about him," Jack said. "And I need to do it as soon as possible."

"I don't see why it can't wait," Skye said. "If you're that close to her, the Rovers have to know it. They'll be waiting for a communication between the two of you."

"They might," Jack said. "But they might not. I told you, they're not always sophisticated."

"It's a risk, though," Skye said.

"Which is why I'm telling you," Jack said. "I can't put this off any longer."

Her lips thinned. His heart was pounding. He could tell from her expression that she knew what else he was talking about. The idyll was almost over.

"We still don't have a plan," Skye said. "I've been thinking about it. We need to hire someone to go after Heller."

Jack had thought of that too. But he didn't want to

take such drastic action. Not yet. They still hadn't finished their research.

"So let's wait," Skye said. "I'm sure she won't mind—"

"She was in a hurry when I talked to her on Krell," Jack said. "And she looked more upset than I'd ever seen her. I *need* to talk to her, Skye. I'm being a bad friend right now. She relied on me, and I am failing her."

Skye stared at him for the longest moment. He could almost see her thought processes. She didn't quite understand what he was talking about, but she was trying to.

"Is something wrong between her and Misha?" Skye asked.

"I don't know," Jack said. "But she doesn't know their entire history together, and she needs to."

"Because…?"

He let out a small sigh. Rikki had told him most of her past in confidence. He doubted she would want anyone else to know, particularly another member of the Assassins Guild.

"Because it might make a difference in a few things she does," Jack said, hoping to leave it at that. "I wasn't really asking your permission. I wanted you to know that I'll be contacting her as soon as we can move the ship near the asteroid belt."

The belt would give them some protection. Their trail would be hard to follow because of the asteroids.

"Then we can go back to what we were doing," he said.

But something in Skye's face told him that going back might not be possible. He reviewed what he had said. She had started to frown when he said he wasn't asking her permission.

"I thought we were a team," she said.

"We are. But we are individuals as well, and I have an obligation to Rikki."

"It could risk your life," Skye said.

He nodded. "Friends do that sometimes. You have, with me."

She let out a small sigh. "What'll happen if you continue to wait?"

"That's what I don't know," he said. "Rikki has her own life. But she relies on me for information. She makes judgment calls because of it."

Skye leaned back for a moment, then shook her head. "In life and in work. You're the information guy."

"You're an information person too," Jack said.

"Only I've never had the kind of friend who needed information from me," she said. She thought for a moment, then said, "It's important to you."

"Yes," Jack said.

"You made it sound like it was more important to her," Skye said. "Don't risk your life on something you don't think important."

It was good advice. He knew that. "I'll keep the conversation short," he said.

"I know," she said. "I hope that's going to be enough."

Chapter 43

Skye gave Jack privacy. She left the entertainment area and wandered, feeling lost. At first she wondered if she were jealous, but she couldn't be, right? She didn't have a real relationship with Jack.

Although she had no idea what she should call these past several days. A vacation? A momentary lapse of judgment?

It didn't feel like a lapse of judgment.

She walked into the galley and made some coffee. Then she took out one of the self-baking cookies she had ordered. They prepared themselves when the stash got low, and the stash had gotten low several times. She hadn't paid attention to her exercise regime or to her diet during this trip.

Of course, she had gotten a lot of exercise. Just not the type she expected.

She almost smiled, and with that near-smile came the explanation for that lost feeling. When Jack talked to Rikki, this trip was officially over. The privacy, the sense of being alone in a vast universe, the way that Skye and Jack had pretended they were the only two humans of consequence anywhere was over.

Real life had intruded again, and with real life came real problems.

And thoughts of how real relationships worked.

She bit into that cookie, tasting molasses, chocolate,

and sugar. It didn't satisfy like it had before. The coffee was done as well, so she had some.

She couldn't check if Jack was done because he had a special communicator that allowed Rikki to contact him, and he carried it with him at all times. He hadn't lost it, even in the chaos of leaving Krell.

He called it the CFA—the Communicator for the Assassinator—which spoke of a fondness between Jack and Rikki that Skye didn't entirely understand.

She was beginning to realize that in keeping herself from friendships, she had kept herself from a lot of warmth, a lot of closeness, and a lot of silly jokes.

She glanced at the time. Jack had said it wouldn't take long. Then he would probably return to work. He hadn't asked for privacy either, although she'd given it to him.

And she did want to know how the discussion went, because it would have a bearing on what the two of them would do next.

She grabbed another cup of coffee, put a few cookies on a plate, and carried it all back to the entertainment center.

The door was open, and Jack was talking. She stopped, about to turn around, when he nodded her in.

He had attached the small communicator to the wall. He was sitting in front of it. He beckoned Skye with a hand that wasn't visible to the tiny woman on the screen.

Skye stayed out of visual range as she set the coffee and cookies down.

"You know, Rik," he was saying, "he seems legit, but I have the sudden urge to kick his ass."

Skye stiffened. Did brothers and close friends respond that way? She knew that lovers did.

"Jealous?" the small image on the screen asked. Her voice sounded tiny and far away. Yet Skye could hear the fondness, and the comfortable banter in it.

"Hell, no," Jack said quickly. "You know what I mean. It's just that he better treat you right. A man has to protect his family and you're all I got."

Skye wondered if that last was for her. Jack didn't look at her as he said it, but his hand was out as if he were waiting for her to take it.

She wasn't going to get close. This was a private conversation, and she felt awkward enough as it was.

"I promise I'll be careful," Rikki was saying.

"You better." Jack glanced at Skye. Outside of the visual range of the communicator he held up a single finger, clearly asking her to wait. It wouldn't be long now.

He opened his mouth, and Skye could tell that he was about to sign off. Then Rikki said, "Jack? One more question."

He leaned back. Something in Rikki's tone didn't sound right. Skye didn't know her and even she could hear it.

"Yeah?" he said.

"You hear any rumblings about the Guild? About someone trying to bring it down?"

Skye suppressed a gasp. She wouldn't have thought Misha was involved in anything. Why would someone like Rikki know about problems at the Guild?

Skye was about to gesture to Jack to ask if she could communicate with Rikki when Jack said testily, "What's he got you into?"

And the moment was lost. Skye wouldn't confide in

anyone using that tone either. Still, she thought maybe she could salvage it by asking Jack if she could talk.

"He hasn't gotten me into anything," Rikki said.

Skye gestured so that Jack could see her. Skye pointed at herself, then raised her eyebrows, asking if she could talk.

But Rikki was continuing. "It's just—I can't talk with you about it over any kind of net. But I was thinking, you know, with the Rovers—"

"I have nothing to do with them," Jack said curtly. "I have to go, Rik."

He had completely misunderstood the gesture. He severed the connection and turned to Skye.

"What?" he said.

"I wanted to talk with her," Skye said.

Jack shook his head. "It wouldn't have done any good. I know Rikki. That last was about something she was finding. She says that Orlinski didn't get her involved in anything, and I believe her."

Skye handed him the coffee. "I do too. But maybe they had information we don't."

"Rikki thought she was being monitored, and you and I are worried about being monitored. I don't think it would have been appropriate to talk with her about it just now."

"You should contact her again," Skye said.

Jack stood, then slipped the CFA off the wall and into his pocket as if he worried that Skye would try to override him.

"Have you thought," he said, "that they're already getting to her?"

"Who is 'they'?" Skye asked.

"The Rovers. She's asking questions about them and the Guild. What made her put that together?"

"Maybe you did," Skye said. "She thinks you're still part of the Rovers."

"Not after that," he said. He sighed, then sipped the coffee. "Thanks for this."

"I think you should contact her again," Skye said.

He shook his head. "It sounds like she and Orlinski are working things out. I just gave them an excuse not to leave wherever they are for a few days."

He said that as if it were important.

"And?" Skye asked.

"And I think we've got to finish this," he said.

"Finish what, exactly?" she asked.

"We have to get Heller off my back and we need to figure out what's going on at the Guild."

"From here?" Skye asked.

He looked at her, and the look was sad. "No," he said. "I think it's time to go back."

Chapter 44

She had known he would say that after talking to Rikki. Skye just wasn't prepared for how it made her feel.

Her breath caught, and the disappointment made her stomach ache. But she kept her expression impassive. She didn't want him to know how startled she was by her own reaction.

"I think we need to meld our research into some kind of chart," he said. "I think that might give us hints as to what's going on. Then we might be able to figure out who to talk to at the Guild."

She nodded. He used the same methods she did, organized, responsible, double checking everything. She still thought it odd that they were so compatible. She had thought before she met him that she—and her methods—were unique to her.

"Then we'd best get at it," she said.

He caught her hand, almost making her spill her coffee. "I'm sorry, Skye. I don't want to go back."

She almost said, *Then don't*. But she didn't. They'd had that conversation. She knew what he was saying. He was saying he was sorry he *had* to go back.

And she understood that. She really did.

"It had to come to an end sometime, didn't it?" she asked. She tried not to sound bitter. She hoped she wasn't sounding bitter. She felt sad too.

"I… hope not," he said. "I mean, this has to end, but we can still…"

He trailed off. She waited. Still what? Sleep together? Be together? Become partners in detection and rove the universe searching for information?

She didn't say any of that.

Instead, she leaned over and kissed him on top of his head. He looked startled. She would wager hardly anyone had ever done that to him.

"We'll worry about what we can still do when we're done doing this," she said. "We have more steps before we're done with any of this. We're not even sure…"

She didn't want to finish that sentence, so Jack finished it for her.

"…that I'll survive it," he said.

She laughed without humor. "I meant to say that we would survive it," she said.

"I'm going to make sure you survive," he said. "You can count on that."

But they both knew that she couldn't. No one controlled the future. And no one controlled people like the Rovers.

But she pretended to agree with him. And then they got back to work.

Chapter 45

THEY HAD FOUND DIFFERENT THINGS ON THEIR research, things they hadn't told each other until they sat at the large gaming table in the entertainment area, the tabletop divided into a dozen screens, each with information flowing across it.

Jack used one main screen in the center to chart all the information. Skye hated to admit that he was better at charting than she was. Faster, better organized, with all kinds of additions that clarified things instead of making them more confusing.

He sat in front of the chart, adding to it as she added information. She wandered around the table, glancing at screens. She also maintained one other screen toward the far end of the table, and that screen scanned for connections that neither Jack nor Skye had seen.

That screen found the thing that nearly made Jack crazy. Apparently Liora Olliver had once been involved with Misha Orlinski.

Jack wanted to let Rikki know right away, but Skye stopped him. Skye normally didn't pay attention to other people's relationships, but she remembered that one. Misha and Liora were mismatched from the beginning. Liora had lorded it over all of the other women that she had been involved with him, and Misha apparently hadn't noticed.

When he did, or when something else happened,

something Skye did not know want to know about *ever* (she believed other people's relationships should be private—extremely private), then he broke up with Liora.

The breakup had been so ugly that Skye avoided both of them. Misha, because Liora stalked him and made nasty comments to any woman who was near him, and Liora because—well, because she had become so very bitter.

She had been so disruptive that the management of the Guild had disciplined her over her behavior. Skye remembered that too, because she had been stunned to see someone else get disciplined and she had also been stunned that the Guild had actually acted against one of its best assassins.

She explained all of this to Jack, who stared at the connection for the longest time.

"And this Olliver woman is the one who hired Heller," he said.

Skye nodded.

"Don't you find that odd?" he asked.

"I find it all odd," she said.

He stood up and arched his back. It popped. Then he reached upward and touched the ceiling. His arms remained bent. She couldn't touch the ceiling if her life depended on it. Not without standing on a chair or something.

"This discipline that she got, was it severe?" he asked.

"Based on what?" she asked.

"I don't know," he said. "I don't know that much about the Guild."

She thought about it. She thought her relationship with the Guild was severe, but she had never been disciplined.

Other people had, though. Some got demoted and were no longer assassins. They got moved to other parts of the Guild. Some were happy to be off the assassin track and probably violated some rule so that they would be demoted and not have to kill for a living.

But people like Liora, they rarely got disciplined, and almost never for something personal.

"She was on an accelerated track," Skye said, thinking out loud. "She was the best at everything, which always made me feel stupid because I was pretty bad at most of it."

"What's everything?" Jack asked.

"You know, shooting, using knives, figuring out how new weapons worked. She could hit targets from a crazy distance, but she preferred to be up close. And if there was a timed test, she often beat the time."

Jack looked down at Skye. She wanted to tell him to sit. This standing made her uncomfortable.

"I thought you didn't pay attention to other people," he said.

"It was hard not to with her. The teachers and judges who weren't very observant always confused us. We look alike."

Jack frowned. "I saw her. She shares your body type, but it's pretty clear that she is nothing like you."

"Not to most of the folks at the Guild. They wanted me to be her. They usually forgot I even existed—until I wanted out, that is. Then everyone knew me." Skye sounded bitter, but she was bitter. No, check that. She was angry. Furious.

And she'd been happy to see Liora disciplined.

"What happened after she got disciplined?" Jack asked.

"She had to go through some sensitivity training or something, I don't know," Skye said. "She couldn't leave the Guild for months. I remember that because I ran into her during that time and wow, was she nasty. I remember saying to Hazel Sanchez, who'd also been in class with us, that the discipline didn't seem to be working."

"And what did your friend say?" Jack asked.

Skye started. She hadn't said that Hazel Sanchez was her friend. "Um, she said that the discipline generally didn't work. It usually pissed people off, and if *she* were in charge, she'd make sure they revamped the entire program."

He pointed at Skye as if she had said that. "There's the link," he said and got back in his chair.

He leaned toward one of the other screens and started tapping at it.

"Is there any way, besides forcing you to remember, to know who got disciplined and who didn't?"

"That's not an easily accessible file," Skye said. "And I don't remember most of who got disciplined. It really didn't matter to me."

"I figured," he said, sounding distracted. "Can we hack into the private Guild files?"

"We'll get found a lot faster if we do," she said.

"Is there a way to figure it out without getting into the private Guild files?"

She sat down beside him. "There is a pattern. Someone is on a career track, then they get yanked off—"

"For months, right?" he said.

"Yeah," she said. "And they get sidelined in the Guild, and then they're never on the same track."

"So this Liora Olliver, she lost her entire career because she had relationship issues."

"They weren't issues," Skye said. "She was stalking him and—"

"You know what I mean," Jack said.

"Yeah, I do," she said. "Liora never got promoted after that. She got passed over for all kinds of assignments."

"And you know that...?"

"Because she bitched about it. She came to me and said that we were two of a kind because we were both bound to the Guild. She had to serve some months doing what they wanted. I told her that we were nothing alike and if she ever said that again, I'd figure out a way to hurt her."

Skye spoke with the same kind of force she'd used when she threatened Liora.

"*You* said that to an assassin?" Jack asked.

Skye raised her chin. "I could do it if someone made me mad enough. I'd be stealthy and I probably wouldn't have physically hurt her. I might've hurt her identity or something, but yeah, I would—"

"I'm just impressed," Jack said.

Skye flushed. Someone else's opinion hadn't really mattered to her before.

"Thanks," she said, knowing the word was inadequate.

He nodded, looking down at the screens, as if what had just passed between them hadn't been important.

Maybe it hadn't been to him, but to her, it was a revelation. She let out a small breath. He was becoming important to her.

She didn't want him to be.

Or did she?

"It's going to take some work to figure out who got

yanked off career paths," Jack said. "These older files are counterintuitive."

She took another deep breath, glad he wasn't looking at her. "Yet, it would all be in the older files."

She kept her head down, then moved to the other side of the table. She didn't want to think about Jack right now. She wanted to focus on this search.

But he was very distracting.

"I think we can set up search perimeters," she said.

"How?" he asked. "It seems to me that being demoted is a personal thing. That whole career track would be something someone would sense, rather than actually experience."

"You are such a Rover," she said.

His head came up quickly. He wasn't smiling.

She held up her hand.

"I didn't mean that as an insult," she said. In fact, she'd meant it as banter. But she didn't say that. "I just meant that you're from an organization that's 'loosely' affiliated. I come from one with rules. There's an actual career track. Look."

She called it up, and showed it to him. The good grades, the high marks on the physical side of things, the internship, the early jobs, and then the successful jobs. Only the most successful assassins got the work that took brains and skill. The rest got pretty routine work, mostly dealing with fairly dumb criminals that couldn't get prosecuted usually for some silly reason.

Only a handful of assassins from each graduating class got assignments of the kind that the Guild was famous for. And after her relationship with Misha, Liora hadn't gotten any of those.

Misha had, though. He had never gone out of favor with those in charge of the Guild.

That had driven Liora crazy as well.

Skye explained all of this to Jack. He studied it as if it were a different language.

"Wow," he said. "It's like the Guild is some kind of government in its own right."

"It is," she said. "Once you're in its sphere, you don't leave."

Or you rarely leave, she thought. She was one of the few who planned to. Even the folks who hadn't done well in her class planned to stay after their early assignments were over. The Guild gave everyone a home, and protection.

Provided they survived their first few years as an assassin.

"That'll help," Jack said. "We might actually have a chance of figuring all of this out."

"Information is always out there," Skye said. "It's just a case of putting it together."

He grinned at her. "Did I say that to you?"

"No," she said with a mock frown. "I've been saying it for years."

"So have I," Jack said, then lowered his head and went back to work.

Compatible. Similar. With the same methods and the same interests. She sighed softly. And he was impressed with her.

His life might be threatened, but she was the one in trouble.

She had succumbed to the ultimate attachment.

She had fallen in love.

Chapter 46

Skye seemed nervous and preoccupied. She paced around the entertainment room, and wouldn't alight anywhere for long. She'd sat next to Jack a couple of times, then popped back up as if ejected from her seat.

He tried to focus on the information pooling in front of him, but he had trouble doing so. Part of him needed to monitor Skye just because she was acting so strange.

And, if he were honest with himself, he also wanted to monitor her because he had been monitoring her all along. She had become his focus. He loved her changing moods, her soft skin, the way that she laughed. He just wanted to spend more and more time with her—and he knew he had ruined that by contacting Rikki.

Not that Skye was jealous. She hadn't been.

He'd ruined it because they had agreed that the outside contact would force them back into the populated parts of the universe. Their time together was over, and they hadn't discussed the future.

He hadn't discussed the future because there might not be one. Or maybe that was just the excuse he was giving himself, because he worried that Skye would tell him that once this entire adventure was over, he was on his own.

She had been so clear from the beginning that she didn't want any attachments. The more he learned about her, the more he realized that she had lived her entire life according to that philosophy, and these past few weeks with him had simply been an aberration.

An enjoyable aberration, but an aberration all the same.

"Okay," he said, trying to focus on the information, "when people get disciplined, sometimes they get demoted, right?"

"Yeah," Skye said. "You find anything?"

"Quite a bit." He already had a list of about twenty names. "Does the Guild do anything to prevent traitors in its midst?"

Skye froze. "That's a big word. Traitors."

"It's what someone would be, right, if they went against a country or a government. Isn't that what we're looking for with the Guild?" Or maybe he was just jumping to the wrong conclusions.

Skye still hadn't moved. She ran a finger along the edges of the screen in front of her. "I guess so, yes. But what would be the goal of these traitors?"

Jack shrugged. "Would they want to overthrow the government of the Guild?"

"We don't call it a government," she said. Then she leaned forward, and started tapping on the screen. "Take a look at this."

She sent more information to him. It was about the death of the former director of the Guild, the man she had mentioned before, a man named Rafiq Zvi. According to the information that Skye just sent Jack, this Zvi had been killed by someone inside the Guild, someone who had gone crazy.

It seemed too easy to Jack.

"Let me check this out," he said.

He dug for a bit to see what he could find. The Guild

records had very little, although they claimed that Zvi had died on Guild property. But the more Jack dug, the more he found references to the nearby city of Prospera.

So he looked in Prospera's records. Apparently, the city had claimed jurisdiction at first because, contrary to the Guild records, Zvi had died in a restaurant in Prospera. The city had investigated a little. Then the Guild informed the city that the Guild would do the investigation.

The city handed jurisdiction over to the Guild with a speed that surprised Jack. Usually police departments were very protective of their own investigations. They also wanted to make sure that a suspicious death got solved properly.

Most of the research he had done for the Rovers early on had been in jurisdictional matters, in figuring out who or what someone could get away with in a particular location. He was an expert in finding out how to avoid jurisdictional problems and when to invite them.

It looked like someone had done the same for this death in Prospera.

He dug a bit deeper, and found a name that had been on his list of possibly disciplined assassins.

"Do you know a Camalla Taub?" he asked Skye.

"Why?" she asked.

"She's the one who got the investigation of Zvi's death moved out of Prospera," Jack said.

"He died in Prospera?" Skye ran a hand over her face. "Wow. I always thought he'd been surprised in the Guild."

"Not from the initial reports," Jack said. It took him some digging to retrieve those reports, but he managed it. "Apparently, he'd been in a restaurant with some old friends. He'd gotten up—to do what seems to be in dispute—and got beaten to death in the back part of the restaurant."

"That's weird," Skye said. "The directors of the Guild come out of the top assassin pool. Do you know how hard it is to kill people like that?"

"Only in theory," Jack said. He really didn't want to know.

"This contradicts every story I've heard about his death," Skye said.

"Weren't you at the Guild at the time?" Jack asked.

"Yeah, and it shook up everyone. But we were awakened the next day, told he was dead, and told that the Council of Governors would elect a new director. It took weeks, and then it got disputed, and finally Kerani Ammons took over. It took her a while to consolidate power since almost half the council had voted against her."

Jack remained silent. He dug a bit more. He felt oddly disturbed. And he wasn't quite sure how to communicate that disturbance to Skye.

Finally, he said, "I know you've learned to think of the Guild in a particular way, but imagine this if it were a country instead of the Guild. The leader dies, and the information about the death is not clear. Someone gets blamed, but that someone might not even have been near the leader when the death occurred."

"Is that true?" Skye asked. "I thought some crazy killed him. Isn't that what happened?"

Her reaction was what Jack had been afraid of as he started this line of thought. He had learned long ago that people brought up in a system had trouble thinking outside of that system, even if they didn't like the system. Since he'd never had any allegiance to any system, he had the luxury of being a free thinker.

"Just go with me on this for a moment," Jack said. "Imagine if the someone who got blamed could possibly be a patsy."

"Damn," Skye muttered.

"And there's a cover-up. No one knows, or the people who do know don't care. To get a new leader, there are a series of hoops that everyone has to jump through, including an election through a limited body."

Skye swallowed hard. Her gaze remained on Jack's. He hadn't moved. He was afraid he would upset the balance between them.

"If you control most of that body, then you get the leader you want," he said. "But if you only control half, it might be dicey. It might take a bit of finesse. It would definitely take more time."

"I'm not sure I like this." Skye clearly understood what he was getting at.

"Ultimately, it doesn't work. The new leader gets chosen but by the wrong half of the council, and it takes a while for that leader to consolidate power. That leader, who hasn't been part of the inside group until now, knows nothing about the cover-up on the other death, and so governs according to whatever laws are in place."

"Laws that include a discipline system that destroys careers," Skye said. She clearly understood what he meant. She seemed both upset and intrigued by it.

Jack was intrigued, but he didn't want to communicate his enthusiasm to Skye. He wanted her to come to the ideas slowly, because he didn't want to have to fight her.

"And that leader will keep people not suited to the job of assassin on the job," Jack said.

Skye backed up, hands out. "I don't like this."

"I know," he said. "But you see where I'm going with it."

"Yeah," she said softly. "Now I understand why you used the word 'traitors.' You think someone is going to assassinate Kerani Ammons."

"And this time," Jack said, "they're leaving nothing to chance."

Chapter 47

It took Skye a moment to absorb what Jack was telling her. She had always assumed that she hadn't fit with the Guild. And because she had assumed that she hadn't fit, she had assumed that the Guild was perfect.

Sure there were people in the Guild who misused it or behaved badly, but they weren't part of the organization. And yes, she didn't entirely believe in the Guild's mission, particularly on a personal level, but she understood how such drastic measures could be necessary in an imperfect universe.

She had never thought that the Guild might be scarred from within.

"So that's what Liora meant when she said that they might not need Heller," Skye said. "He was third because they have two other methods of killing Kerani Ammons, and if those fail, he gets to step in."

"It's speculation," Jack said. "But it's the kind of speculation I would act on if I were researching this for a client. The information about the previous director tilts the rest of this in the direction of another assassination."

Skye sat very still. *Another assassination*. She hadn't really wrapped her brain around the first one. Rafiq Zvi had died in a murder—by Guild definitions—killed by a crazy member of the Guild.

But if Jack was right, then Zvi had been assassinated:

deliberately targeted with the idea of deposing him, and changing an entire system.

Not the kind of assassination that the Guild usually did. The kind of assassination, in fact, that the Rovers were heading toward, the kind that Jack wouldn't do.

The unethical kind. If, of course, you could call any assassination ethical.

Maybe *illegal* might be a better term. The kind of assassination not sanctioned by all those agreements between all those governments. The kind that occurred when one government tried to influence another.

"So," Skye said slowly, "you think that the members of the Guild who had been disciplined are doing this?"

"Disciplined and disgruntled." He rested his hands near one of the screens. "Has anyone ever tried to recruit you?"

She hadn't expected that question. "How would I even know?"

"You probably wouldn't or you would have answered me immediately." He was talking as if this were normal. Maybe in his world, it was.

She felt shaken. She had to concentrate to focus on what he was saying.

"You would have had conversations with someone—or a bunch of someones—about how much you disliked the Guild or how the current ruling body isn't working well or what you were willing to do to get out of your contract."

"Oh, hell," Skye said. "I've had conversations like that all the time."

Only she hadn't had *conversations*. She had the openings of *conversations*. She had shut down the topic, usually because she figured her opinions were no one's business but her own. Besides, most of the people who talked with her weren't people she liked much.

No one she liked had ever had a conversation like that with her. Was that just her gut? Or had she forgotten the conversations with people she liked?

Or was she seeing everything in a paranoid way now? Was Jack right? Were all of those conversational gambits just a way to feel her out, just to see if she was interested in joining a conspiracy? To see if she was willing to be a traitor to the Guild?

She had hated the Guild so much that she never saw herself as part of it, so she never rebelled against it in an organized way. She was so against any attachments that she never even thought of the other people who were having similar issues.

If she had thought of them, would she have banded together with them?

"Skye," Jack said gently. "Has anyone tried to recruit you?"

She couldn't answer that, not definitively. And she was an information person. She believed in definitive. Definitive made sure the right target got assassinated, not the target's twin brother or the person that the target tried to slip his guilt onto. Definitive meant that innocents went free and the guilty got punished, and no one got falsely accused.

She was all about definitive.

So no matter what, she couldn't answer Jack's question. She hadn't thought she was being recruited into a band of traitors, so to be definitive, she would have to answer no. But she was also oblivious. She hadn't even realized that such recruitment was possible, that people would want to conspire against the Guild.

If someone didn't like the Guild, then they could just wait until the end of their employment or repayment contract and leave. She hadn't thought there would be any other way.

But Jack's theory made sense to her, in that gut way that she trusted.

"Skye?" he asked again.

She got up and went to his side of the table. She tapped on one of the screens, making the list that he had compiled holographic. She hit one other part of the screen so that the hologram included images of the people who had been disciplined.

Her mouth fell open. She closed it, then bit her lower lip.

He had twenty names on that list. Sixteen had spoken to her at odd times. Sixteen. And a few of them had done so in such a way that she remembered thinking afterward, *That was weird*.

Jack watched her. She could actually feel his patience, as if it were a live thing. He was waiting for her to figure something out.

She had one more thing to do. She opened another holographic window and tapped on it, looking up vacation days from five years ago.

Fifteen of the names had the same date. And then again, each year. She didn't have information for this year because that would be in the Guild's current records, and to get those records, she would have to hack into the system.

She closed the screens, sat back down, and put her face in her hands. She was shaking.

The Guild hadn't been a safe place for her, but it had been understandable—at least, she had thought it had been understandable. Everyone in their place, everyone with their assignments, people who had moved out of their place had either succeeded or screwed up. She had never thought of anyone cheating or gaming the system, because she hadn't believed it was possible.

She figured all of the bad people would get caught. And those with questionable skills or a questionable commitment to the Guild, like she had, would get shunted aside in favor of better candidates.

Jack placed a tentative hand on her back. Then he rubbed gently, not in a sexual way, but in a soothing one. He probably thought he knew how upset she was.

Oddly, she was upset about the broken rules and about the misunderstandings. Not that these people had formed a conspiracy against the Guild.

The Guild didn't treat everyone well. It was only a matter of time before someone rebelled.

Someone other than her.

But she had never expected the rebellion to take this form.

People from within, killing to obtain their desires. Surely, the Guild should have foreseen this? How had it missed the conspiracy?

She raised her head and tapped the screen one last time. Jack's hand remained on her back, soothing and warm. She didn't try to shake him off, which was unusual for her. His touch wasn't a distraction at all, and she found his nearness comforting.

"That's it," she said to herself. "They control the information."

"What?" Jack asked.

She looked at him. "You're right. There's a group and there has been for years. They set this up a long time ago, and they meet off-site at least once a year. But the key is that a lot of these people got demoted into what's called The Office. They handle routine things, like the security for Guild members and vacation days and financial transactions. They do some investigating, mostly background of potential candidates for the school, and they have their fingers in a lot of the Guild's management."

"Do you think this conspiracy extends beyond these people that I found?"

"It would have to, wouldn't it, to have part of the Council try to vote their own candidate in as the Guild's director." She rubbed a hand over her face.

She and Jack had spent so much time here, while Liora and her people were planning an active assassination. For all that Skye knew, it could be all over already.

Or about to happen.

It sounded like they had real plans, major plans, with at least two backups.

"We have to get this information to the Guild," Skye said.

"If you don't know which people are working together," Jack said, "how are you going to know who to trust?"

Great question, especially since she'd missed so many cues already. She would ask Jack, who seemed to have a very good sense of other people, who to trust, but he didn't have decades of experience with them.

"I guess we take this information to the director," Skye said, "and let her figure out what to do."

Jack was silent for a moment, as if he were considering what to say next. Finally, he nodded his head just a little.

"And what if we're too late?" he asked softly.

Her heart twisted. She cared more than she thought she did.

"I don't know," she said. "I guess we'll figure that out when we get there."

Chapter 48

THERE WAS NO QUICK ROUTE FROM THEIR LOCATION IN the NetherRealm to Kordita, the planet where the Assassins Guild made its home. Even with their speedy ship, it took four days of solid travel.

Jack got his lovemaking on the cockpit floor, mostly because neither he nor Skye wanted to leave the navigation system unmonitored, particularly after that explosion near Zaeen. The lovemaking wasn't as exciting as Jack had hoped it would be.

Instead, like all of their interactions these days, it had a touch of sadness. They were still deeply attracted, and the sex was wonderful, and inventive. But it no longer felt new. It felt instead like the kind of sex people had after they had already broken up.

Jack tried to approach the topic a dozen times, but always elliptically. And he had started to learn that Skye wasn't good with subtlety. Perhaps that was why she hadn't understood the conspiracy recruitments when they happened.

She didn't believe that people could think differently than she did, so when she was confronted by someone with a competing (but unarticulated) agenda, she simply ignored it, or failed to comprehend all of the subtext.

It wasn't that she was dumb, it was that she lacked an interest in others that appeared in situations like that.

They had maybe a half a day to travel to get to

Kordita when Jack decided to be as blunt as he possibly could. By then, they had finished all of the research they could do with the records available to them. They had decided to make a risky hack into the Guild's database when they were still in the NetherRealm. That hack had lasted less than ten seconds and had garnered most of the Guild's current information.

They had sorted through it on the rest of the trip here, but now they were done. Mostly, all they had gained was more confirmation that the people they suspected were worth their suspicions.

Skye sat in the pilot's chair. Lately, she'd been doing hands-on flying because she worried about the proximity of some other ships. She said she paid better attention when she actually manipulated the controls herself.

She had done the bulk of the flying on the return trip. One of them had to monitor to make sure they weren't followed, so when she needed sleep, he spelled her. During those times, he used the autopilot and did research nearby.

This meant that the two of them were on different schedules, so they hadn't even had a chance to sleep in the same bed.

Jack missed it.

She had the screens open, so that she could see everything around them. He usually didn't pay much attention to anything outside of a ship, but he did lately. And he was noticing just how much extra traffic there was here. It was as if they had left an unexplored part of the galaxy and arrived in a part that was running out of room for ships and humans.

Jack sat at his research station. The chair had become

familiar to him, but it didn't allow him to see her unless he swiveled toward her, which he did now.

"Skye," he said. "Can I ask you something?"

She was staring at the navigation board in front of her. From this distance, it looked like a bunch of multicolored dots moving in a variety of directions.

"It's kind of important," he said.

Kind of. As in not entirely. He mentally kicked himself for the hedge.

"All right." She tapped something, then raised her head. Her eyes were a bit glazed. He was surprised to note the shadows under them. Had she been working that hard?

He supposed so. He had too, but he always worked hard. He rarely thought about it.

"It's about us," he said. He had never used that word before, *us*, and it made him nervous.

A small frown creased the spot just above her nose. He wanted to caress the frown away, but he was too far from her. He had initially thought of moving to the copilot's chair before having this discussion, but was now glad he hadn't. He needed the distance. He wanted to focus on the words, not on that magical physical pull between them.

"We haven't talked about the future," he said.

She shrugged. He didn't like the reaction, but he pushed forward.

"I initially worried that talking about the future was wrong because there was no guarantee that I'd have one," he said. "But I think if we present this information to the Guild, and they deal with Heller and by extension, the Rovers, I'll be fine. I'll be able to make choices. And so will you."

She didn't say a word. For a moment, he thought she would turn back toward the navigation panel in front of her. He wasn't even sure she understood him.

"I don't have friends, Jack," she said. "Most people would consider that a warning sign."

A warning sign of what? He almost asked the question, but decided not to get sidetracked.

"I think you do have friends," he said. "You just haven't noticed."

Her lips thinned, but that flat expression remained on her face.

"Besides," he said, "I'm not talking about friendship here."

Her frown grew deeper. "We're loners. We work separately. We come from different cultures."

"And we've had a hell of a run these last few weeks," he said. "We get along really well."

"Because of the sex," she said.

The words stung him. He hadn't thought that. He wondered how she could.

"No," he said. "Even without the sex. We've talked about a lot of things, examined a lot of things, spent quiet time together—"

"And you think that'll last past this trip?" she asked.

Now he was feeling defensive. "Don't you?"

She shrugged again. "I've never been in this situation before."

And it sounded like, from her tone, that she didn't want to be in the situation now.

Still, he pressed on. "I would like to continue spending time with you."

That sounded too vague.

"I'd like some kind of relationship," he said.

Less vague.

"Maybe even something perman—"

"Jack," she said, her voice cold. "I don't make attachments. I thought you knew that."

Then she turned around and went back to the navigation panel as if nothing had happened.

His heart ached. He'd never really felt like this before, as if he'd been gut-punched when no one touched him.

"I'd like you to make an exception," he said.

She didn't respond. He thought about repeating himself, but knew that she'd ignore that as well.

Maybe he hadn't been unclear earlier. Maybe she had just been ignoring him, hoping he wouldn't continue to bring the topic up.

She had made herself very clear from the beginning. A one-night stand. She had said she liked him, but nothing more. No words of love during lovemaking—or rather, sex. And she didn't make attachments.

He did. She had known that.

But apparently, being the kind of person she was, she either hadn't noticed or hadn't cared.

He turned his chair back toward the research screen, but he couldn't concentrate. He'd never been in this situation before. No woman had interested him like Skye. He hadn't ever felt this way about anyone.

He loved her.

And apparently, she did not love him back.

Chapter 49

If this trip had taught her anything, it was that she knew nothing about people. Skye bent over the navigation panel, pretending that nothing had happened. She felt Jack's gaze on her back and she knew when he had turned away.

She had a gut sense of people, but only as it pertained to her. Were they safe? Were they honest? Were they people she needed to spend time with?

Whether or not they were into something bad or good, it didn't matter if it didn't concern her.

She'd been thinking about the conspiracy for days, knowing that she had probably missed a hundred clues, primarily because she hadn't cared about the future of the Guild. She had only concentrated on leaving it.

And now this, with Jack. She had been very clear. She didn't make friends. She wasn't warm and cuddly. She was brittle and breakable and she wasn't going to change. Eventually, he wouldn't find her intriguing. He would find her irritating, and he would leave her one day just like everyone else had.

The best way to avoid that was to avoid the attachment.

No one came back. Everyone left.

How she felt about him didn't matter because he would never return the emotion. He might think he loved her, but he didn't. He was only responding to the sexual connection and once that faded, then he would move on somewhere else.

He was talking about a future now, but once they had survived all of this—once they had made it to that future—he would want out.

Everyone did.

Her fingers kept missing the edges of the screen. She finally had to stop trying to work the navigation panel and flatten her hands against her thighs. She needed to get ahold of herself.

I don't have friends, she had said to him.

And he had said, *I think you do have friends. You just haven't noticed.*

Could that be true? How could she have friends if she hadn't noticed? Weren't friends like pets or children? Didn't they require care and feeding and constant attention?

The fact that she didn't know these things meant that she wasn't attachment material. She had purposely not learned any of it.

But she did care about some people back at the Guild. The idea of them getting caught in the crossfire of whatever might happen disturbed her more than she could say.

Just like the idea of Jack getting killed disturbed her. That was why she had joined him in the first place, even after that spectacular one-night stand. She wanted to know he was surviving out there, living his life.

Was that friendship? Or was she just being selfish?

And how could she tell the difference?

She wanted to ask him, which was rich in irony. He was the only person she trusted to tell her how friendship worked.

And she was going to walk away from his.

Only he'd been clear: he hadn't wanted friendship. He wanted "some kind of relationship." He wanted something "perman—" She had interrupted him, because she hadn't wanted to hear the word *permanent*.

She hadn't wanted to contemplate it. It would be too tempting. Like chasing after her parents after they dumped her time after time. At some point, she had to learn the lesson.

No one wanted her. No one would stick with her. No one would want something permanent. Not after they got to know her.

Not even the Guild wanted something permanent. They just wanted her to repay the investment they'd made in her. That was all.

Well, when she gave them this list, she would consider the investment repaid.

That thought gave her strength. She sat back up and forced herself to pay attention to the board.

A flashing light in the far corner caught her attention. The flash was faint, almost nonexistent. She tapped it.

The ship's scanner said, *Ship-sized object. No registration. No identification. Scans failing. Hands-on analysis might be possible. Hypothesis could be derived from component parts.*

She had never seen a message like that before from any ship. She frowned at it, figuring it out.

Was she seeing something in stealth mode? Or something else?

"Jack, have you seen anything like this?"

He moved from his research chair to the copilot's chair. The chair groaned underneath his weight.

"Yeah," he said. "Some really sensitive navigation panels constantly scan images, and as the panel understands what it has seen in the past, it puts it on the screen."

She let out a small breath. "You mean like a ghost image, not an image of what's really out there? A reflection of what had been there?" she asked. Then she frowned as she contemplated that idea. "Well, that would explain the message."

"What message?"

She moved that message to his screen. He swore when he saw it.

"Let me find this," he said. His tone sounded urgent.

"What are we looking for?" she asked.

"More images just like this," he said.

"You think there's an army of these things?" she asked.

"No," he said. "I think this is an old image that the scanning system is trying to understand. Something made it visible to our systems just for a second. We need to figure out what that something is and scan for it."

"I can do that." She knew this ship's systems really well now. She tapped the screen and made sure the computer started looking for the signature it had found before. She told the computer not to worry about what it was, just where it was, and where it had been.

The computer gave her a secondary screen, with a map of ghostly images, all the same size.

"Shit," she said softly.

"What?" Jack asked.

She imposed their ship's path onto the ghostly images. The images matched.

"We're being tailed," she said.

"How is that possible?" Jack asked.

"That's not the question to ask at the moment," Skye said. "The question to ask is how do we lose the tail?"

"Evasive maneuvers?" Jack asked.

She glanced at him sideways. "You've never flown a ship, have you?"

"Not without autopilot," he said.

"The tail knows where we are. They're tracking our signature. It doesn't matter if we fly in circles, they'll still find us."

"So," Jack said, "how *do* we lose them?"

She swallowed hard. "I don't think we do."

Jack turned toward her, surprise on his face. "Why not?"

"We're not far from Kordita. They know where we're going or can guess. We land, and we just keep going. I can lose someone on foot. Can't you?"

Jack nodded, but he looked preoccupied. "I can lose most people," he said. "But not everyone."

She had to sound strong. She smiled at him. "The good news is that this isn't 'everyone.' It's someone."

"Or a group of someones," Jack said.

"And we have no idea if they're after us or the *Hawk*."

"I thought the *Hawk* wasn't stolen," Jack said as he used his fingers to expand the images on the screen.

"I don't think it was," Skye said. "I checked the registration as best I could. But you never know. And the last time we got chased, we were chased because of the ship."

She felt odd saying that. She'd never been chased before she met Jack. She'd never been in the middle of anything like this before she met Jack.

He was maneuvering the images on the screen. "It's not the *Hawk*," he said softly.

She glanced over, saw a series of little ghost images, and couldn't quite make sense of them. "How do you know?"

He pointed to the first image. "That's not long after we hacked into the Guild's database."

"They've been onto us since then?" she asked.

He nodded. "Maybe it's the Guild."

"The Guild doesn't operate that way," she said.

"Not for its members. But what about outsiders who tap in?"

It sounded logical, but it didn't feel logical. "I don't know," she said.

"Well," Jack said. "Let me do what I can to find out."

Chapter 50

Jack dug into the computer system. He had a sick feeling about that ship, and he tried to ignore it. If he worked off of preconceptions, he might make mistakes.

That was the last thing he needed to do.

He found the ship's silhouette, and let the *Hawk* plot the ship's trajectory. Then he continued to dig.

The *Hawk* continually revised the images on the screen, and he didn't like what he was seeing. The other ship kept getting closer and closer—not in real time, but in the past. Only he was just seeing it now, because the tracking was catching up to the ship, and that wasn't good. It meant that the ship had probably slowed down.

And if that ship followed the *Hawk*'s trajectory, then that meant it was really close.

Jack sent that data back to Skye but kept working. He needed to find out whose ship this was. If it belonged to the Guild, then Skye would deal with them. She would apologize, explain the situation, and find a resolution.

If the ship belonged to someone he and Skye didn't know, then Skye's plan of going straight to Kordita and playing a ground game made sense. They were heading to the Guild, and no strangers got into the Guild. Jack wasn't even sure he would be able to.

But he worried that the ship belonged to a Rover, and if that were the case, then he and Skye were in deep trouble.

He paused for just a moment as a thought flitted across his brain. Then he realized that he had missed something obvious.

He went back into the information the computer had sent him, and looked for images of the ship before it went into stealth mode.

It took some back-tracing, but he found it.

"Got you, you bastard," he said softly.

"What?" Skye asked.

"Nothing," Jack said. He wanted her to be focusing on their trip. "You got the information I sent you, right?"

"Yes," she said. "I'm trying to speed the recalibration up. I'm worried that this ship is much closer than we think."

He was worried about that too. He looked at the configuration of the ship before it went into stealth mode, selected the image, and told the computer to find that ship in all the various registries.

The ship was smaller than Jack expected, the kind of ship only one person or two people used, which didn't reassure him. He wanted to see a larger ship, something owned by a corporation or the Guild. He didn't want a fast-moving stealth ship that could sneak up on something larger, like the *Hawk*.

While the computer searched registries in various sectors, Jack did one other thing. He hacked into the system of the store where he and Skye had purchased the *Hawk*. He had set up the hack before leaving, figuring they might need more information.

At the time, he had been worried that the *Hawk* was stolen and being resold. He wanted information at his fingertips: if someone trailed them again and tried to attack them for something the *Hawk*'s original owner had done, he wanted to know who the original owner was.

He hadn't expected to use the same hack to determine if anyone else had looked at the records.

No one outside the store had, but the records were accessed a few days after Jack and Skye left Zaeen. And then someone had dug into Skye's identity.

"Skye," Jack said, "did the Guild issue the identity that you used to buy this ship?"

"Why does that matter?" Skye asked.

"Because I want to know how breakable the identity is," Jack said.

She shrugged. "If you're good, you might be able to figure out that it came from the Guild. But you won't be able to go beyond that."

If you were good, you wouldn't need to go beyond that. Hell, if you weren't even marginally good. If someone had looked at Krell's security feeds, saw Skye and Jack together, realized that they had stolen the *Rapido* together, then that someone could trace both Skye and Jack. They had been a presence on Zaeen, but they hadn't been there long.

Long enough to be on security, though. Security that could easily be sold to someone with cash and a determination to find them.

Even someone who usually hired spies and investigators to do his dirty work could follow this trail, if he were determined enough.

Jack didn't like how he was thinking. It was too close to a preconception.

Then the computer pinged at him. The ship following

them had been part of a bulk buy from a sector so far away that it took nearly two months to travel from there to here. That wasn't what caught Jack's eye, though. What caught his eye was this: The ship was registered to a familiar name.

One Jack had invented. He had created the corporate identity, he had filled out all of the documentation, he had even set up the bank accounts.

That ship was part of a Rover buy from two years ago.

He tapped the screen so that the computer would show him the image of the person who had flown that ship out of its last port.

The man frozen in the two-dimensional image was slight, with scruffy brown hair. He wore the same jacket that he had worn on Krell.

Heller.

"Oh, shit," Jack said. They were in deep trouble now.

Chapter 51

A WARNING LIGHT APPEARED ON THE NAVIGATION panel. Skye checked it as Jack cursed beside her.

He probably had the same thought she did; they'd been boarded.

She activated a part of the *Hawk*'s exterior usually used only as a ship approached a port, to identify and dislodge anything that might have attached itself to the exterior during flight.

The docking hooks near the cargo bay lit up. Something had attached itself—and space debris usually didn't use docking hooks.

"We've been boarded," she said.

Jack cursed again. Then he stood so fast that he banged his knees on the console. "I'll take care of it."

"Take care of what?" she asked. "There could be a dozen people down there."

He looked down at her, his face pale. "There isn't. At most, there are two or three."

"And you're going up against two or three people?" she asked. "I'm just going to speed up and get us to Kordita as quickly as possible."

"No," he said. "As soon as I go below, you're going to seal off this level. Separate the environmental system from the rest of the ship. Lock out anyone who tries to access the cockpit."

He knew something. He wasn't telling her everything.

She felt a wave of anger run through her. Nothing infuriated her more.

"You know what's going on," she said.

"Yeah," he said. "I traced the ship. It's small, and it belongs to Heller."

Her breath caught. Heller? On board? How was that possible? And Jack was heading down to greet him? Alone?

"I'm going to separate the *Hawk*'s environmental system now," she said. "If he put anything into it, I can scrub it. Then I'll just get us to Kordita."

"No," Jack said. "Heller's not the kind of assassin you're used to. He doesn't care who dies. He's probably attaching some kind of explosive to the interior of the *Hawk*. Then he's going to leave, and no one will ever know what happened. We certainly won't. We'll be dead."

"He may have already done that," she said.

"And I'll disable it," Jack said.

"You know how to do that?" she asked.

He shook his head. "Do you?"

"We learned how to make bombs, not how to take them apart," she said. "And it was mostly theory, because bombs rarely take out only one target."

"Exactly," Jack said. "This ship is the middle of a shipping lane. Heller doesn't even care if someone else's ship gets destroyed because of his bomb. I'm going down."

She caught his arm. "I'll get the *Hawk* away from everything. I'll separate us off from the rest of the ship. He'll leave. And then we can get the bomb together."

"No," Jack said. "Because that allows him to go free.

He'll go after your director. He'll go after all those government contracts. He'll kill lots of innocent people."

"Starting with you," Skye said.

Jack shook her off. "I'll be all right."

"It would be better if I went," she said. "I'm the one with assassin training."

"You're the one who *failed* assassin training," Jack said, his tone harsh. "I'm going. Stop arguing."

"But you won't know what to do," she said.

"That means Heller won't know what to expect," Jack said.

He bent down, cupped her face in his hands, and kissed her so thoroughly that her toes curled. She grabbed at him, feeling oddly desperate, wondering if she could seduce him into staying.

Then their lips separated, but he didn't let go of her face.

"Here's what you don't know," he said softly. "I love you. I will always love you, no matter what happens. And I do want something permanent with you. But if this is all we ever have, I'm happy we've had it. My life is so much better with you in it. Thank you."

Then he turned quickly, and let himself out of the cockpit.

She was shaking, his words echoing in her ears.

"Dammit, Jack," she said, wishing he could hear her. "I love you too."

Chapter 52

As Jack took the ladder down to the lower levels of the ship, he hoped Skye was tracking him. He couldn't communicate with her—he had to bet that Heller was monitoring the comm system, as well as the ship's elevator. Which was why Jack had crammed himself into the engineering ladders, designed only for times when the elevator wasn't working well.

He barely fit in the rounded hole that the designers had carved into the middle of the ship. The rungs of the ladder were set so that it would be easy for someone Skye's size to go down quickly.

He kept getting tangled up in his own limbs. But he was moving as fast as he could, and as quietly as he could.

Jack hoped Skye switched the environmental system immediately. He wouldn't put it past Heller to poison the ship's atmosphere and then leave. That would be the easiest and most efficient way to kill them.

It would also be cowardly.

And somewhat stupid, because eventually someone would find the ship with the bodies on it. The sector government would get involved and figure out that there was no reason to kill Skye and Jack except simple murder. The Assassins Guild might actually seek retribution.

Heller wasn't dumb. He probably knew all of that, which was why Jack was gambling that Heller wouldn't do that.

Of course, Heller might change the atmosphere, then set a bomb. That would be smarter, particularly if the bomb had a timer. Heller could get far away, and no one would know exactly what happened.

If Jack were a betting man, that plan was what he would have put money on. Heller would do his best to kill them, and then dispose of the evidence.

But Heller thought he had time. He figured neither Jack nor Skye knew that Heller was after Jack.

Jack hoped the information would give him an advantage.

Because he wasn't sure what the hell kind of advantage it would give them. He was an untrained guy, going up against a trained assassin. If he got too close, Heller could just break his neck.

Jack paused on the lower level. Skye had brought a laser pistol on board. She kept all of her things in the main master suite one level down from the cockpit. He eased off the ladder onto that level.

He had to hurry. He slipped down the hall, listening hard for unusual sounds, hoping that Heller hadn't somehow made his way here.

The master suite was at the far end of the corridor—better views from the portholes on the edge of the ship—and he cursed that. He wanted to get in and out as rapidly as possible.

Each second seemed to take an hour. He reached the door to the suite, opened it, and dashed inside.

The pistol wasn't near Skye's research area. She kept everything neat, which he usually appreciated. Right now, though, he wanted a messy desk with her clothes strewn on the floor, and the laser pistol on top of everything.

Instead, he had to search drawers and closets until he found it.

It was inside one of her coats, as safe as it could be in this haphazard collection of clothing and stuff she had accumulated on Zaeen.

He grabbed the pistol, examined it to make sure he knew how to use it, then set the safety and jammed the entire thing in his belt. He didn't have time to finesse anything.

He had to find Heller, and he had to do it fast.

Chapter 53

For the first time in her life, Skye hated being alone. She paced the cockpit, wishing it were bigger just so that she had more area to walk in. She had all of the screens up as holograms, and she monitored everything.

Monitoring was all that she could do.

She had sped up the *Hawk* as fast as it could go, hoping that she might get to Kordita before anything bad happened. Jack would probably tell her not to do this, but she had hopes that Kordita's space cops would be able to help her before the *Hawk* exploded and took other ships with it.

As she had sped up the *Hawk*, she had also separated the environmental system of the cockpit from the rest of the *Hawk*. She had realigned all of the *Hawk*'s navigational and engineering controls to the cockpit and sealed that realignment with DNA identification and a living hand confirmation. She had locked down this level.

No one, not even Jack, was going to get up here without her help.

She tried to watch what was happening on the video security system, but apparently Heller had shut that down the moment he crawled into the cargo bay. He had entered alone—she saw his scrawny form ease the bay doors open—and then the video went off, as did the heat signature monitoring.

Somehow he had done that without tripping any

alarms up here. If this ended well—when this ended well—she would figure out how he did that.

Right now, she kept an eye on the only monitors she had—the heat signatures on the lower decks outside of the cargo bay. The video security got shut off everywhere, but the heat signatures remained everywhere except the cargo bay.

So she could keep an eye on Jack—at least at the moment.

The security system had registered him as a little red dot, which she would have found amusing if it weren't so stressful. Nothing about Jack was little—not his body, not his brain, and certainly not his courage.

Damn him for that courage.

It was going to get him killed.

And then she really would be alone.

She watched the red dot hesitate near the next lower level, and for a moment, she worried that Heller had found Jack. Then she realized that she would see Heller as a heat signature if he were outside the cargo bay.

Jack was clearly contemplating something else.

And then she realized what it was. He had stopped one floor down and run toward the master suite.

She knew what he had gone for.

Her laser pistol.

And that broke her heart.

He hadn't had the lessons she had, the training she had. He probably didn't know that superior firepower meant nothing when facing off with a good assassin, or even with a better trained opponent.

When she'd been training, she'd gone into several simulations with a laser pistol—as the only person armed in the room—and she had been disarmed and fake-killed within seconds. Once she'd actually sprained her arm trying to wrench the pistol away from her opponent. Her trainer had later told her that had that been a real fight, the opponent would have broken her arm, and then broken her neck.

"Jack," she whispered.

He was going to leave her. Only unlike her parents, unlike everyone else in her life, he wouldn't leave intentionally. He would leave because Heller would kill him.

And then everything that Skye had done these last few weeks, everything she had tried just so that she would know that Jack existed somewhere in the universe, all of that would be for nothing.

He would be dead, and she would be alone.

If she survived whatever else Heller managed to do.

And right now, she was out of options. She had done all that Jack had asked and more.

All she could do was wait.

Chapter 54

HELLER WASN'T EVEN TRYING TO BE QUIET. HE BANGED around in the cargo bay, humming as he worked.

Jack glanced at the bay's monitors on the outside of the door, but noted that Heller had shut everything off. There was no way to monitor what cargo was in the bay—which was what the monitors were for—and no way to track who was inside.

But shutting all of that off left the door open—it was one of those safety regulation things—and that allowed Jack to hear what was going on.

From the sounds of it, his assumptions were correct. Heller was setting up a bomb.

It was, Jack had to admit, the best way to go up against a member of the Assassins Guild, particularly if you had no idea whether or not she was a trained assassin.

Jack took a deep breath. He only had one shot at this. He would have to override the controls outside of the door, then shut the door, and then shut off the atmosphere entirely. Without oxygen, Heller would die.

It wouldn't be pretty, but it would happen relatively fast, and then Jack could go in and try to disable that bomb.

He wished he were a better engineer. He wished he had had time to familiarize himself with all of the controls on this ship. Instead, he'd familiarized himself with Skye. He didn't regret that, but he'd had a few other hours to himself. He could have used them more efficiently.

Or, at least, he would have if he had known that he would be in this situation. He had never thought Heller would come after him directly, but it made sense.

Heller wanted him gone. Heller had tracked him out of the sector, where no one would have known if Jack had died.

Heller had then followed him here, and if Skye hadn't seen that ghost image, he would have killed them both—and whoever else was nearby on the shipping lanes when that bomb went off.

Jack's hands were unbelievably steady. His heart wasn't. It pounded against his chest like a prisoner trying to get out. He moved quietly and quickly, and wished he were more resourceful.

And that was when he realized all of the sound from the cargo bay had stopped.

Either Heller was done with the bomb or Jack had done something to alert Heller.

Neither scenario was good.

He grabbed the laser pistol from his belt, unhooked the safety, and eased toward the door. Then he peered in. Heller had stopped working and was looking at a light that had gone on above him.

That light must have been what alerted him to Jack's presence.

Jack had only a few more things to do before he finished rerouting the circuitry. He couldn't do those things one-handed.

He had to make a quick decision: he had to finish the work, because that was the only way he could fight Heller like an equal, or he had to try to shoot Heller.

Jack decided to finish the work.

Now his hands were shaking. He couldn't make a mistake and yet, half of what he was doing was guesswork. He finished, praying it would succeed.

As he stood, he realized that he hadn't heard anything from inside the bay for a long time.

He made his way to the door, trying not to breathe loudly. He leaned in, and saw Heller about ten yards from him, weapon out, scanning the entire area.

And Heller's weapon wasn't a laser pistol. It was a laser rifle, the kind that could shoot so fast that the victim probably never even saw the shot coming.

Jack resisted the urge to call him and taunt him.

Instead, Jack did something he had never done before.

He pulled out the laser pistol and fired, aiming straight for Heller's heart.

Chapter 55

The shot missed. Instead of hitting Heller in the heart, Jack hit him in the leg, knocking him down.

Jack had been hoping for a kill shot. He had thought it his only chance of making it out of this alive.

Instead, he'd wounded Heller, and made him mad.

Heller propped himself up and turned the rifle toward Jack. Jack sprinted to the side and slammed his hand on the controls, as red laser shot after red laser shot banged out the door.

"Shut, shut, shut," he said, urging the door to close. He heard more shots, realized they were coming faster and they were nearer than they had been before.

The door groaned and then started to move. Jack crept toward it, and shot through it, staying away from the opening. Shots from Heller's rifle went past him.

"You can't beat me," Heller yelled.

"I have no idea why you think I'd try," Jack said.

The door was moving too slowly. The shots had stopped, and Jack heard scraping, coming closer.

Jack knew what that meant. Heller was trying to get out. If he got out of that cargo bay, he would kill Jack easily.

Jack continued to shoot, hoping that the door would close all the way.

One shot went wild and burned a smoking hole in the floor. And that was when Jack quit shooting. He didn't dare make holes in that door, and he didn't want to give Heller ideas either.

More shots came out.

"Let's talk, Jack." Heller's voice sounded closer than it had before.

"About what? Your desire to kill me?"

"You can still work for us, forget about all that other stuff—"

The door slammed shut, and Jack ran back for the controls. He fumbled, then managed to get the environmental controls to respond.

He hesitated for just a moment—if he shut off the environment, he would be killing a man—but that man would kill him, Skye, and anyone else in his path.

Jack flicked the controls off, and then monitored them, hoping Heller was too far away to get to the control panel. Jack didn't want Heller to turn the environmental systems back on.

Shots hit the door, but didn't break through.

Jack held his breath. He'd have to move out of this corridor and shut it down too. He ran, stumbling a little. And managed to get farther down toward the elevator.

Then he realized it didn't matter if he used the comm.

Shots broke through the door, creating holes. That was all that Heller would need. Holes would provide oxygen and a way out.

Jack went for the ladder, slamming on the comm as he did.

"Shut off the environment on this level and vent the oxygen," he said. "Do it now."

He hoped the message got through.

He hoped Skye wouldn't care that he was here.

He hoped she listened, because if she didn't, Heller would win.

Chapter 56

SHOTS. THE ENTIRE COCKPIT WARNED HER OF THEM. Shots in the cargo bay. Someone was using a laser rifle on that level, and Skye knew that someone wasn't Jack.

Skye stopped pacing and went to her chair. She wasn't sure what she could do, but she wanted to be ready.

And then she realized there was one thing she could do. She knew where Heller was. She knew where he wasn't.

And he wasn't on board his ship.

She turned on the exterior program that separated objects from the *Hawk*. She scraped that ship off the side of the *Hawk* as if it had never been. Then she monitored it. If it spun uselessly away, no one was on board.

If it righted itself, then Heller had companions.

Because no one left an autopilot running if a ship was attached to another ship.

She swallowed, watching Heller's ship spin away.

If it spun in the right direction, it would become Kordita's problem. She sent out a message, though, warning about loose space debris in the area. That should protect some other ships.

Then Jack's voice echoed in the cockpit.

"Shut off the environment on this level and vent the oxygen. Do it now."

She hit the comm panel. "Jack! Jack!"

But he didn't respond. And she cursed.

If she shut off the environmental control, she would kill him too.

She glanced at the red dot that was Jack, saw it was on the ladder going off that floor. On the floor, near the cargo bay, another red dot appeared.

Heller.

Shit. He was coming for Jack. No wonder Jack wanted the environmental controls off.

She sealed the level, hoping the seal wouldn't impact Jack on the ladder. Then she shut off the environmental controls to the entire floor.

She wanted to close her eyes, but she didn't. She had to see if Jack made it.

She had to see if he survived.

Chapter 57

"You son of a bitch!" Heller shouted. "I'm going to make sure that your death *hurts*."

His voice echoed from the floor below. Jack kept climbing, slower than he wanted to. He tried pulling himself up two rungs at a time, his hands sore.

No sign that Skye had heard him. No sign that she had shut off the environmental controls.

Jack was trapped. Once Heller got to this part of the ship, he would shoot upward, and Jack would die. It would probably be painful.

And then Skye would die, and so would everyone nearby.

He tried to go faster. Maybe if he got to the next level, he could shoot down at Heller.

But Jack was a terrible shot, and Heller killed people for a living. Jack had only had one chance, and he had blown it.

He got to the next level, and pulled himself out of the engineering circle. Then he leaned over the edge, pistol pointed downward, and waited.

And waited.

And waited.

Heller hadn't said anything for several seconds. And Jack couldn't hear him moving below.

Jack finally rolled over, got up, and checked the security system. One red heat signature on the floor below him, and it wasn't moving. In fact, the red was fading.

Was that possible? Was the heat fading away? Did it get that cold that fast in an area without oxygen?

For a guy who loved being in space, Jack was truly clueless about the deadliest parts of it.

He slammed his hand on the comm. "Skye?"

"Jack! Oh, my God, are you all right?"

"Yeah," he said, although he hadn't done an inventory. He could move. He could talk. That was enough. "Did you shut off the environmental controls on that floor?"

"Yes," she said. "It's sealed off."

"And you vented the atmosphere?"

"Yes," she said.

He let out a small sigh of relief. Then he said, "You have to scrape off the ship. Make sure no one else boards."

"Already done," she said.

"God, you're marvelous," he said, and meant it.

He glanced at the heat signature. It was so light as to be indistinguishable.

"Do you have a temperature reading from down there?" he asked.

"You don't want to know," she said.

"How long will it take him to die?"

"Not long," she said. "And if you're thinking of going back down, it won't be pretty."

"I have no choice but to go down," he said. "There's a bomb down there."

Skye was silent for a moment. "I can help," she said.

"You know that building a bomb is different from dismantling one," Jack said.

"Yes, but at least I know what the components are," she said.

She had a point. Jack let out a small sigh. Still, he didn't want her down here.

"Tell you what," he said, "I'll turn everything on when I get there, and you can talk me through it."

"Jack, it's better if I come down," she said.

"No," he said. "You might have to open the cargo bay doors. It'll be better to sweep me and that bomb into space than it would be to have it explode on the ship. I'll hook everything back up."

She was silent. He could tell she was thinking about it.

"Can't I do that from below?" she asked after a moment.

"No," he said, even though he had no idea if that were true. "Is he dead yet?"

"I don't know," she said, "I'm not watching it. I don't like watching someone die without an atmosphere. It's worse than drowning or suffocating. It's the worst way to die."

Jack knew that, but he was a bit stunned that Skye, who had told him she didn't get grossed out by anything, was squeamish about this. Of course, anyone who had seen someone die in space without oxygen or a pressurized cabin never wanted to see that again.

"But," Skye said into Jack's silence, "even if Heller isn't dead, he won't be in any shape to come after you."

No kidding. And that would be even worse. Parts of Heller would have already been so badly damaged that he probably couldn't move.

Jack didn't want to think about it either, but he had to.

"All right," Jack said. "Turn the environmental controls back on. I'm going in."

Chapter 58

It took longer than Jack expected to get back down to the cargo area. The ship wouldn't allow him access until the environment was human-friendly. That meant oxygen at the proper mix, and temperature somewhere above freezing.

He could feel the clock ticking with each wasted moment. He had no idea what was going on with that bomb, and he worried that it was ready to blow.

Finally, the ship let him into the floor below. When he reached it, he was stunned to see ice on the floor and the walls. The ice was slick and starting to melt, but he had to be careful.

Apparently, he and Skye had had the humidity higher than usual in the ship, and the moisture had become ice as the air leached out of this part of the ship.

He came across the rifle first. It had slid away from Heller's body. The body itself was gruesome. He was glad that Skye didn't see it. He hoped she never would.

He wasn't sure he would ever forget it.

He made his way—gingerly—to the open door to the cargo bay. He stepped inside and went to the interior controls first, turning the security video feed back on.

"Got me?" he asked.

Skye's voice floated around him. "Yes. Are you all right?"

He wasn't about to assess his feelings at the moment. "I think so," he said. "Can you see the bomb?"

"No," she said, "but there's equipment on the floor about a dozen feet to your left."

He walked over there, carefully again, and saw it. The bomb was large, hanging off one of the empty cargo containers, right in the center of the room. He couldn't tell what kind of bomb it was or even if it was active.

He swallowed hard. "Found it," he said. "Follow my finger."

He pointed at the bomb, and hoped she could focus in somehow.

"Got it," she said. Then she was silent. He wasn't sure if she was contemplating what she saw or if he had lost a connection somehow.

"Skye?"

"Yeah," she said. "I think it's not active. But I need you to do a few things."

She outlined them. He didn't understand why she needed that connection checked or a particular chip located except that she had a hunch about the bomb itself.

He was glad she talked him through the process. If he had come here alone, he would have had no idea what to do.

"Why can't I just pull it off the container?" he asked.

"Because then it'll go off."

He glanced at the cargo bay doors. "What happens if I jettison it?"

"And another ship hits it?" she asked.

"Can I jettison this thing after we have dismantled it?" he asked. "There's always space debris."

"Yeah, there is," she said. "I just sent out a warning

about Heller's ship as debris. I figure it's large enough. Other ships can avoid it, and Kordita can deal with it when they want."

Jack peered at the bomb.

"Then let's jettison this thing as well," Jack said. If he survived dismantling it. If it didn't go off now.

"Okay," she said. "Let's get to work."

Chapter 59

Thank heavens, the bomb was pretty standard. Skye had unsuccessfully tried to build one half a dozen years ago for one of her classes. She understood the principles, and in that case, she had deliberately screwed up the execution. She hadn't wanted to build a bomb ever, just like she hadn't wanted to kill someone ever.

Only she had broken that vow, hadn't she? By turning off the environmental controls and venting the atmosphere on that lower level, she had killed Heller.

And really, she should have regretted it.

But if she hadn't, Heller would have murdered Jack—and relatively quickly. Since she had to choose between Jack and Heller, she didn't even have to think about it.

She chose Jack.

It took fifteen minutes to make certain that the bomb wasn't active. Jack didn't want to send it into space, but Skye did. She didn't want it on the *Hawk*.

Jack thought Heller wasn't that bright, but Heller had managed to follow them from Krell to Zaeen and back here. He'd also managed to shield his ship in such a way that they almost didn't catch it.

If they hadn't had that lucky break, then they would be dead by now. And so would others.

"That should be it," Skye said. "Let me know when you're out of the cargo bay."

"You're going to have to seal off this level again," Jack said. "The door into the bay is ruined."

He didn't say that Heller ruined it, but that was what happened.

She felt oddly calm about it all, and wondered if that was her assassin training.

"Let me know when you're out of there," she said. "And leave the door to the cargo area open."

"Why?" Jack asked.

"Cleanup," she said, unwilling to say more. She had scanned the corridors as the video surveillance came back online and she had seen just enough of Heller's body to know she didn't want to see any more. Better that it get jettisoned into space along with some of the empty cargo containers.

"All right," Jack said, and signed off.

She made sure everything was locked down. She watched his heat signature, so that she wouldn't have to see that hallway again. Jack took the elevator up to this level, and let her know on the comm that he was clear.

"Go ahead," he said.

She locked down the lower level, then shut off the environmental controls. Then she opened the airlock and the cargo bay doors. For a moment, she thought they weren't going to work. Then she realized that doors were moving slowly because they were going through the system that Jack had jury-rigged. Apparently Heller had shut down the direct controls to the outside doors and the airlock.

Still, everything opened, and the *Hawk* acknowledged the change in pressure. It didn't lurch like that other ship had or even move. This ship was in good shape. But it told her that something had gone wrong in the cargo bay—at least from the *Hawk*'s point of view.

From hers, the worst of it was over.

The door opened to the cockpit and Jack stumbled in. His hair was messy, and his shirt was torn. His pants had tears in the knees, and he had scrapes on his elbows.

She had never been so glad to see someone in her life.

She launched herself out of her chair and into his arms.

And all of the panic she had felt, all of the fear, all of the worry, surged through her. She had to blink hard to keep herself from tears.

That made her angry. She wasn't a woman who cried for any reason.

Still, she clung to him, and he clung back.

She had no idea how long they held each other.

"I thought he was going to kill you," she said.

"I told you I'd be back," Jack said.

"You also gave me one hell of a good-bye speech."

He leaned back so that he could see her face. His looked vulnerable. Then he grinned. Her Jack, always a glass-half-full kinda guy.

"I did, didn't I?" he said. "I meant every word."

Then he kissed her.

Or he tried to, because she moved her head just enough. This time, she wasn't going to miss her chance to speak.

"About that thing you asked me earlier," she said.

"About the bomb?" he asked, and he was serious. She had no idea what he was referring to.

"About a relationship," she said. "A permanent one."

His expression froze. "What about it?"

"Yes," she said. "Yes, yes, yes, yes."

"I thought you didn't have attachments," he said.

She nodded. For the first time in her life, going back on something she said didn't feel like a retreat. It felt like she was moving forward.

"I thought I didn't either," she said. "Then you went down to that cargo bay and I realized I was attached already."

He didn't smile. "You can still disengage."

She shook her head. "I can't. I'm in love with you."

He stared at her as if he hadn't heard her. Then he whooped and spun her around the cockpit. She tucked her feet in, afraid she'd hit something important.

He pulled her close and this time, when he tried to kiss her, she wrapped her arms around his neck and kissed him back.

Chapter 60

THEY HAD TO DO A LOT OF TALKING WITH THE authorities on Kordita. They had jettisoned a ship, some cargo (with a half-finished bomb), and the remains of a person just outside of Kordita's space boundaries. But Skye's status as a member of the Guild got them through all of the questioning and made most of the problems go away.

They were even able to get Jack into the Guild, but that had nothing to do with Skye. That had to do with Rikki and Misha, who vouched for Jack. It seemed that Rikki and Misha had stopped an attack by Liora Olliver, and saved Director Kerani Ammon's life in the process.

The director had been injured in the attack, and she was healing. The Guild itself was a great place for relaxation, which Skye always thought ironic. Beautiful stone buildings, well-maintained gardens, perfectly controlled atmosphere.

She always thought of it as an excellent way to hide the violent training that occurred inside the walls.

Because Skye didn't know who to trust, she had demanded to see the director alone. The director's apartments were beautiful, airy and light, with lots of arched windows and multicolored carpets. The director herself rested on a divan, a light blanket over her feet.

She had an angular face and dark black hair. Skye had never been able to guess her age.

The director had already figured out that there was a conspiracy, but she was grateful for the names. She also appreciated the warning about the remaining attacker who was at large.

"Jack and I can figure out who that is," Skye said. "It would take research, but I suspect we'll find the person who got hired."

The director smiled. "The trail should be relatively easy to follow," she said. "Between the research you've given me and the research my people have done, we should find this last threat. The threat we hadn't known was this man you and your friend Jack eliminated. I thank you for that."

Skye let out a small breath. She wasn't used to being told not to do something from the Guild.

"Then what do you want me to do?" she asked.

"You are free to do what you want," the director said. "With this, you have satisfied your obligation to the Guild. We no longer have the right to tell you what to do."

"I'm *free*?" Skye asked. She'd never expected to hear that, especially two years before her contract was over. "Really?"

"Yes," the director said, "and before you ask, we will give you documentation confirming this."

Skye sat down even though she hadn't been invited to. Her legs no longer held her. "Why?"

The director smiled at her. "You've done ever so much more than we expected of you. We would love to keep you, but I know how much you hate it here. So go, with my blessing, and enjoy your life."

Those words were foreign to her, at least in that context. *Enjoy your life?* Really? People did that?

"You have a fantastic partner, and you work well together. Now it's time to step into your future," the director said.

Skye's heart lifted. Was this what it meant to be a glass-half-full person? This joy inside her?

"Thank you," she said. Then she stood, and reached for the director's hand. "Thank you, thank you, thank you."

The director smiled. "No thanks needed. You have already done more for us than we could ever repay."

Skye had no memory of leaving the room. She did remember trying hard not to skip down the stairs to the garden where Jack waited for her.

"I'm free," she said as she approached the white bench he sat on. His head popped up over some blooming birds of paradise, and his feet nearly kicked some greenery nearby.

"Free?" he said.

"I no longer work for the Guild," she said.

He took her hands and pulled her down beside him. "How fascinating," he said. "I no longer work with the Rovers. I'm free too."

"The director told me to enjoy my life," Skye said, still marveling at that.

Jack's smile faded. "Can you?"

She understood his sudden seriousness. She squeezed his fingers. "I realized I've been going about living all wrong. I've been worried about losing something I never had, rather than enjoying something I do have."

"What does that mean?" he asked.

"I didn't make attachments because I was afraid they'd go away. I had no idea how wonderful they are." She looked at their threaded fingers. "How did you learn how to have attachments when you have no idea who your parents are?"

"Rikki," Jack said. "She helped me through the dark times. You had to go through those times alone. But I'll be with you for any dark times in the future."

"Will there be dark times?" Skye asked.

"There always are," Jack said. "But they're not so dark when you share them."

She leaned her head on his shoulder. "I thought I only deserved one night with you. And now I'm going to get a lifetime."

"Are you ready for that?" he asked.

"Oh, yes," she said. "I'm ready. And we're free to choose where we spend that lifetime. We're not bound to anyone."

"Except each other," Jack said.

She grinned at him. She couldn't believe the happiness that filled her.

"Except each other," she agreed. And she knew that would be more than enough.

Read on for an excerpt from the first book in the Assassins Guild series

Assassins in Love

Available now from Kris DeLake and Sourcebooks Casablanca

HANDS FUMBLING, FINGERS SHAKING, HEAD ACHING, Rikki leaned one shoulder against the wall, blocking the view of the airlock controls from the corridor. Elio Testrial leaned against the wall at her feet. She hoped he looked drunk.

Things hadn't gone as planned. Things never went as planned—she should have learned that a long time ago. But she kept thinking she'd get better with each job.

She completed each job. That was a victory, or at least, that felt like one right now.

The corridor was wide and relatively straight, like every other corridor on this stupid ship. Every floor looked like the last, which had caused problems earlier, and all were painted white, as if that was a design feature. She didn't find it a design feature. In fact, it was a problem feature. Because any dirt showed, and blood, well, they said blood trailed for a reason. It did.

So far, though, she'd managed to avoid a blood trail. Of course, she'd thought about avoiding it, back when Testrial really was drunk. And because she thought about avoiding it, she had.

But there was no avoiding this damn airlock.

Her heart pounded, her breath came in short gasps. If

she couldn't get a deep lungful of air, her fingers would keep shaking, not that it made any difference.

Why weren't spaceships built to a universal standard? Why couldn't she just follow the same moves with every piece of equipment that had the same name? Instead, she had to study old specs, which were always wrong, and then she had to improvise, which was always dicey, and then she had to worry that somehow, with one little flick of a fingernail, she'd touch something which would set off an alarm, which would bring the security guards running.

High-end ships like this one always had security guards, and the damn guards always thought they were some kind of cop which, she supposed, in the vast emptiness that was space, they were.

Someone had fused the alarm to the computer control for the airlock doors, which meant that unless she could figure out a way to unfuse it, this stupid airlock was useless to her. Which meant she had to haul Testrial to yet another airlock on a different deck, one that wouldn't be as private as this one, and it would be just her luck that the airlock controls one deck up (or one deck down) would be just as screwy as the controls on this deck.

She cursed. Next spaceport—the big kind with every damn thing in the universe plus a dozen other damn things she hadn't even thought of—she would sign up for some kind of maintenance course, one that specialized in space cruisers, since she found herself on so many of them, or maybe even some university course in mechanics or design or systems analysis, so that she wouldn't waste precious minutes trying to pry open something that didn't want to get pried.

She cursed again, and then a third time for good

measure, but the words weren't helping. She poked at that little fused bit inside the control, and felt her fingernail rip, which caused her to suck in a breath—no curse words for that kind of pain, sharp and tiny, the kind that could cause her (if she were a little less cautious) to pull back and stick the offending nail inside her mouth.

She'd done that once, setting off a timer for an explosive device she'd been working on, and just managed to dive behind the blast shield (she estimated) fifteen seconds before the stupid thing blew.

So she had her little reflexes under control.

It was the big reflexes that worried her.

"Need help?" Male voice. Deep. Authoritative.

She didn't jump. She didn't even flinch. But she did freeze in place for a half second, which she knew was a giveaway, one of those moments little kids had when they got caught doing something wrong.

"I'm fine, thanks," she said without turning around. No sense in letting him see her face.

"Your friend doesn't look fine." He had just a bit of an accent, something that told her Standard wasn't his native language.

"He's drunk," she said.

"Looks dead to me," he said.

She turned, assessing her options as she did. One knife. (People were afraid of knives, which was good. But knives were messy, hard to clean up the blood, which was bad.) Two laser pistols. (One tiny, against her ankle, hard to reach. The other on her hip, obvious, but laser blasts in a corridor—dangerous. They'd bounce off the walls, might hit her.) Fists. (Might break a bone, hands already shaking. Didn't need the additional risk.)

Then stopped assessing when she saw him.

He wasn't what she expected. Tall, white-blond hair, the kind that got noticed (funny, she hadn't noticed him, but then there were two thousand passengers on this damn ship). Broad shoulders, strong bones—not a spacer then. Blue eyes with long lashes, like a girl's almost, but he didn't look girly, not with that aquiline nose and those high cheekbones. Thin lips twisted into a slight smile, a *knowing* smile, as if he understood what she was doing.

He wore gray pants and an ivory shirt without a single stain on it. No rings, no tattoos, no visible scars—and no uniform.

Not security, then. Or at least, not security that happened to be on duty.

"He's drunk," she said again, hoping Testrial's face was turned slightly. She'd managed to close his eyes, but he had that pallor the newly dead sometimes acquired. Blood wasn't flowing; it was pooling, and that leached all the color from his skin.

"So he's drunk, and you're messing with the airlock controls, because you want to get him, what? Some fresh air?" The man's eyes twinkled.

He was disgustingly handsome, and he knew it. She hated men like that, and thought longingly of her knife. One slash across the cheek. That would teach him.

"Guess I've had a little too much to drink myself," she said.

"Oh, for God's sake," the man said as he approached her.

She reached for the knife, but he caught her wrist with one hand. He smelled faintly of sandalwood, and that, for some reason, made her breath catch.

He slammed the airlock controls with his free fist.

The damn alarm went off and the first of the double doors opened.

"What the hell?" she snapped.

He sighed, as if she were the dumbest person he had ever met, then let her go. She did reach for the knife as he bent at the waist and picked up Testrial with one easy move.

She knew that move wasn't easy. She'd used an over-the-shoulder carry to get the bastard down here, after having rigged the corridor cameras to show footage from two hours before. Not that that did any good now that this asshole had set off the alarm.

He tossed Testrial into the airlock itself, then reached inside and triggered the outer door. He barely got his hand back into the corridor before the inner door closed, protecting them from the vacuum of space.

"What the hell?" she asked again.

The man gave her a withering glance. "He was dead, you were going to toss him out, and then you were going to go about your business as if nothing happened. I just helped you along a little."

"And now every security agent on the ship will come down here," she snapped.

"Yeah," he said. "But it won't be a problem."

"It won't be a problem?" she asked.

But he already had his arm tightly around her shoulder, and he dragged her forward. The movement felt familiar, as if someone had done this to her before.

Except no one had ever done this to her before.

"C'mon," he said. "Stagger a little."

"What?" she asked, letting him pull her along. Her hand was still on her knife, but she didn't close her fist around the hilt. Not yet.

"Do you know any drinking songs?" he asked.

"Know any… what?"

"*Stagger*," he said, and she did without much effort, since he was half-carrying her, not allowing her feet to find a rhythm.

They stepped onto the between-decks platform, which she loathed because it was open, not a true elevator at all, and he said, "Down," and the stupid thing jerked before it went down, and suddenly she was on corridor cameras.

"Do you know any drinking songs?" he asked again.

"No," she said, ready with an answer this time. "I don't drink."

"No wonder you lack creativity," he said and added, "Stop," as they passed their third deck. He dragged her down the corridor to the airlock, and slammed it with his fist.

Another alarm went off as the inner door opened, and he reached inside, triggering the outer door.

"What the hell are you doing?" she asked again.

"Is that the only question you know?" he asked.

"Just answer me," she said as he turned her around and headed back toward the between-decks platform.

"Weren't you ever a teenager?" he asked.

"Of course I was," she said.

"Then you should know what I'm doing," he said.

"Well color me clueless," she said, "because I don't."

His eyebrows went up as he looked at her. "Color you clueless? What kind of phrase is that?"

"The kind of phrase you say when someone won't tell you what the hell they're doing."

"Watch and learn, babe," he said. "Watch and learn."

He took them to the platform again, and as it lurched downward, he pulled her toward him using just his arm and the hand clutching her shoulder. A practiced move, and a strong one, considering how much resistance she was putting up.

He held her in a viselike grip, and then, before she could move away, kissed her. She was so startled, she didn't pull back.

At least, that was what she told herself when he did let go and she realized that her lips were bruised, her hand had fallen away from the hilt of her knife, her heart was pounding rapidly.

That was a hell of a kiss, short but—good God, had she ever been kissed like that? Mouth to mouth, open, warm but not sloppy, his tongue sampling hers and hers, traitor that it was, responding.

"Yum," he said, as if she had been particularly tasty, and then he grinned. He was unbelievably handsome when he smiled, and she didn't like that either, but before her addled brain figured out what to do, he added, "Stop," as they reached one of the lowest decks.

He propelled her forward with that mighty arm of his, and she tripped stepping from the platform into the corridor, which was a good thing, since a male passenger stood near the platform, looking confused.

The passenger, middle-aged, overweight, tired, like most everyone else on week three of an interstellar cruise, peered at them.

The man beside her grinned, said, "Is this the way to the lounge?" and then kept going.

The male passenger said, "What lounge?" but they were already too far away to answer him.

They reached yet another airlock and the handsome man still holding her hit the controls with his fist, setting off yet another alarm and doing his little trick with the doors.

This time he kept going straight, swaying a little, knocking her off balance.

"Too bad you don't know any drinking songs," he said. "But then, you don't smell like booze. Enhancer, maybe? Too many mood elevators? No, that doesn't work. You're not smiling."

They rounded a corner, and came face to face with three terrified security guards, standing in three-point formation, laser rifles drawn.

"Stop!" one of them, a man as middle-aged and heavyset as that passenger, yelled. He didn't sound nearly as in control as Rikki's companion had when he told the platforms to stop. In fact this guy, this so-called guard, sounded dangerously close to panicking.

Rikki stopped, but the man didn't and neither did his arm, so he nearly shoved her forward, but she'd faced laser rifles before, and had even been shot with one, and she'd never forget how the stupid thing burned, and she wasn't going to get shot again.

"Ah, jeez, Rik," the man said, and she jolted. The bastard knew her name. Not the name she was using on this cruise. Her *real* name. "Let's go."

"I said stop," the guard repeated.

"*You*," the man said, turning to the guard, and slurring his words just slightly, "are too tense. C'mon with us. We're heading to the lounge."

"What lounge?" the female guard asked. Not only was she the sole female, but she was the only one in what

Rikki would consider regulation shape. Trim, sharp, but terrified too. Her rifle vibrated, probably because she wasn't bracing it right.

Amateurs.

"I dunno what lounge," the man holding Rikki said. "The *closest* lounge."

He grinned as if he had discovered some kind of prize, and if she didn't know better, she would've thought he was on something.

"You've gotta be kidding me," the third guard said. "Is that what this is all about?"

"I dunno," the man said, "but you sure got a lotta doors leading to nothing around here. Where's the damn lounge? I paid good money to have a lounge on each floor and I been to—what, hon? Three floors? Four—"

He looked at Rikki as he said that and pinched the nerve on her outer arm at the same time. She squeaked and hopped just a little as he continued.

"—and we ain't found no damn lounge anywhere. I wanna drink. I wanna enhancer. I wanna burger. Real meat. You got real meat on this crappy ship?"

The first security guard sighed, then lowered his rifle. The other man did the same, but the woman didn't.

"Oh for God's sake," the female security guard said to the guard in front. "You gonna let them get away with this just because they're drunk?"

"I'm not drunk," Rikki said, and the man pulled her close again so that she had to put a hand against his waist to steady herself.

He tried to kiss her again, but she moved her face away. "She's not drunk," he said rather grumpily, "because we can't find the damn lounge."

The front guard shook his head.

"They opened three airlocks," the female guard said.

"They're *passengers*," the male guard hissed at her.

"Reckless ones," the female guard said.

"What's your room?" the guard asked.

"Um..." the man said, his hand so tight around Rikki's upper arm that he was cutting off circulation. "B Deck, Something-something, 15A?"

"If you're on B Deck, it would be 15B," the female guard said.

The man extended his free hand. "'S on here," he said, and to Rikki's surprise, let them scan the back of his hand to get the code upscale passengers had embedded into the skin so they didn't have to carry identification.

"B Deck," the female guard said to the others, "Section 690, 15B."

"Suite," the male guard hissed again. "Expensive."

Rikki tried not to raise her own eyebrows. She had a cabin, K Deck, without a view. Cheap.

"We'll take you to a lounge," the male guard said to the man holding Rikki, "but we're going to have to fine you."

"For taking me to a lounge?" He sounded indignant. "Jus' tell me where to go."

"I'd love to," the female guard said.

"No," the male guard said. "We'll fine you for the airlocks."

"Not interested in a damn airlock," the man said. "Wanna lounge."

The second male guard shook his head. "I need a new job," he said softly to the woman.

"Good luck with that," she said back to him.

"I've got your information," the male guard said to

the man holding Rikki. "I'll be adding 6,000 credits to your account. Two for each airlock you opened."

"Didn't open no damn airlock," the man said.

"We'll talk about it when you're sober," the male guard said.

"Don't plan to be sober anymore this entire trip. Too damn dull." The man glared at him. "You said lounge. Where's the damn lounge?"

"This way," the guard said and headed off the down the corridor.

The man holding Rikki lurched after him, dragging Rikki along. She tripped again, this time because her toe caught the man's heel. He was doing that on purpose, but she didn't argue. She was slightly breathless from the strangeness of it all, and from the way he held her.

The other two guards followed a good distance behind, clearly arguing.

The first guard led them to an actual elevator, in the main section of the ship. Four other passengers stood inside, three women, one man, all older than Rikki, all better dressed. They eyed her as if she lowered their net worth by factors of ten.

The man holding her grinned at them. It was a silly, sloppy grin, and it made him seem harmless. "You goin' to the lounge too?" he asked.

She realized as he continued to slur his words, all trace of that accent was gone.

The four passengers leaned against the walls and looked away, wanting nothing to do with him.

They got off on the main level, but the guard led Rikki and the man to B Deck and took them to the B Deck–only lounge.

"It's exclusive," he said to the man. "Just touch the door with your fist, like you did with the airlocks."

She stiffened. The man holding her had ID embedded in his hand. They had known who he was from the moment he hit the first airlock.

That was why she stayed below decks. Cheaper. No identification required.

He grinned at the guard and gave him a mock salute. "You need a favor, friend, I'm there for you," he said, then slapped his palm against the door to the B Deck lounge.

The guard nodded, almost smiling himself. "You won't say that tomorrow when you look at your accounts."

"Hell, I got enough. Should tip you, really," the man said.

"No, you shouldn't." The guard was smiling now. "Enjoy your evening, sir."

The guard stepped back as the door slid open. The man staggered inside, pulling Rikki along. The noise startled her—conversation and music, live music, and a view. The entire wall was clear, showing the exterior of the ship, darkness, pinpoints of light, patterns she didn't recognize.

Full tables, filled with overdressed passengers, laughing, talking, a few waving drinks. Some people at a roulette wheel to the left, others at a card table to the right, some sitting on couches, leaning against each other, listening to the music.

No one noticed as Rikki and the man holding her entered.

"Thanks," Rikki said, starting to pull away, but he held her tighter.

Are You In Love With Love Stories?

Here's an online romance readers club that's just for YOU!

Where you can:

- **Meet** great *authors*
- **Party** with new *friends*
- **Get** new *books* before everyone else
- **Discover** great ***new reads***

All at incredibly BIG savings!

Join the party at DiscoveraNewLove.com!

Wickedly Charming

by Kristine Grayson

He's given up on happily-ever-after…

Cinderella's Prince Charming is divorced and at a dead end. The new owner of a bookstore, Charming has given up on women, royalty, and anything that smacks of a future. That is, until he meets up with Mellie…

But she may be the key to happily-right-now…

Mellie is sick and tired of stepmothers being misunderstood. Vampires have redeemed their reputation, why shouldn't stepmothers do the same? Then she runs into the handsomest, most charming man she's ever met and discovers she's going about her mission all wrong…

"Grayson deftly nods to pop culture and offers clever spins on classic legends and lore while adding unique twists all her own." —*Booklist* starred review

"I love this take on an old story… Exceedingly endearing…"
—*Night Owl Reviews* Reviewer Top Pick

Utterly Charming

by Kristine Grayson

He could be her own personal Prince Charming if only dreams did come true…

Mysterious, handsome wizard Aethelstan Blackstone hires beautiful, hardworking attorney Nora Barr to get a restraining order to protect Sleeping Beauty from her evil stepmother. But if Sleeping Beauty is supposed to be his soul mate, then how come he's becoming bewitched by Nora?

And when Nora finds herself baby-sitting a clueless maiden from the Middle Ages, avoiding a very wicked witch, and falling hard for a man whose magic she doesn't believe in, she begins to think that love itself is only a fairy tale…

"Grayson uses smooth prose and humorous, human characters to create a delightful, breezy tale perfect for anyone who truly enjoys happy endings." —*Publishers Weekly*

"This is another fascinating tale! I love how Kristine Grayson adds twists to the fairy tales that we all know and love!"
—*Bitten by Books*

Thoroughly Kissed

by Kristine Grayson

Sleeping Beauty has sworn off kissing...

Emma awakens to an entirely different world than the one she lived in a thousand years ago, and although she's the real Sleeping Beauty, her life is no fairy tale. After parting ways with her supposed Prince Charming, she's determined to be a normal girl—she hides her magic and swears off kissing strange men.

But her gorgeous boss Michael knows there's something unusual about Emma, and he thinks she's as infuriating as she is beautiful. Now Emma needs to teach Michael a lesson, which means mastering her magic. She knows she's flirting with danger, but after one look at Michael's perfect lips, all she can think is, "What's another thousand years...?"

Welcome to the fractious fairy tale world of Kristine Grayson, where the bumpy road to happily ever after is paved with surprises...

"Charming and engaging, the story moves quickly and fluidly. A sweet love story makes this a perfect beach read for hopeless romantics." —*Publishers Weekly*